The Sorceress of Scath

Lloyd Arthur Eshbach

A Del Rey Book

BALLANTINE BOOKS • NEW YORK

A Del Rey Book
Published by Ballantine Books

Library of Congress Catalog Card Number: 87-91875

ISBN 0-345-32464-1

Manufactured in the United States of America

First Edition: August 1988

Cover Art by Darrell K. Sweet

To the memory of the masters of fantasy and science fiction of a bygone day whose stories fanned the creative fires in me in the days of my youth: Edgar Rice Burroughs, A. Merritt, Francis Stevens, Homer Eon Flint, H. P. Lovecraft and E. E. "Doc" Smith

CONTENTS

Return to Lucifer's World

Seeking some trace of his vanished brother in the Scottish Highlands, Alan MacDougall discovered a long-abandoned tower. In it he found an ancient scroll, a Druid sword, and a golden armlet in the shape of a two-headed serpent. When he slipped it on, everything seemed changed. Beside him stood his lost brother, now strangely turned to Cinel Loarn, a leader of the Sidhe or Little Folk. And the previously bare walls of the tower now bore four bronze portals. The first showed a road leading to a beautiful city.

Once through the portal, he was attacked by a band of men, to be saved by Taliesin—the ancient Bard of Celtic myths—who told him that this was Tartarus, a world created by Lucifer for the Daughters of Lilith, now gone. It was peopled now by men and Celtic gods who all died on Earth fourteen centuries ago, re-created here to eternal boredom.

That night he seemed to hear telepathically Danu, Nuada, and other gods discussing him. They knew he had come to Tartarus without dying, through the Gate they had long sought. Some wanted to force him to tell. But Danu, queen of the gods, forbade that.

Nevertheless, he was soon attacked by minions of the evil gods and forced to flee to the Hall of the Dead, a Forbidden Area, where he saw stored bodies reanimated to replace any who were killed in fighting or accidents. Then the Bard told him the scroll had revealed that finding the Gate would do others no good, since any doomed to Tartarus would quickly wither to dust beyond the Gate. But none would believe that. Evil gods, mad Dalua and Balor of the Evil Eye, hated and envied him bitterly. He survived only because he learned that the armlet gave him strange powers, such as invisibility and shape-changing.

Then he discovered a Golden Tower, invisible to others, in another Forbidden Area. He was welcomed by Ahriman, lieutenant of Lucifer, and was shown a model with which Ahriman could control everything and everyone in Tartarus.

On his return, he found that the gods were starting a war over who should force the Gate secret from him. He fled, with Dalua and Balor behind, and managed to reach the Gate and plunge through. Balor came behind. But Cinel Loarn and the Sidhe were waiting. Their swords killed Balor as he peered through the portal.

Alan recuperated from his adventure with the kindly Cameron family, resolved never to return to Tartarus. There he found himself falling in love with Elspeth Cameron. And there he learned that the heads of the armlet were Queen Inanna and Lord Enki, who had been gods to the ancients of Assyria, Babylon, etc., though they were really Dark Angels who had fallen with Lucifer. Now Lucifer had doomed them to dwell in the armlet.

Despite his resolve, Ahriman forced Alan to return to the tower and go through the second portal. This time, he found himself in Ochren, the gloomy Underworld of Celtic myth, unsuspected by the inhabitants of Tartarus. Taliesin joined him, brought by the god Nuada. But Beli, god of the Underworld, also tried to gain the secret of the Gates. They escaped, but were captured by Arawn. Again, despite the powerful illusion spells of Arawn's Druids, they escaped to the castle of Manannan, Celtic god of the sea. Manannan seemed friendly, but soon proved to be working with Beli and Arawn.

Alan shape-changed to the form of Manannan and stole the god's boat, the *Wave Sweeper*. Manannan pursued on his wonder horse that could run across the sea.

Once again, Alan was drawn to the Tower of Ahriman, where Ahriman told him he was of royal blood and destined to a great destiny in Lucifer's scheme. When Alan told this to Taliesin, the Bard seemed to believe that Alan might be of royal descent. If so, the Stone of Fal in the Great Temple would prove it. The gods were already convening there, but they could go invisibly to the Stone.

When Alan sat upon the Stone, it began screaming loudly—a most unwelcome sign that his blood was royal. Hearing it, the gods came running, and Alan was stabbed in the back. Near death, he suddenly found himself transported through the Gate by Ahriman.

When he regained consciousness, he was healing in bed at the Cameron farm, brought there by the Sidhe. He resolved again never to return—but there were still the third and fourth Gates waiting!

CHAPTER 1

The Third Gate

Alan MacDougall opened his eyes to the heavy darkness of his bedroom. He was suddenly wide awake, senses alert. What had disturbed his slumbers? He listened intently, feeling somehow that he was no longer alone.

He heard only the rain, wind-driven, striking the window with a soft, stealthy sound. The clouds had rolled in slowly during late afternoon, and before dusk the sky had become a lowering gray blanket that seemed to rest heavily on the surrounding hills. The rain began with darkness, thin, soft, steady, almost soundless, little more than a falling mist, and had continued thus through the long evening. The wind had risen and the rainfall intensified while the Cameron household slept.

Carefully, scarcely breathing, Alan sat up, bringing into view the faint glow filtering under the door from the ceiling light in the hallway. That feeling of another presence in the room persisted.

Minutes dragged by as he sat unmoving, telling himself that he must have been awakened by a dream. A pajama leg was twisted annoyingly around one knee, but he made no move to adjust it. Now he became aware of a faint, rhythmic pulsing, and realized it was his own heartbeat. He tensed as, faint in the swish of the rain, he heard the creaking sounds that could always be sensed in an old house if one listened intently enough. Finally, when the endless minutes passed with nothing happening, disgusted with himself, he decided to get up and flick on a light to dispel his imaginings. He flung back the covers—then froze, his breathing checked, his eyes widening, and his pulse racing.

A heavy mist came between him and the single line of light, slowly dimming it, then blotting it out altogether! Oppressive silence fell; even the slithering sound of the rain was gone. Without warning, a smothering cloud of blackness engulfed him.

MacDougall leaped erect, arms flailing, a terrified cry frozen in his throat. The black cloud thickened, clinging, shutting out the world. He writhed and twisted, striking out against nothing, becoming aware of something evil and revolting, seeming to merge with his very being; and into his mind poured a flood of thoughts, hate-filled, savage. Out of the wells of memory rose a panorama of the faces, mocking, deriding, and taunting, of those who had been his enemies in the Other World.

They were the harpy features of Morrigu; Balor of the Evil Eye; dark, mad Dalua; cadaverous Caermarthen; Arias the Druid who had lashed him with his whip; Pryderi the jailor; Arawn, King of Ochren; Beli of the Dragon; Manannan, god of the sea; and finally the gloating face of Semias the Druid who had thrust a knife into his back.

They seemed to be reeling around him, faster and faster, laughing hideously; and with their dizzying dance they drew closer and closer, their gyration seeming endless; and wrath and hatred mounted within Alan MacDougall. Their spinning slowed and crept to a halt;

before him he saw Semias, now lying face up, his white throat bare and inviting.

Alan's fingers clutched that throat and his grasp tightened, all his dark hatred venting itself in the action. Dimly he was aware of fingers tearing at his clawed hands.

"Alan—Alan!" A choking gasp penetrated the veil of black savagery that held MacDougall in thrall, heard only in his mind.

Elspeth! Like an electric shock, horror swept through him. He tried to wrench his hands free. His fingers seemed locked about the soft neck. Appalled, he dragged them away. Elspeth? What had he done? What madness had seized him? He glanced wildly around. He was in her bedroom. She was staring up at him, gasping, massaging her throat. Again he heard the drumming of the rain and he saw the subdued light coming through the open doorway, realizing the nightmarish black cloud was gone.

"Darling—darling!" Whispering, MacDougall dropped to his knees beside the bed. The words tumbled out. "What have I done? How—Elspeth—have I hurt you? Something horrible possessed me, an evil black thing. I thought Semias lay before me—I felt hatred that could not be mine—"

The girl reached out and laid her fingers on his lips, managing to speak, her voice faint. "I am not really hurt —only frightened near to death. I saw that blackness like a cloud—and I know it was not you. Sorcery—from the Other World. But go—go! No one else must know about this. Tomorrow we'll—talk."

Numbly MacDougall struggled erect, his thoughts in turmoil. He moved out, through the hallway and into his own room. Even as he softly closed his door, he heard a shrill, frightened cry, then childish sobbing; David's voice coming from the room between his and Elspeth's.

Still dazed, the new shock held him for seconds; at

the sound of footfalls in the hallway he flung open the door, emerging just as Elspeth came from her room, and Norah, the housekeeper, thrust her head through her doorway across the hall. There was a thud as Duncan Cameron's plaster cast struck the floor. The man appeared a moment behind the others. All converged on the eight-year-old's room.

Elspeth reached it first. As she switched on the light, the lad sat up and covered his face with his hands to shut out the sudden glare. Moments later he flung wide his arms toward his sister.

"'Speth!" he cried. "I had a fearfu' dream about ye! I canna tell it—"

She put her arms around him and hugged him close. "Now, now, laddie—'tis all right. You'll tell me in the morning."

Just as his father entered, David asked, "An' ye'll stay wi' me till daylight?"

Norah, her small, wiry frame lost in a tentlike gray flannel nightgown, snorted her disdain. "Bad dreams, i'deed! An', Duncan, dinna ye say 'twas my cookin' brought it on. Nightmares come to us a'. An' us standin' here i' the nicht when we should be asleep."

"No' your cookin', Norah," Duncan Cameron growled, "but your fillin' the lad's thoughts wi' heathen superstitions. Dyvid, lad, are ye a' right?"

"Aye, faither—wi' Elspeth by me."

Gradually quiet settled over the Cameron household. Alan had not spoken and he was glad no one seemed to expect him to speak. There was silence in his room but tumult in his mind and heart. Knowing there would be no more sleep for him that night, he stepped into his slippers, put on a robe, and seated himself beside the window. There was too much to think about. In view of what had happened, he would have to be ready if another onslaught came from whatever had attacked him.

His thoughts were disordered, in a ferment. Could

this have been a dream, a wild nightmare? Impossible. It had been too real. That cloud of blackness was unlike anything he had ever imagined or encountered in Tartarus or Ochren, a frightening thing, revealing his vulnerability. He felt in memory the clinging, suffocating evil, like an alien entity with its dark, twisted illusions and outpouring of hatred.

The darkness began preying on his imagination, and he arose and opened the door wide. Seated again, he stared unseeing at the oblong of dim light, the awfulness of what had happened impressing itself on his mind. He could almost feel his hands about Elspeth's throat. He shuddered. Nothing that had happened in the Other World had shaken him as this had. There the attacks had been directed against *him*; this was using him to harm, perhaps kill, another—and worst of all, the girl who had saved his life, the girl, he admitted to himself, whom he loved.

Anger, cold bitter anger boiled up within him. A picture formed in his mind of carefully groomed black hair, full, too-red lips, and gem-hard blue eyes. Ahriman! It had to be Ahriman, smooth-talking, superior, disdainful Ahriman. Oh, he himself was not that black cloud, but it was his doing. Someday there would be an accounting. Alan grimaced, then ground his teeth. There was no denying the power of Lucifer's lieutenant, but even he must have a vulnerable spot.

His thoughts returned to Elspeth. How fortunate— and amazing—that he hadn't injured her. He frowned as he stared into the dark flood drumming against his window. It seemed impossible that he had not hurt her. Had he been restrained, the purpose behind the attack other than her death? Certainly if he had exerted the strength of his hands even for a moment there would have been damage. Had she been minimizing her distress? Still, she had seemed to be herself when comforting David. And what must be her state of mind as she lay beside her young brother in the next room? He pressed his hands against his temples in mental misery.

What could be the motivation, the reason behind the attack, if not Elspeth's death? There was only one logical purpose—to speed Alan's return to the Other World. If there was any truth in the idea that he was to fulfill Lucifer's prophecy—though it still seemed preposterous—pressure might be exerted to make him go back. No question, he had fully recovered from his wound, though maybe not all his strength. But his real reason for staying at the Cameron farm was his wish to remain with Elspeth and his distaste for confronting whatever lay behind the third Gate.

Now there could be no further delay. He could not risk another night in this household, facing the possibility of a renewed attack. Eventually he'd have to go back into that alien realm. The golden armlet clung as tightly as ever to his arm, and most assuredly the serpent-gods were still with him. He touched the massive gold band with its twin jeweled heads, feeling the serpent form and reptilian scales through his sleeve.

Lord Enki and Lady Inanna! He directed a thought into the armlet. "Lord Enki, where were you during my recent trouble?"

There was faint derision in the answer. "A rather silly question, I should say. You know we are always with you, though for the last thirty of your sleeps you have ignored us completely. Not that we objected. It gave us freedom to pursue other concerns. This trouble you refer to—?"

In swift thoughts MacDougall related what had happened, including his ideas about the possible motive for the attack.

The Lady Inanna commented, "It does indeed sound like the clumsy work of Ahriman, and, in view of the failure of the assault, your analysis of his purpose seems logical. There is also the possibility that your subconcious restrained you. Is there any action you wish us to take?"

Action? Not at the moment. Alan ended the mental dialogue. He reached to the little table beside his bed, groped for and found his wristwatch. In the dim light he could not be sure, but it appeared to be twenty past four —a long time until daylight, especially with the overcast sky.

He thought again of Ahriman and of what he had said about Alan's future during their second conversation. That had been very little, as he recalled it—some reference to the prophecy of the Scroll, of his being a descendant of royalty, of a possible ancient pact, and the Persian's refusal to show him his models of the lands beyond the other two Gates, making veiled comments about its being unwise to foresee the future. Nothing, actually. The implication was clear, however; he would visit the lands beyond those portals.

For obvious reasons he had no desire to return to Ochren. Tartarus was more inviting, especially with Taliesin there, but that didn't seem to be in the scenario —if he admitted he was part of Lucifer's plan, whatever that might be. And undeniably, he was curious. The strange jungle seen through the third Gate bore no resemblance to anything in his experience.

He thought again of the crying out of the Stone of Fal in that fantastic temple of crystal, the sound which supposedly identified one of royal blood; it had been a startling experience, ending ironically with a blade plunged into his back.

He thought of David's nightmare, the terrifying dream involving Elspeth. What had it been? A startling possibility struck him. Could David somehow have seen—been shown—the ghastly spectacle of Alan choking his sister? If so, he would surely talk about it. That was a devastating thought. Most likely it was something entirely different, he reassured himself. Whatever it was, he'd know in a few hours.

Slowly the minutes passed; and despite his efforts to shut out the thought, memory of the enveloping black cloud persistently returned. He repressed a shudder and tried to think of it dispassionately. The blackness had been intangible, formless, yet somehow sentient. He felt again the impression of a merging, as if whatever it was sought to enter, to penetrate, and to control him. And it actually had taken over his thoughts, had controlled his actions, and had led him without his knowledge into Elspeth's bedroom. By sheer will, he shut out the thought.

He considered the day ahead. This was Sunday. He'd be driving the Camerons to the Free Kirk in Kilmona as usual and joining them in the service, of course. Afterward there would be a midday dinner, and he'd somehow arrange to be alone with Elspeth, unless, after this night, she'd avoid him. He thrust aside the possibility. They'd *have* to talk. Afterward he'd leave, ostensibly to pick up the gear he had left in the old stone tower and perhaps, he would say, to spend a few more days in the hills. Inevitably there would be questions which he wouldn't be able to answer, especially if the rain continued, but that couldn't be helped. He looked out through the window, noticing that the rain had returned to the gentle drizzle of the evening before.

At last the sky in the east grew lighter. With the coming of dawn, the long night ended; and with daylight, the rainfall ceased, though the sky remained overcast. Stirrings followed. Norah was first in the familiar routine. After she had descended to the lower floor to begin preparing breakfast, Duncan Cameron moved into the bathroom. Following him came Alan's turn, the order that had been established by the head of the household when MacDougall had become strong enough to care for himself. Elspeth followed, with young David the last to descend. Alan's final day at the Cameron farm had begun.

His visualization of the morning, based on past Sundays, was accurate except for the one rather startling detail of David's dream. David had tried to speak of it at the breakfast table, only to be silenced by his father; but while they were preparing for church he made another attempt. MacDougall was relieved to learn that he was not involved in the lad's nightmare. David had seen Elspeth imprisoned in a wooden cage formed of dry branches, with faggots heaped all around; and when the wood had been set aflame he had awakened, screaming. It was a strange dream to form in the mind of an eight-year-old child. Strange, indeed. Could Norah have said anything to stimulate such imaginings?

After the midday dinner, Alan went to his room and changed into his black outfit, the one he had had tailored to his specifications for his adventuring into the Other World, now carefully cleaned and repaired, with all bloodstains gone and the rent from the dagger almost invisible. From the dresser drawers he retrieved all the contents of his pockets, again distributing them through the jacket and cape.

Returning to the family group, he announced his plan to climb into the Highlands to rescue the rest of his gear, adding that he might do a bit more exploring. This brought forth a chorus of objections; but eventually, with a generous lunch provided by Norah, he managed to leave, asking Elspeth to walk with him part of the way.

At first there was little conversation, both of them acting restrained. MacDougall's thoughts were a mixture of rebellion and regret over the necessity for his leaving, of angry frustration because of his involuntary involvement in an impossible adventure, and especially embarrassment because of the events of the night. Finally he made a somewhat hesitant reference to his nightmarish attack, to be silenced quickly. One hand tightened on his arm.

"Say no more, Alan. We both know that could not have been you, as we both know there can be no future for us until this matter is resolved. The forces involved are very strong, beyond anything human, and they are evil powers. You—we—somehow I feel I, too, am a part of this—we are pawns in a game far vaster than we can imagine. They are evil powers; but there are powers for good as strong—stronger. And good will overcome." She smiled up at him, but her eyes remained solemn. "Trite? I know, but I feel it strongly. So has it been and so shall it be."

All too quickly they came to the hillock where the upward climb began and they halted, to stand face-to-face.

"Well, darling, I guess we have to say farewell. You know—"

"Alan," she interrupted with sudden resolution, "I see no reason why I shouldn't climb the hill with you. I'd like to see this ancient tower, this *broch* with its Gates. Also," she added with a warm smile, "this gives us a little more time together."

"I should have thought of that," MacDougall responded as, with hands firmly clasped, they faced the slope, dark and forbidding in the somber gray of the cloudbanks. Together they started across the expanse of moor and heather, studded with clumps of yellow gorse, heading toward a stand of white-trunked birches.

During a period of silence that followed, MacDougall mentally addressed the gods imprisoned in the armlet.

"Lord Enki and Lady Inanna, will you guide us to the tower on the hilltop? Last time I made this climb I missed it." Bitterly he added, "I am ready to play puppet again while Ahriman pulls the strings."

"Have no fear," Lady Inanna answered silently. "We will keep you on course." Slyly she added, "It would never do for you to get lost in company with your Elspeth."

At that instant Elspeth spoke. "Will I hear the singing blades? During your illness, you spoke of their chiming."

Alan listened. There were no sounds save those of their own making; even the birds were silent in the heavy air. "It seems unlikely. Cinel Loarn may not know we're here, else I suppose he'd greet us."

There was little conversation during the rest of the climb. MacDougall became aware that he was not quite as fit physically as he had thought, and Elspeth seemed to sense this. He made the final steep ascent into the oak grove on dogged determination alone; and as they halted before the round gray stone tower, he sank to a seat on a boulder to rest and catch his breath. He offered the girl his canteen; after she drank, he took a refreshing draught. Together they surveyed the area. Elspeth remained standing.

"I don't like it," she said suddenly, her voice low and her gaze fixed on the rough stone tower.

Surprised, Alan looked at the familiar scene. On his right rose the rock cairn he had erected over the cadaver that had once been his brother Malcolm; Little Mac, who had inexplicably reappeared later as Cinel Loarn, leader of a band of the Sidhe, survivors from the enchanted past of Britain. The *Shee* evidently had borne Alan's inert and bleeding form to the Cameron farm after Ahriman had brought him back from Tartarus through the Gate.

The blanket of clouds concealed the tops of the tallest oaks, in some places dipping to touch the rocky earth with sodden gray wisps. The only audible sounds were the muffled murmur of the mountain brook, somewhere behind them, the rustle of wet leaves, the spattering of raindrops dripping from the foliage, and the distant cry of a curlew. He repressed a shiver, scowling. It seemed a fitting day for his departure. And he didn't like it, either.

"I mean the tower." Elspeth's voice and manner expressed revulsion. "It's evil, Alan. Enchanted—though that isn't quite the right word." She looked at him apologetically. "Remember, I'm a Scot and there are times when the sight is upon me. I wish you had never seen that gray tower."

"But then," MacDougall objected with a half smile, sliding from the rock and putting his arms around the girl, "I might never have met Elspeth Cameron."

With sudden fervor she clasped him tightly, their lips meeting. And high and clear through the woodland sounded a distant childish voice:

"Elspeth! 'Speth, where are you?"

Startled, the girl drew back, exclaiming "That's David! He must have followed us." For an instant she frowned in vexation, then shook her head resignedly. "I should have known." She lowered her arms and gently pushed Alan away.

"Go," she said, then forced a rueful smile. "I don't want David to see you vanish into a stone wall. I don't really fancy the idea myself. I'll tell him you've already gone." She called out, "Here I am, David! I'm coming." And to MacDougall, "Farewell, my darling. Be careful —as best you can." As her brother's cry was repeated, she turned and walked swiftly in the direction of the sound. "Coming, David!"

MacDougall stood grim-faced, then called, "Farewell, Elspeth." Turning away, he crossed to the entrance of the *broch*. With his powerful flashlight beam showing the way, he passed through the low doorway and tunnel into the central chamber of the tower. He circled the walls of the now-familiar room with his light. He saw four yard-wide portals and stared wonderingly at the round bronze disks with their serpentine hieroglyphic design, visible to him through powers imparted by the golden armlet.

There was something strange, something unexpected

...and suddenly he knew what it was. He had left all four Gates open when he had passed through the second one into Ochren. He had been returned through the first Gate by Ahriman, unconscious and at the point of death. Who had closed the Gates? Ahriman? It seemed unlikely. Then Cinel Loarn, who had been his brother Malcolm?

Aloud he exclaimed, "Cinel Loarn!"

Instantly the leader of the Sidhe stood visible before him. About three feet tall, athletic, and with dark hair sheared at shoulder length, he was a handsome figure in his garments of leaf-green leather, bearing his inevitable gleaming bronze shield, with his sheathed sword at his side.

"Greetings, Alan. We watched you approaching, but since you were not alone, I thought it unwise to strike our shields, even though Elspeth and I have spoken— while you were ill."

"While I was ill," MacDougall repeated, deeply moved. "If it had not been for you and your band taking me to the Camerons I would have died. Thank you, Malcolm."

The little man gestured, palms up. "We could do no less. And are you now returning to the Other World?"

"Yes, through the third Gate. I bow to the inevitable. I feel somehow that this experience won't end until I have visited the four lands." He thought of the closed portals. "Cinel Loarn, did you close the Gates after I returned?"

"Yes. I felt they should not remain open and unwatched."

"Then you can see them?"

"Of course." He looked surprised. "Else how could we guard them? And we will keep watch again until you return." With the last word and a wave of his hand, the Chief of the Sidhe vanished.

For a moment MacDougall stared into emptiness. He

could never cease to marvel. His brother now one of the Sidhe, a people out of mythology that should not exist. Neither should a magic serpent armlet, nor these portals into an ensorcelled world. He shook himself mentally. Things were as they were. To the business at hand, Mac-Dougall, he told himself.

He examined the rest of the room, the great fireplace, the two narrow openings leading into chambers on each side, and the great oaken table at his right. All as he had left it.

Not quite all! He saw a great, dark stain on the flag-stone floor just below the first Gate and instantly real-ized its source—his own blood, pouring from the knife wound in his back. He traced the trail of dark drops across the floor and out through the short corridor, see-ing a single small sandal print repeated in a fading trail leading to the exit.

He thought of another bloodstain he had seen on the wall and floor following that abortive attempt of Mor-rigu, the goddess of war, and her "hoodie" crows to crowd through the portal only to be slashed by the swords of the Sidhe; those bloodstains had vanished within hours.

He turned his attention to the room where he had left his backpack and hiking clothes. His sword, would it be there? He had been wearing it at the time of his return. The Camerons had not mentioned it, nor had he seen it during his stay at the farm. He found things as he had left them, and with his gear lay the weapon in its ornate silver scabbard, evidently placed there by the Sidhe. Smiling his satisfaction, he strapped it around his waist. He was not a skilled swordsman, but the blade seemed to be a necessary part of his equipment. He was ready for his return to the Other World.

Back in the central chamber, MacDougall considered the four portals. Should all be opened? He had gone into Ochren and had returned through Tartarus. Had the first

Gate been closed... Quickly he opened all four gateways, revealing the diverse lands, then shut off his flashlight beam to see each scene by its own light.

Tartarus appeared, its chill auroral beauty a frame for the crystalline perfection of Falias, the City of the North, with its gemlike temple from which he must have been plucked by Ahriman's magic powers. Ochren was the dark and ugly island of eternal twilight, land of illusion, and dwelling place of the gods of the Underworld.

He passed the third Gate with scarcely a glance, moving to the fourth portal. Soon he would learn more about what lay beyond it, in all likelihood, than he wanted to know, unless—for a breath he entertained the thought— unless he skipped the third and passed through the fourth gateway. Certainly it was more inviting, showing a beautifully groomed formal park with snow-white walks, silver-roofed follies, and a great marble castle. He grimaced. With the thought came a strong feeling of negation. The Gates, he somehow knew, had to be entered in order.

He returned to the third Gate and studied the unearthly scene. It appeared as he remembered it. There were the same massive, grotesquely twisted trees with their skin-smooth, ivory bark and slender, dangling pink leaves, fluttering incessantly like nervous, downward-pointing fingers. Through the canopy of leaves he could see the strange red and white auroral sky. The undergrowth had not changed—tangled bushes, pallid creepers, vines, and fleshy cacti, some thorn-armored and others bearing bulbous pink fruits and unfamiliar flowers.

As he studied the scene, he thought, What are you waiting for? Quit stalling. By this time Elspeth and David should be halfway down the hillside.

As if to refute the thought, he heard the boy's insistent treble, close to the tower.

"But, 'Speth, maybe he's in the *broch*. We should

look even if it is dark." So the lad's curiosity had prevailed.

Dark? Of course. Their eyes were blind to the glow
coming through the gateways. But Alan could be seen
even in the half-light, should the boy enter. He looked
intently at the scene beyond the portal, seeking signs of
activity; seeing none, he stooped and stepped through
the portal.

Vertigo, barely noticed, passed in a moment, and
MacDougall stood motionless, senses alert to every impression of his surroundings. Unlike Tartarus or Ochren,
where silence dominated, here arose a faint but endless
blending of sounds: a humming as of multitudes of bees;
constant stirrings in the underbrush; and the rustling and
soughing of a million leaves, though Alan could feel no
trace of moving air.

Even more prominent than the sounds was the cloyingly sweet scent that permeated every breath, like a
combination of an exotic incense and a clinging perfume.
Yet oddly, there was none of the tropical heat one normally associated with this sort of jungle.

The third impression was intangible, psychic rather
than sensory, that of evil and danger lurking everywhere.
As if—wild thought—this massed woodland were a living entity, the motion and sound and smell that of something sentient, something that resented his presence. He
had entered this land reluctantly; his impressions of the
forest served to intensify his gloom and resentment.

But he was here, and there was no changing his mind.

He had not moved; now he turned and looked behind
him. He had to mark the gateway. That was no great
problem, with fleshy trees crowding in everywhere. Directly beyond the ghostly outline of the tower rose a
twisted trunk; drawing his sword, he cut away a sliver of
bark, exposing the white wood beneath. Notching a tree
to right and to left and one facing the Gate itself completed his task. But he took one more precaution.

"Lord Enki and Lady Inanna, will you keep the position of the Gate in mind? My marking will have no value if I can't find the trees."

"Of course, though you should start improving your own sense of direction."

Mentally Alan scoffed. Maybe he had such, but it was not something he would trust. Time to move, MacDougall, he told himself. But where? The jungle looked the same in every direction. It was almost impossible to move through the heavy undergrowth, leaving travel a matter of going where the jungle permitted. Doggedly he drove ahead, his progress painfully slow. Too bad he didn't have a machete.

A sudden thought struck him. No machete—but he had a sturdy sword! Maybe that was not the best treatment for its edge but... Drawing the blade again, he found it an effective aid in clearing the way. Using it sparingly, as much as possible confining it to the thorny cacti, which spattered wetly under the blows, he began to make progress. At last the undergrowth thinned and he seemed to be approaching the edge of the thicket. After wiping his blade on a broad leaf, he thrust it into its sheath.

Abruptly the nature of the forest changed, almost as if a line had been drawn. The skinlike trunks and dangling pink leaves ended; ahead, beyond a stretch of tall grass, lay what must be an orchard, its ancient trees standing in uniform rows.

And busily picking purple, plumlike fruit were women, a score or more scattered among the trees!

Marveling, MacDougall peered through the last screening bushes. He hadn't known what to expect in this land, but certainly not this. All of the pickers were dressed alike in garments suggesting full-cut coveralls of coarse gray fabric, drawn in at wrists and ankles. Their hair, cut to shoulder length, was without ornamentation. Each was equipped with a long pole, at the tip of which a wire arch spanned a cloth cup that fed into a long sleeve, down which the fruit slid to fall into a three-foot-wide four-wheel cart, where the lower end was fastened.

Alan observed what appeared to be three guards, also women, standing idly by, each with a sword suspended at one side, with a quiver of arrows at the other. Each had a steel bow arched diagonally above one shoulder, the bowstring crossing between the breasts. Single bronze breastplates covered the left breasts; the right ones were bare. Highly polished, round, bronze shields completed their armament. In addition, they wore light-fitting trousers of iridescent green and over them short white tunics.

Their hair, like that of the pickers, was square-cut to shoulder length and unadorned. But strikingly, each wore about her neck a heavy gold chain, suspended from which was what appeared to be a dark-blue carved ornament.

Should he make his presence known? He didn't know why he was here, and sooner or later he'd have to make contact with someone.

He heard a rustling sound behind him and at the same instant felt something hard and sharp prodding his lower back on both sides. A woman's low-pitched voice said sharply, "Walk out into the open. And make no movement toward your weapon."

Obediently MacDougall stepped out on the turf, the pressure on his back unchanged. He thought of invisibility but instantly decided against it. Disappearing might bring a violent reaction from what he assumed were sword points; besides, these Amazons aroused his curiosity. It was stupid of him to let them creep up on him, though not surprising since he had moved through the brush with the stealth of an elephant.

As they emerged from the jungle, Alan saw the three guards with the pickers suddenly come fully alert, fitting arrows to their bows and aiming at him.

When they were well out of the woods and in the full light of the aurora, the same Amazon commanded, "Turn around slowly." There was no warmth in the tones.

Carefully Alan obeyed, curious to see his captor—no captors; there were two. There was silence while each inspected the other. Dressed as were the other three, both women were unusually handsome, one a freckled redhead and the second green-eyed with dark-blond hair. And both wore the large, curiously wrought pendants of lapis lazuli suspended from gold chains, each bearing a fanciful carving of a catlike female face that was grotesquely human. The blond was the speaker. Alan saw awakening interest and wonder appear on her face.

"What new trick is this?" she demanded coldly. "Appearing as a man—"

"*Appearing* as a man!" MacDougall exclaimed. "I *am* a man, a visitor from another world. And I can't say much for your hospitality."

"A man—you must be jesting! None has ever set foot on the Isle of Scath. We have seen no man during all the ages since we awakened here. You mean you are not one of—them?"

"Them? I have no idea who 'they' are, but I assure you, my manhood has never been questioned. This is the third land I have visited in your world, and on each I have been met with drawn swords."

"Your name?" the Amazon asked, her manner changing. "And this Other World you speak of—?" The sword points did not waver.

"I am Alan MacDougall," he replied promptly. "I came into your land through an enchanted Gate. And I would see whoever rules here."

"You shall. You shall." There was a hint of regret in the voice. "This is a matter for Queen Scathach." The blond Amazon motioned toward the other women; with the puzzled pair behind him, MacDougall crossed the meadow to the fruit trees.

All activity had stopped as pickers and guards alike watched their approach. One of the other Amazons called out, "What have you found, Brendah? One of—them?"

"He says he is a man and that he comes from another world."

The guard uttered a short unpleasant laugh. "He'd have to hail from another world to dare to visit Scath."

"I am reporting to Queen Scathach," the one called Brendah commented. "This is not for us to deal with. Shall we?"

As on a signal the five Amazons formed a circle with Alan in its center. Each grasped her golden-speckled, purple-blue pendant with one hand and held her shield before her with the other, forming a mirrorlike circle of polished bronze. They closed their eyes. For a fleeting instant MacDougall thought: Now's my chance to go invisible. But why should he? He wanted to meet this ruler—Queen Scathach they had called her—and learn something about prime authority in what appeared to be a feminine world.

The five held their positions rigidly, as did the fruit gatherers; the only movement was the dancing aurora reflected from the circle of shields. Slowly that image changed, fading, disappearing, to be replaced by a misty gray. Fascinated, MacDougall watched as a life-sized face began forming on each shield. Not reflections of a face; it was as if the actual countenance looked out of each shadowy gray disk. The face solidified, became crystal clear—and MacDougall caught his breath.

It was a lovely face, but an awful loveliness, sublimely beautiful, but of a dark sublimity. How could anything be so startlingly lovely, yet seem so evil? There was an uncanny familiarity about it, as if sight of it had stirred old, forgotten memories—memories of lives lived long ago, perhaps the source of that impression of evil.

Strangely, the words of Ahriman came to Alan's

mind: "Who knows what kind of pact may have been entered into in the centuries long gone? Or what promises made?" It seemed as if this Queen Scathach had been part of that past.

Her dark eyes caught and held his gaze—large eyes, deeply set, widely spaced, faintly shadowed, with irises almost as black as the pupils and long curling lashes. She had thin, gracefully arched brows, skin of delicate ivory, high cheeks, faintly rose tinted, strong features, and a wide mouth, full-lipped, crimson, amorous, and with a faint hint of cruelty in its curve. Her high-piled hair, raven black, bore a gold tiara set with sparkling emerald-green gems. Like the Amazons, she wore a carved lapis pendant, the same human-feline blend, but thrice the size of the others.

He thought of the Dresden-doll beauty of Darthula, Princess of Gorias, and of the warm and winsome loveliness of Elspeth Cameron. Neither was here. Rather, he saw power and strength on a face eternally youthful but subtly bearing the stamp of ages, a face alluring, yet somehow awakening hatred.

All of this flashed through Alan's mind in seconds, to be followed by growing wonder at the look appearing on Scathach's face. The imperious stare, as he watched, was replaced by dawning recognition and by unbelief mingled with incredulous delight.

"Tell me—what is your name?" The voice was oddly resonant, that of one born to command, and it seemed to come from the very image before him.

The Amazon called Brendah answered rapidly, "Highness, he is a man who calls himself Alan MacDougall, and he says he has come from another world. We caught him in the thicket—"

"Quiet!" Queen Scathach interrupted impatiently. "He may answer for himself."

Suddenly irritated, MacDougall exclaimed, "She speaks truth. And if you are ruler of this land, you need to instruct your subjects on how to greet visitors. I have come here to meet you, but I will do so at my convenience. And I expect to receive the respect due me."

The image on the shield seemed hardly aware of Alan's words, her expression growing dreamlike, as if she saw distant scenes.

"It has been so long, " she said, wonder in her voice, "but at last you have returned to me. What matters a name! You have had many names through the ages." Sharply she addressed the Amazon leader. "Brendah, bring him to me. At once! And see that no harm befalls him, as you value your life." Like a switched-off television picture, the face of Scathach vanished, and again the bronze shields cast back the dancing lights of the aurora.

Four of the Amazons ranged themselves in a curving line behind MacDougall, the leader taking a position directly ahead of him. Respectfully she said, "Will you follow, my lord? As you heard, the Queen wishes to see you." With a curt "We leave" to the pickers, they started through the orchard along a well-worn path between the fruit trees, the gray-clad workers trailing behind them in single file, each dragging her own cart.

Alan followed willingly enough, glad to have the opportunity to consider what had happened. The vision of Queen Scathach and her reception of him, the semi-recognition on his part and apparent full recognition on hers, had been totally unexpected. He knew he had never seen anyone like her; yet he could not rid himself of the feeling that he seemed to know—rather, to have known—her somewhere or sometime.

He scowled. More of this strange meshing of unrelated matters, this uneasy fitting of pieces into a pattern. Abruptly the visit to the Queen had lost its appeal. His jaw clamped shut and he stared at the back of the Amazon named Brendah. Not so docilely would he be led into Scathach's presence. This time around, he'd follow his own course of action. His cooperation thus far should have served to throw his escorts off guard. If opportunity came, he'd disappear. He'd meet the Queen at a time of his own choosing.

The orchard ended and they entered a stand of trees somewhat resembling chestnuts, the similarity borne out by the many clusters of thorny burrs visible overhead. The path continued through this grove, dark and shaded by the thick spread of leaves above them.

"Brendah," Alan called, "can you tell me—are these nuts harvested, as are the fruits in the orchard?" He was curious, but at the same time felt he could further establish his seeming cooperation.

She half turned, then answered, "Yes, as we harvest other nuts and fruits to feed all who dwell in the realm of Scathach."

"Are you the only group of harvesters?"

"Oh, no! There are many of us, scattered through all the groves and orchards stretching across the middle of Scath. There are none close to us at the moment."

"And can you tell me why it is necessary for armed guards to be with the fruit pickers? Or are they prisoners who might escape?"

"Not prisoners. We are here to protect them. There are beings in the woods who would harm them, beings who are forever enemies of the Queen."

"You mean whatever you call—*them*?"

"Yes. They are vicious, and we must always be alert for their attacks."

He thought of the Queen's directive. "Where you are to take me—is it nearby?"

Brendah uttered a short laugh. "No, indeed. It is too far to walk. Horses are tethered at the edge of the woods. Two of the guards will ride double to provide a mount for you. The pickers, of course, always walk since they have their carts."

MacDougall suppressed a chuckle. Strange thinking. Too far for Amazons to walk, but not too far for pickers to pull their loads of fruit. He tried to secure additional information about the "vicious" beings, but the Amazon evidently had said all she intended saying.

The nut grove ended and the path led into another stretch of forest, not as impassable as the jungle that held the portal, but thick enough to provide shelter. Time to escape, MacDougall decided. He watched for a logical spot.

At last he saw what he sought, a narrow opening into the forest suggesting a path. A few feet past the spot, he worked the magic of invisibility, dashed around the four rear guards, then moved stealthily along the path past the pickers and their carts. With his disappearance the startled Amazons cried out and the column halted.

"What happened?" Brendah demanded.

At the same moment Alan crawled under the rearmost cart and crouched there motionless.

After noisy protestations that said nothing, the frantic search began, even the pickers joining in. MacDougall grinned in sympathy. How did one find an invisible man? As he had expected, the path was searched, an Amazon following it for a considerable distance before returning.

"Not in there," she said with certainty. "There's not a sign that anyone has passed through, not a leaf disturbed."

Watching, Alan waited for a time when none was close to him, then stood up. He selected several of the larger fruits from the cart and hurled them into the brush up ahead as far as he could throw. An old trick, but it worked, drawing all attention in that direction.

After a period of fruitless searching, the column moved ahead, leaving MacDougall standing unseen in the middle of the road. He watched until he heard Brendah call loudly for the other guards to return. When they formed a circle with shields held before them, clutching their pendants, he decided it was time to move. They were reporting his escape. With utmost stealth, he moved along the path into the woodland.

CHAPTER 2

Amaruduk

This was a rather normal-appearing forest, nothing like
the area surrounding the Gateway. The air carried just a
trace of the cloying sweetness of the jungle, and the endless humming and rustling were greatly subdued. He
didn't recognize the trees, but the leaves were leaves,
though the pallid green of the auroral world. For a time
little of the sky could be seen, but red still dominated.

Gradually the undergrowth thinned out and the woodland became more parklike. The contour of the land
changed, became undulating, somewhat hilly, and the
startling aurora shone through the treetops. He began
making excellent progress through the woods.

Progress toward what? Toward nothing, but away
from that domineering Scathach who seemed to think
she had known him and who ordered him about as she
would one of her guards.

Occasionally he halted to listen for sounds of pursuit;
but, though now and then he heard rustling in the brush,

there was no indication that the Amazons were anywhere near.

He saw a suggestion of movement ahead and stopped short. It was not movement exactly, but the appearance of a misty light framed by the forest. It was a subdued glow like a giant full moon haloed by luminous mist. Like—suddenly he recognized it—like the shields of the guards just before Scathach's face formed. And like them, in the mist now appeared that unforgettable countenance.

The face turned to right and left as if searching—searching, Alan was sure, for him. He felt sudden doubt. Could the Queen see through his invisibility? The eyes passed him with no indication that he had been seen. And as the face appeared, so it disappeared. Very interesting, MacDougall thought. The appearance itself was fascinating. A projection of the Queen? Whatever the method, behind it lay sorcery.

He continued on his way through the thicket, but had not gone more than thirty feet when, from behind him, he heard the vibrant voice of Scathach. Turning, he saw the triumphantly smiling face surrounded by its halo of light.

"Foolish of you, Alan MacDougall, to try to elude me. Though invisible, you could not avoid disturbing the bushes. I shall summon Brendah and her warriors." The smile became faintly mocking, gently derisive. "Do not carry your game too far or perchance I may lose patience." Again the image vanished.

Exasperated, Alan MacDougall stared at the spot just vacated by the projection. Sorceress, indeed! He scowled, more determined than ever to visit this Queen when he chose and not before.

He began a winding, zigzag course through the forest, avoiding any consistent direction, trying to avoid touching bushes and lesser growths to conceal his passing. When he thought about what he was doing, his anger grew, his Scots stubbornness taking over. This flight was silly—but he'd be damned if he'd let himself be caught!

Twice more he saw the projection of Scathach overhead, and once she spoke: "There is no use," she said impatiently, "in your seeking to escape me. It is only a matter of time until my warriors arrive; and any movement will reveal your position."

After this last appearance of the Queen's image, Alan remained motionless for what he thought must be all of ten minutes; when finally he moved, he sighted an opening in the hillside. Well concealed by undergrowth, it suggested the entrance to a cave, and so it proved to be.

Carefully Alan crawled behind the bushes, into an opening barely large enough to admit him. The floor of the cave, sloping steeply downward, was leaf-covered and dry. In the dim light, he saw that it widened into what appeared to be a small room, hardly natural in formation. He thought of his flashlight but decided to put off exploration until he had rested.

Rested! He slumped against the wall just inside the entrance. He was tired, and no wonder. From the time he left the Cameron farm he had been on his feet, with only a short break at the tower. He had hacked his way through a jungle and had hiked, it seemed, for hours through this forest. He was thirsty, hungry, and tired. His canteen and Norah's lunch would satisfy the first two, and time would relieve the last.

As he ate he thought of Tartarus and Ochren and his experiences there; inevitably there formed in his mind a picture of the short, rounded Bard, Taliesin—balding, with a fringe of white hair over his ears, twinkling brown eyes under heavy white brows. Taliesin had been Alan's companion in adventure, the only one he could depend on, his only real friend in the world of Lucifer. The Bard would want to know that he had returned to his world— more, that he had survived the murderous attack of the madman, Semias. And maybe Taliesin would want to join him!

He stared blankly into the shadows. Should he call on the serpent-gods to help him reach across the miles? He had done so in the skeleton-jail on Ochren and had been told he had the ability within himself. And later, without help, he had communicated with the Bard across the width of the island. Was distance a factor in telepathy? He'd soon know.

He closed his eyes and centered his thoughts on the Bard, trying to visualize the total man.

"Taliesin, this is Alan MacDougall."

There was an immediate response, the familiar thought pattern expressing incredulous joy. *"Alan—it is good to hear from you! I tried to reach you several times, feeling eventually you would return—if you lived. You are in Lucifer's world?"*

"Oh, yes; but not on Tartarus or Ochren. This is the Island of Scath, the land beyond the third Gate."

"And have you fully recovered from your wound? I really feared for your life, though I could not believe that Semias had slain you."

"Fully—or perhaps not quite all my strength."

"You said the Island of Scath. There was a Dun Scaith in the old days."

"Yes—a world of women, apparently, ruled by Queen Scathach. Plus their enemies whom I have not seen, but who apparently are not human."

"Scathach. I once knew of a Scathach who taught Cuchulainn his magic. She was famous through all the lands as a sorceress of surpassing powers and as chief of a band of warriors of savage ferocity, all women. But," he concluded abruptly, *"you can tell me all about it when I get there."*

"Then you are joining me?" Alan responded eagerly.

"You couldn't keep me away. I will get one of the gods to help me."

"Not Nuada. I'm sure he resents my being in his world."

"No, more likely the Dagda. But come I shall. I'll call you when I have made arrangements. Until then—it is wonderful to hear from you again." And Taliesin severed the mental ties.

MacDougall grinned with satisfaction. He needed the Bard's wisdom, knowledge, and counsel, and had come to depend on him. Besides, Taliesin was good company.

As he stowed away the leftovers of his lunch and took a last swallow of water, Alan considered his next move. He felt like stretching out on the leaves and taking a nap, which, of course, was out of the question. Before anything else, he should examine the cave. He reached for his flashlight, gazing toward the black depths, wondering what, if anything, might be there. Suddenly he checked all movement, peering intently into the darkness.

He saw a dim glow forming about thirty feet away and about ten feet below his eye level. The light grew brighter, a palest green, fuzzy, not clearly defined, suggesting a fluorescent light without a glass container. It seemed suspended in midair, floating free. It hovered at the base of a slope, near the top of what appeared to be the beginning of a tunnel large enough for him to walk through.

Momentarily he thought he glimpsed a gray-robed, male-appearing figure only slightly more clearly defined than the light; he gained the impression of a tall, swarthy being, somehow twisted, shoulders sloping, one arm longer than the other, grotesque in the greenish glow. Instantly the view clarified, and the visitor bore no resemblance to what Alan thought he had seen, a trick, probably, of uncertain light.

Oddly, though the newcomer was masculine, Mac-Dougall did not think of him as a man even at first sight. Like Ahriman the Persian, he was more.

As tall as Alan, physically more massive, there was

something about him that suggested regal power. Perhaps it was the face. A dark complexion, night-black hair, light beard, heavy brows, a large Semitic nose, and cold black eyes—no single feature, but the totality, suggested royalty. His single garment, a voluminous silken amber robe reaching to his ankles, was gathered at the waist by a broad gold belt; dangling from it on his left was a curved shortsword in a gold, turquoise-and-carnelian-inlaid scabbard. Amber-thonged leather sandals encased his feet.

His first words were mockery as he spoke in low, vibrant tones. "If I could not work a better invisibility spell than that, I would not try. Who are you?"

Annoyed, but returning to visibility, Alan demanded, "And who are you to ask?"

For an instant the other's face grew darker with anger; then, with evident effort, he forced a smile. "There is no reason for us to quarrel. You wish to elude Scathach the Sorceress, hence I am your friend. Come, join me. I wish to aid your escape from the one who falsely claims to rule this island."

He stepped to one side and bowed. "There is much to tell, and here we are too close to the Witch's searchers."

Mentally Alan shrugged. Why not? He didn't want to meet the Queen of the Amazons—at least, not now; and he had to get acquainted with the people here. He moved quickly down the slope.

Side by side, the two started along a tunnel cut through clay, about eight feet high and six feet wide, its floor of gray flagstone. The strange green light moved with them, hovering above their heads.

"Tell me your name," the amber-robed one began. "You cannot deny it; you are not of this island. You were seen as Scathach's guards ambushed you. I have been here forever, it seems; and no new face has appeared during all those ages except replacements for Scathach's slain. You could not be one of these. They are always women."

"What of your slain? Or do none die?"

The dark face smiled grimly. "None ever die."

Despite the strange answer, MacDougall decided. "I am Alan MacDougall, and I have come from another world, what you may have known as Alba, land of Celt and Druid."

Silence greeted Alan's statement, to be followed by a muttered, "Scathach's land." Then came a question. "And her time?"

"No, not her time. Probably fourteen hundred years have passed since her day in my world."

His companion turned swiftly and clutched MacDougall's shoulders, his eyes burning brilliantly from their shadows.

"You mean you have come from the land of the living? Through the portal?" There was an eagerness, a consuming hunger in his manner as he awaited the answer.

Startled, Alan removed the grasping hands and stepped back. How could this being know of a portal? But—why not? The gods of Tartarus had inborn knowledge of a Gate into the Other World. Was this a god? He wished now he had been less forthright, but there was no possible retraction.

"Precisely. From the land of the living."

He heard a sharply indrawn breath; and they walked on in silence while the other seemed to be considering matters.

Almost absently he finally said, "I am Amaruduk, once King of Kings and God of gods. There is much to tell, but not until we reach the circle." He lengthened his stride, staring fixedly through the tunnel. Keeping pace, Alan tried to remember their course, but found it impossible as they crossed intersecting passageways, strode around curves, and even seemed to reverse their direction. He caught glimpses of moving lights in branching corridors, indicating the presence of others, but he saw no details.

At last they halted in what appeared to be a sort of underground amphitheater, literally a circle cut out of the clay, thirty-five to forty feet wide. He thought of the Trolls under Findias on Tartarus with their incredible tunneling through rock. This appeared to be entirely of clay; it was still a fantastic job. Of course, with more than a thousand years—

"This is the center of Scath," Amaruduk commented. "From here tunnels lead to every part of the island, including Marduk. We shall sit."

As MacDougall joined him on one of a series of massive wooden seats along the wall he glanced hastily around and saw eight tunnel entrances equidistant from each other, with seats between them; but he had trouble keeping his gaze from a sort of massive monolith at the middle, dimly seen in the glow of the single green light.

His guide seemed amused as he saw Alan's fascinated attention, but he made no comment. A surrealistic sculpture in dark-green bloodstone with its red mottling, it seemed to twist and writhe in the fuzzy radiance. Alan tore his eyes away and looked at his companion.

"What I am about to tell you," the latter began, "has not been given voice for ages. There is a reason for my doing so now as you shall see.

"In the long and long ago there was a land called Sumer, and there men called me Amaruduk, and I was King of Kings and God of gods. The tens of thousands worshiped me. Amaruduk, firstborn of Ea, god of the watery abyss, creator of heaven and earth was I.

"Later, in Assyria was I Merodach, and in Babylon I was Marduk, and everywhere was I Bearer of the Tablet of Destinies, the high god above all high gods. Slayer was I of the monstrous Tiamat. Power was mine from Ninurta, and Nergal and Zababa and Nabium and Sin,

Shanash and Adad. Power none had ever known before.

"In Upshinaku the gods gathered joyfully to proclaim my victory and to declare that my words might never be changed, and that what I did might never be altered. So they gave me the scepter and the throne and the insignia of royalty. All power among the gods was mine. Even the Wise Lawgiver proclaimed that I would raise up or bring low, my utterance was truth, and none among the gods should transgress my bounds.

"Yet through one failure that was not really mine I was cast down, I was brought low, and the Lord of Light sent me here, and here have I been through the timeless times."

The speaker became suddenly vehement. "But not forever will I remain here! As one of the Host my powers still are great." With black eyes burning into MacDougall's he demanded, "How did you enter Scath?"

"I walked," Alan answered soberly.

Amaruduk glared, then tried to cover his annoyance. "Why you of all those among the living?" He started at a sudden thought. "You have not—*died*?"

Alan shrugged and smiled. "No, I have not died. And why I have been chosen to visit what I call the Other World, I have no knowledge whatever."

"But this is not the first time." It was more assertion than a question.

Alan temporized. "What makes you think so?"

"Because you are too calm. You show little surprise."

"This is my third visit," he agreed.

"To Scath?" Amaruduk exclaimed doubtfully.

"No, this is the third island. But a wide sea separates Scath from Ochren and Tartarus."

Amaruduk's eyes narrowed as he stared speculatively at MacDougall. He didn't seem surprised. "I have always been certain that this island was not alone on this quiet sea. The Messenger had to come from somewhere.

Tell me, is there on one of these islands a—a god, tall, with black hair and intensely blue eyes?"

Ahriman obviously, MacDougall thought; but the Persian had never claimed godhood. "I know of no god who answers that description," he said. "Not Balor, nor Manannan, though both are tall—"

"Gods who are not gods," Amaruduk scoffed. "Later I would learn more about these other islands and their dwellers. But now, tell me—has none returned, none gone back to your world with you?"

MacDougall repressed a chuckle. The crux of this matter. "None. There have been attempts—quite fatal. Even for gods."

The self-declared God of gods attempted a warm smile. "Friend MacDougall, I believe I have devised a way for me to visit the Other Side, and successfully. A way to our mutual benefit."

Alan made no attempt to hide his skepticism. "How?"

"A way with no effort on your part. And the powers that would result for you are fantastic. God powers at your disposal."

Silently Alan waited, narrowed eyes steady. He felt his hackles rise. He thought he knew what was coming. Both stood up as Amaruduk spoke.

"Share your body with me, just for a visit. Skills you cannot conceive will be yours. Skillful spells. Total invisibility. Miracle powers. New sight to discover treasures long lost. Untold wealth. Think, friend Alan—"

For a moment MacDougall met the other's intense gaze with a blank expression, then looked down as if considering. His thoughts raced, a cold fear rising within him. A god from Sumer, the ancient land of Lady Inanna and Lord Enki. Who knew the powers of this Amaruduk, or the limitations? Could he indeed enter the body of another and share its tenancy? He thought of Balor, god of the Fomorians, and his expelling the spirit of a newly awakened Norseman to take possession of his body; and this was certainly a greater power.

A phrase the god had used crystallized in his mind. "As one of the Host my powers still are great." A startling idea. By Host did Amaruduk mean the *Heavenly* Host? Alan sought to gain time.

"Then you are what men call a demon?"

Amaruduk bristled with sudden anger. "Not a demon! We deny the term and all it suggests. I am one of the Host of Heaven who chose to follow Lucifer during the Great Confrontation. Our Master is the Mighty One, the Lord of Light, the Son of the Morning. Not demons! But if you must have a name for us—angels will do. Or better, gods.

"We are not men. We are neither male nor female. Or if we wish, either male or female. Or both. We are gods."

Impatiently MacDougall responded, "Gods, gods, and more gods! Everywhere I turn in this world I meet gods. In my land we have an expression, 'A dime a dozen,' which denotes things of little value. The term seems to fit the gods of Lucifer's world."

Amaruduk's eyes narrowed to slits as he growled, "You go too far. I told you what I did because I had thought to favor you with an opportunity to share tenancy in your body when I use it to return to your world. Now you will be—displaced!"

MacDougall's muscles grew rigid as dread lanced through him. He thought of Balor; but far more frightening was remembrance of the invasion of an alien power in his bedroom at the Cameron farm. The black presence that had led him unknowingly into Elspeth's room, to choke her...

His breath caught in his throat as the being before him became misty gray, expanding, darkening, becoming cloudlike. Abruptly the amorphous globe of light dimmed; as near darkness fell, the living black cloud flowed over and enveloped MacDougall in a suffocating embrace. Again he felt that horrible *merging*, that feeling of duality; and into his brain poured alien thoughts, a phantasmagoria of exotic scenes, of ancient splendor of multitudes in battle, of flowing blood, of dark temples where worshipers knelt, and of human sacrifices. Above all, of power—power over life and death—demonic thoughts not his own, rising in another mind.

The tenor of the alien flood changed, became centered upon his expulsion; an utter negation, a total rejection, a strongly willed command that he leave! Leave his own body? An appalling, indescribable sensation, frightening...

He fought back desperately out of fury and indignation and fear, resisting with all his strength.

"Lord Enki and Lady Inanna!" In panic Alan sent the thought. "I need help. One from Sumer—"

The Lady Inanna answered instantly; and MacDougall had never before been aware of such intensity of feeling, such fury in her thought. "We know, and are ready for the Lord Amaruduk! Ready, indeed! Not now does he have the might of the gods of Sumer behind him!"

Strength gigantic poured out of some inner well of power; and sudden release came, all pressure gone, the suffocating presence as if it had never been. The nearly formless light, now dim and feeble, hovered near the center of the circle, wavering erratically. Below it, sprawling near the base of the bloodstone monolith, lay the motionless figure of Amaruduk, staring dazedly at MacDougall.

But now it was not the regal god he had been dealing with; rather, it was the darkly twisted individual with sloping shoulders and mismatched arms he had viewed dimly during the forming of the light. The real Sumerian, Alan thought, and the other form the result of shape-changing.

Interminably, it seemed, they held their positions, though in fact only seconds could have passed. Tides of relief poured over Alan. Obviously the repulsion of the demon had been the work of the serpent-gods; but the violence of the effort, the physical force behind it, were most unusual. *His* energy had not set the attacker reeling, since there was none of the draining—it had to be that of Amaruduk himself! And the loss of energy had prevented his maintaining his changed form or even his suspended light.

"You win this time." A harsh, discordant voice came from the god as he struggled erect. "A setback, but no more. Not defeat." He grimaced savagely. "Find your own way out of this maze—if you can."

Instantly pitchy darkness fell, and with it, silence, save for Alan's own breathing. Reacting instantly, he found his flashlight and sent its beam around him. The clean light was a comfort, though there was still something disturbing about this chamber. Perhaps it was that monolith; its shape was repelling even in the brighter light. And what of Amaruduk? His assailant was gone, unless . . . An answer came unasked from Lord Enki. "Not invisible. He has transferred himself elsewhere." In relief Alan grasped the armlet.

"Lord Enki and Lady Inanna, my heartfelt thanks for coming to my rescue. I fear I was losing that struggle with this god from Sumer, if such he was. This one who claimed to have been God of gods."

"He was indeed," Enki answered, "and of Babylon and Assyria, even as he said. His troubles started when Darius became King. Men turned from Amaruduk, who was then called Marduk; his own priests betrayed him, following a new god not of Lucifer's choosing—Ahuramazda—and the Lord of Light, greatly displeased, evidently sent Amaruduk here. Condemned him, it appears, to the twisted form you saw.

"There was a time when he was known as King of the

Gods. This was in the long ago before even Sumer rose to power in the world. This was the time of Lachmu and the goddess Lachamu; and Anshar and his consort Kishnar. And Tiamat the Great Serpent lived in the deeps. This was the first physical form of the Lady Inanna.

"And because the gods feared Tiamat and her powers, they chose Amaruduk, the youngest among them, to do battle with the Serpent of the Deep. To him they gave all their combined powers. And Amaruduk slew Tiamat and treated her body shamefully."

The thought of Inanna came, freighted with frigid wrath. "Now he stands alone! Now he is but one, without the powers of the many gods, and exiled to an island of women. Not now is he King. And he shall feel my might."

Mentally MacDougall groaned. "This world was bad enough when I had to contend with the gods of ancient Britain. Now appear the deities of Sumer—and I suppose of Babylon and Assyria and Egypt!"

The Lady Inanna expressed surprise. "Why do you find this strange? Think you Lucifer's domain is limited to one time and nation? In the island you call Tartarus are there not Norsemen and Ch'in? And after all, those like Danu and Nuada and Balor are not gods as we are. They are mortals with some magic skills who were given god powers through men's worship. We who chose to follow the Shining One from the Beginning are the only gods worthy of the name."

Alan felt a sudden chill; he tried not to think of what the statement implied. Changing the subject, he asked, "Which tunnel shall I follow to find the nearest exit? Without your help I would find the task as difficult as Amaruduk thinks it."

"One moment while we investigate." In seconds the Lady Inanna directed, "Follow the fourth entrance at your right. Turn left at the first intersecting corridor. There you will find a ramp."

Briskly MacDougall started out, glad to leave the monolith, his thoughts involuntarily returning to the demonic attack. Too close for safety! He preferred attacks like those of Balor and Morrigu who tried to follow through the Gate. Again he saw the twisted god glaring up at him from the floor.

"Lord and Lady," he asked, "when you cast off Amaruduk, did you, as I suspect, use his own strength?"

Amusement was in Inanna's reply. "Indeed. Through what he was attempting, he was vulnerable. And he never knew what smote him."

"And you once were Tiamat?" MacDougall was puzzled. "Your earliest form, you say. What of those goddesses you have claimed who came after your and Lord Enki's imprisonment in the armlet? Surely there must have been such, since Sumer was a very ancient land."

The Lady Inanna seemed somewhat vexed. "You have placed limitations upon us that do not exist. True, we have been confined to this armlet since my escape from the World Below, because the Lord Enki and I upset the division the Lord of Light had established. But on occasion he has given us special assignments, utilizing our abilities for tasks of his choosing. You must recall there were times when you sought Enki and he was busy elsewhere. After all, during the millennia, there have been wearers of the armlet who knew little of its powers; and there have been times when it lay in forgotten tombs amid crumbling skeletons until searchers were led to its resting place. A lot has happened during forty-five centuries."

Again MacDougall felt his flesh crawl. Why had he ever touched that infernal jewel? But enough of such thinking. There remained one troublesome question that had been gnawing at the back of his brain since the vanishing of Amaruduk.

"Can you explain the incredible coincidence of my hiding in the only place where I could encounter this one-time god of Sumer? He seemed to know about the Gate and was not really surprised at my saying I came from the land of the living. It's unbelievable."

Lord Enki seemed amused. "Not coincidence at all. Not the only place, either. Your capture by the woman was observed by one of Amaruduk's own guards and was reported to him. Your escape also was seen; and he knew where you were hiding. We told you when he vanished that he transferred elsewhere. With that power, no matter where you had concealed yourself, he would have appeared before you.

"As for his lack of surprise when he learned from whence you came, he knew you were none of his, nor did he think you were one of Scathach's. So when he heard the truth, it was not too surprising. As for the Gate—this was knowledge preplanted in his present brain."

As he continued through the tunnel, MacDougall tried to keep his thoughts away from Inanna's revelations, especially the fact that the dwellers in the armlet, supposedly his servants, were actually demons! The thought of their being mythical gods had not been half as disturbing. He grimaced into the shadows. Semantics, Mac. Snap out of it. Not a thing has changed.

He came to the cross-tunnel and in short order found the ramp. Following it led into a dense clump of bushes. Again invisible, he found a cleverly concealed passageway opening into the forest. At its edge he paused, peering through the screening brush, alert for signs of the Amazons or the projection of Scathach overhead. He could sense nothing disturbing the tranquility of the scene. On the verge of leaving his concealment, he thought of the powers of the armlet.

"Lord and Lady, are those Amazons nearby? I hear nothing, but your sight reaches far beyond my hearing. Even you, of course, cannot predict where Scathach will appear."

Seemingly annoyed, Inanna commented, "We *can* predict that in a very short time two warriors will pass within sight and hearing of this spot."

MacDougall's lips moved in a silent "Damn!" It seemed they could smell his whereabouts. Nothing for it but to wait until they had passed. Two of them. Hmmm. So they had divided into two or perhaps three separate groups. He grimaced. They thought so little of his powers of resistance that two should be able to capture him.

He heard the pair approaching. At the moment they seemed unconcerned about stealth. An idea formed suddenly. Why not follow in their tracks? They couldn't see him, and if Scathach tried to trace him through moving brush, she'd attribute the motion to the two. Swiftly, but without undue commotion, he intersected the path of the two who had captured him in the first place, Brendah and the redhead, and fell in behind them. He heard the redhead speaking:

"I suppose you know we are getting close to the Grove of Spirits. It is not to my liking. Nor will I enter it. Strange things happen there."

"I like it no better," Brendah answered somberly. "We'll pass along its edge. No place in the Grove for him to hide." She gave a sudden impatient exclamation. "I keep forgetting—he's invisible. This is so stupid. How can we expect to find him? He could be in sight of us right now and we could not know. Yet search we must. He escaped with me in charge, so I must face Scathach if we fail. It would mean lashing—or worse." There was a note of despair in her voice.

As they continued on their course, with Alan following undetected, the character of the forest changed. It was gradual, a stunting of trees and bushes, tapering until the forest merged into a narrow expanse of yellow-green turf. The grass formed a band about twenty feet wide, and the open space ended at a stand of great trees, close set and straight-stemmed, with only grass between them. The grove suggested a park, except for the crowding of the trees. This must be the Grove of Spirits.

The Amazons edged away from the Grove, even avoiding the shade of the wide-spreading branches, walking instead through the shorter brush. Alan followed at their heels. Here was nothing to reveal his motion if Scathach should be watching.

As she was!

MacDougall saw the rounded, misty glow, this time set against the veils of aurora. The face of Scathach followed.

"Brendah"—her voice came sharply—"you are not trying. He must be in this vicinity. The Three Sisters tell me so. Do not look for him; look for movement of the bushes. And when you find him, stay with him. Make no attempt to overcome him—he must not be harmed—but don't let him escape again. Just report to me immediately."

"What if he has gone into the Grove?" Brendah's companion asked. "There are no bushes there. And—and we don't plan to hunt him among the Ghosts."

"There would be tracks in the grass, but this need be no concern to you. If he enters the Grove, he will leave very quickly." She emphasized the phrase: "*Very* quickly!" Then she added, "And separate, you two. No reason for your searching together." Finally in a harsh voice to Brendah, she ordered, "Do not fail."

The projection vanished. Evidently, Alan thought, he had not been noticed.

"Head to the north," Brendah directed, "and I'll continue east toward the Well of Darkness."

As they moved away, MacDougall remained where he was, staring into the Grove of Spirits. So he'd leave very quickly if he entered! Interesting. Nothing unusual about its appearance. Gloomy and shadowed as one would expect with big trees crowding each other, their leaves hiding the sky, which had not been overly bright to start with. Ghosts, spirits in Sheol, Lucifer's domain. Logical enough, though he had become accustomed to the dead having new bodies. There was one striking exception; from the depths of memory came a mental picture of a swirling, tortured cloud of endlessly whispering spirits in the pit of Annwn on dark Ochren, and he felt a chill as if a frigid wind had passed over him. He caught himself listening, but heard only the faintest trace of a pervasive humming.

Deliberately, MacDougall strode across the stretch of open turf and entered the Grove. Immediately he became conscious of an eerie feeling, a disconcerting impression that he was being watched from every side, as if his invisibility were no longer effective and countless eyes were fixed upon him. Absurd! His imagination must have been stirred up by Scathach's comments; even the name of the place was doing its part.

The feeling persisted, even intensified; and Alan could not avoid thinking of the other times when he had felt unseen eyes watching. Better get out of here! He scowled. And prove the Sorceress correct? This was ridiculous. Certainly, after all he had experienced since that day ages ago when he'd first put on the armlet, to be disturbed in anticipation by supposed spirits was absurd.

Defiantly he stalked deeper into the woods and looked for a comfortable seat. He found a tree with a slightly slanting bole and plenty of grass at its base and seated himself to await developments. As he did so, he realized his invisibility had gone. Trying to restore it, he felt a strong negative force of opposing wills. The myriad watchers resisting?

The serpent-gods, of course! They could help.

"Lord Enki and Lady Inanna, I feel unseen eyes upon me. Will you help me see the watchers—these Ghosts— if they are really there?"

"We thought you'd never ask."

MacDougall blinked to clear away a momentary mistiness; then, as the veil lifted, he stiffened in vast surprise.

Before him stood three wraithlike figures, leaning over as if examining him. At his sudden movement they floated back, halting a few feet away, seemingly poised for flight. Through the tenuous substance of the three he could see the trees beyond them; and now he saw other ghostly figures peering around tree trunks. There was something dreamlike in all of this.

As he became more accustomed to the strangeness of the spectacle, he began noticing details. The wraiths were lovely women, long-haired, clad, it seemed, in the thinnest veils of palest green, as wraithlike as themselves. Ghostlike, yet clearly defined. Now he understood how this Grove got its name.

Moving very slowly, Alan stood erect, trying to avoid disturbing the denizens of the Grove. Even so, some of those peering from behind trees vanished, to reappear timidly moments later.

"Who are you?" he asked quietly.

There was no response; only their falling back showed that they were aware of his speaking. He tried again, resulting in another retreat. Crossing his arms, he leaned against the tree and stood unmoving, waiting. Slowly at first, then building up to a flood, the wraiths appeared, coming from every side; and then something happened that shocked him utterly.

At his elbow suddenly appeared one of the amorphous beings, *not* coming from around the tree but emerging from the tree trunk itself. There could be no mistake.

Dryads! Of course. Ghostly forest dwellers living in the trees! He knew little about dryads, though it seemed to him they came out of Greek mythology. Inclined to laugh at this new fantasy that he was accepting, Alan shuddered when his eyes met those of this newest arrival. Never had he seen such eyes, pupilless and utterly without life. Soulless.

The dryads continued moving, floating toward him, approaching from every side. It was a disturbing spectacle, literally hundreds of the wraiths coming from the depths of the forest, crowding closer; but how could there be anything menacing about beings without material substance? In spite of himself Alan felt a pang of apprehension. He thought of Scathach's remark and of the Amazons' obvious fear of the Grove.

Abruptly all motion ceased, the wraiths as one staring fixedly into vacancy, suggesting a motion-picture still. They held their position interminably, as if listening; then as one they resumed activity. But not as before.

Those on one side began closing in on him and on the opposite side, backing away, opening a path through the woods. Their purpose was clear; they were intent on moving him—somewhere. Alan's first impulse was to resist, to stay where he was, but somehow the thought of contact with the ghostly dryads, if indeed contact were possible, repelled him.

As they drew closer, he realized there was a total lack of expression, a zombielike blankness on their faces. Suddenly he felt an urgent desire to be far away from this Grove of Spirits. He looked around for an avenue of escape. There was none, short of pushing through that enveloping mass of wraiths, and he shrank from that.

As the strange movement ended, MacDougall's eyes widened in unbelief. They had entered a vastly larger outdoor counterpart of the underground circle! It was an arenalike clearing in the heart of the Grove, as level as a tabletop, covered by a carpet of grass. At its center towered a massive stone monolith carved out of red-splattered green bloodstone, a grotesquely malformed image that repelled and fascinated at the same time. A crimson flare of light from the aurora bathed its crown, somehow suggesting a wash of blood. Obscene, Alan thought, though he could not have told why the thought formed.

With the engulfing wraiths he entered the open area. Still yielding to the ghostly flow, he began to circle around the clearing, at the same time circling the great carving. Something icy seemed to clutch the pit of his stomach, and a feeling of helplessness began to grow. There was something uncanny about all that was happening and about the total silence that prevailed.

Silence? He became aware of a barely audible drumbeat, rhythmic and almost subliminal. And he and the masses of wraiths began to sway with the beat. Almost subliminal? With a shock MacDougall realized that he really heard nothing, that the sound, the rhythm had formed in his mind. It seemed to permeate his very being.

The tempo quickened with the passing moments, and the flow and gyrations of the circling wraiths kept pace with the rhythm, as did he. A part of him seemed to say, This is a nightmare; it can't be happening. But just as surely, another part knew this insane thing was taking place.

And now, like instruments in some ghostly orchestra, other sounds, a cacophony of rhythmic discords added their voices to the bedlam. Swiftly the volume of the silent sounds increased, multiplied, and swelled until MacDougall thought his head would burst. It was as if every mad note of every rock band he had ever been exposed to were suddenly to repeat its sound within his brain. And hypnotically, insanely, the hellish beat transferred itself to his feet and body, impelling a wildly careening course around that repulsive monolith.

Even as he swayed and gyrated, he seemed always to avoid touching the dancing wraiths, all swaying to the same wild tempo.

The monolith! It was closer, the circle narrowing. And as he moved around the carving, MacDougall's eyes seemed to be opened to the beauties in the figure that had eluded his earlier sight. His eyes became fixed on its splendor; it became an all-enveloping entity of power and glory.

The beat had slowed and the sounds had faded, as did the movements of the ghostly company. Silence fell, all motion ended, and Alan became dimly aware that he was kneeling at the base of the great bloodstone figure. Into his brain poured a flood of thoughts dredged out of some forgotten reservoir of evil, as if every foul desire, every dark impulse, long repressed, were about to be granted. He felt a cold paralysis creeping up through his body, enveloping him like a dark cloud, seeping into him.

"Amaruduk!"

Violently the name lanced through his mind. The thought was Inanna's, and it was filled with rage.

"MacDougall, awaken! Open your eyes."

Alan reeled erect to face three tightly bunched demons at the base of the monolith, Amaruduk at their center. He caught a glimpse of baffled fury on the latter's face; then they were gone.

Groping for understanding, MacDougall turned to look at the dryads. They were in confused retreat, fleeing swiftly in every direction, vanishing into the trunks of surrounding trees. In moments the last one had disappeared, and Alan stood alone, the monstrous statue towering above him.

Still semidazed, he stalked away from the grotesque figure, trying to clear his brain. Echoes of the bedlam of sounds passed through his mind, sounds that he knew had to be totally mental. Whence had they come? Perhaps the serpent-gods could explain.

"Lord Enki and Lady Inanna, during that crazy dance with the dryads—"

Derisively the serpent-god interrupted, "Dryads! No dryads, these. They are the life essence of the Daughters of Lilith, given shelter through the ages by the Lord of Light in these trees to await the day of restoration to their bodies. And obviously they are subject to every command of such as Amaruduk."

Into Alan's mind flashed a vision of the crystal-clear boxes stacked on the top level of the Hall of the Dead outside of Falias, each holding a wraithlike body of a beautiful woman. The bodies of the Daughters of Lilith, according to legend as Taliesin had told it, fathered by the angels who had been cast out of Heaven with Lucifer.

"He does not yield easily," the Lady Inanna continued. "He thought to weaken your defenses by an indirect attack. Had I not interfered, he might well have succeeded. The sounds you sensed—you actually heard nothing—were stored in your own mind, and through his—rather, through the collective minds of the Three— were transmitted to the spirits. The task of Amaruduk's helpers was the control of the spirits, while he concentrated on you." Amusement crept into the serpent-goddess' thought. "You acted very strangely."

MacDougall felt his cheeks grow hot, and his resentment at the demon Amaruduk flared. He must have been giving a bad imitation of a frenzied teen-ager at a rock concert. Not that bad, he hoped. Hastily he changed the subject.

"This grotesque mass of rock—what is its excuse for being here?" he asked caustically.

There was restraint in Lord Enki's reply: "One does not question the form in which the Son of the Morning chooses to present himself. For the Daughters of Lilith this is a constant reminder of his presence. As it is—and as is the one in the circle below—for those who assemble here."

A stab of dread flashed through Alan at the answer, emphasizing as it did the constant Luciferean presence in everything in this world and pointing out how alien his armlet-companions really were. Resolutely he shut out the thought.

"How do I get out of this grove? I've had enough of Amaruduk. I'm ready to meet Queen Scathach." He thought of Brendah and the warning of the Sorceress. "Lead me to the Well of Darkness. I'll let Brendah recapture me. I've caused the girl enough grief; and that way I can ride."

With swift, sure strides, following the course implanted in his mind by the serpent-gods, he left the Grove of Spirits. As he reached its edge, there burst into his mind the unmistakable thought of Taliesin.

"Alan! I've been trying to reach you, only to meet a strong block. Behind it I could sense wild confusion. Are you all right?"

"There's no problem now," MacDougall responded with forced calmness. *"Are you ready to join me?"*

"Indeed. I have the help of Credne. Dagda preferred staying in Falias. Visualize where you are, and we'll be on our way."

Credne, the Bronze-Master who had dropped him outside Falias on their way to the Bard's home. He hoped that wouldn't happen to Taliesin over open water!

Closing his eyes, Alan centered his thoughts on his surroundings, creating a mental picture with himself at its center, holding it to the exclusion of all else. Minutes passed; he opened his eyes at the sound of a familiar, joy-filled voice at his elbow: "Alan! A sight to gladden the heart."

"Taliesin, my friend!"

Spontaneously they embraced. As the Bard stepped back, holding MacDougall at arm's length, another voice said diffidently,

"Good to see you looking well, Alan MacDougall. And now I must return."

Facing the Bronze-Master, Alan asked in surprise, "At once? Don't you wish to see something of this island, Scath?"

The slender, wiry Credne shook his head, his straggly

red beard wagging decisively. He held out his hands, indicating his metal worker's apron. "Gobniu awaits my return. We are working on a particularly fine sword, and the metal needs my attention. I helped the Bard of Bards in his need. So—farewell!" And abruptly he was gone.

"Well—" MacDougall began, then switched hastily to mental address. *"Quick, Taliesin—invisible, don't move, and say nothing.*

"Scathach!"

CHAPTER 3

In Scathach's Tower

The dark beauty of the Sorceress took form against a nimbus of misty radiance a hundred feet away, hovering over the edge of the forest. The invisible watchers remained motionless as her projection moved about over the area, then rose skyward, slowly shrinking and finally disappearing.

"I don't think we were seen." MacDougall sent the thought. *"But we'd better play it safe. She sometimes returns at a nearby spot."*

"Something new," Taliesin commented, *"that image appearing in the sky. But that is the Scathach I knew, a mistress of magic. Not a goddess, but a power in the old days with her sorceries and her warriors."*

"And certainly a power in Scath, the Queen ruling over a country of women; though Amaruduk contests her claim to be ruler of all the island."

"Amaruduk?" The Bard's thought expressed sharpened interest.

"*Yes. A one-time god of ancient Sumer. To me, a demon.*"

"*I once knew an Amaruduk—*" Taliesin's thought seemed hesitant. "*Very long ago.*"

"*It would have to be* very *long ago*," Alan observed. "*Five or six thousand years ago, in fact. Of course, there could be two Amaruduks.*"

"*There could be.*"

The mental interchange died on this note; and Mac-Dougall finally said aloud, "It's probably safe to move now, though we'll remain invisible. Since both of us can see beyond invisibility we will have no trouble in staying together."

As they started out, MacDougall suddenly chuckled. "You must be wondering why I am hiding from Scathach and what this is all about."

The Bard's eyes twinkled. "The question occurred to me, and I was somewhat puzzled, but I decided you'd explain eventually."

Quickly, switching to telepathy for convenience, Alan summarized what had happened since his passing through the third Gate. He tried to cover everything, though he glossed over the more painful details of the attack in the Grove of Spirits.

"So now you understand why I'm hiding. I plan to go to Scathach, but I'll let Brendah guide me. I won't give the Sorceress the satisfaction of having a part in my capture."

"So Amaruduk tried to—possess you," the Bard said gravely. "Not a matter to be treated lightly. Fortunate that you had help. I should like to speak with this Amaruduk."

Their course led for a long time along the grassy boundary of the Grove, then veered to the left into an ordinary woodland. For a substantial distance, the nature of the forest remained unchanged; then the way began to slope, as if they were entering a hollow. The very atmosphere changed subtly, a damp mustiness becoming evident. There was something oppressive about the place—not that anything Alan had previously encountered had been bright and cheerful.

The spaces between the trees widened as the slope grew steeper, more of the scarlet auroral light penetrating the net of leaves, but somehow the unnatural gloom became more oppressive. The bushes thinned to give way to bloated cacti that, fortunately, were sufficiently wide-spaced so that, despite the multitude of thorns, they could continue on their way. These in turn were displaced by fungi of strange and grotesque shapes and enormous size. It was a veritable mycologist's paradise —or nightmare—with cones and fans, domes and spheres, umbrellas and formless blobs of sickly yellows and gray-blues, and of pallid flesh tones and bloody reds on every hand. An unnatural silence held this grotesque land in thrall.

"Lucifer's creation is quite varied," MacDougall commented, "as if he were displaying his versatility."

"A sage observation." The Bard's tones were solemn. "A constant attempt to prove he is not second best, but doomed to failure because he can only reshape matter already created."

Again silence fell.

Underfoot, dank mosses formed a vast carpet, growing upon a spongy mat of decaying matter of uncounted centuries. Each step sent up a swamp-breath of mephitic fetor that rose to mingle with a pervasive, faintly repulsive fragrance like that of a mortuary.

Alan became aware of the haze and the tendrils of mist so gradually it was only as vision was obscured that he realized its presence. It was not the solid fog that Taliesin had conjured up to hide their entry into undersea Murias, nor the utterly blinding barrier raised by the Druids of Beli in the underworld of Ochren. Rather, it was like the wisps of vapor rising at dusk from some hidden Highland stream, gradually thickening in small areas, and, as they strode through it, swept aside by the air of their passing.

The forest ended, only the giant fungi, many waist-high, continuing. The slope leveled off and their way lay across a flat expanse. The tendrils of mist thickened into a fuzzy fog, shutting out some of the aurora's rays. The deepening darkness and obscuring of sight prevented MacDougall's seeing the woman until he was almost upon her.

It was the Amazon, Brendah. She sat upon a stone wall, staring disconsolately into the mist, her shield on the wall beside her. Apparently she had been crying. She had not heard their approach.

"It's Brendah, the leader of the Guards," Alan silently observed. *"I'll give myself up to her while you, obviously, remain unseen. I'm sure we'll head for the horses where there should be five mounts, since none of the searchers would dare to leave without me. You've ridden an invisible horse before."*

MacDougall moved stealthily away until he was sure the fog hid him; then, again visible, he walked toward the girl. When he saw her stiffen with awareness and hastily wipe away tears, he said casually, "Hello, Brendah. Fancy meeting you here."

The Amazon sprang to her feet, staring wide-eyed, drawing her sword and exclaiming, "Alan MacDougall at last! I can hardly believe—"

"Put up your sword," Alan directed. "You won't need it. I've decided to let you guide me to your Queen. I've proved my point—I go to her when I want to—and I've seen enough of this thicket and the beings it conceals."

"You mean it?" The words came tumbling forth. "How can I thank you? I would never have dared to return to Scathach—" She hesitated. "If you mean what you say—and you do!" She smiled with delight. "I think in you she has met her match."

"However," Alan continued, "I must take one precaution. I don't want you reporting this to the Sorceress as you were instructed. May I have that jewel of yours?"

Instinctively Brendah clutched the lapis pendant, then with a smile unclasped the chain and relinquished the link with Scathach. "Better you have it, then I cannot be blamed for my silence."

"Before we go," MacDougall said, glancing about, "what is this lovely spot you selected for a resting place?" Knowledge, any knowledge, could be of use later on.

She looked at him uncertainly, then, recognizing his facetious intent, turned and indicated the area beyond the low stone wall. "This is the Well of Darkness, or so it has always been called. From it flows all the water of Scath, except of course for the surrounding sea."

Alan stepped to her side and looked where she pointed; he fought a sudden wild impulse to grasp the wall and hang on.

He seemed to be looking into the black heart of this world, down through a tremendous vortex of swirling waters, a great bore all of thirty feet across, utterly dark, absorbing rather than reflecting the aurora. A miniature black hole, the absurd thought came unbidden. There was something hypnotic about the spectacle; with a physical effort, he wrenched his gaze away.

Involuntarily he looked back—and unbelievably only about four feet below him he saw dark water swirling swiftly as it rose from the depths, but no longer threatening to engulf him. Strange, that illusion. The stone wall on which he leaned encircled the well, left and right sides opening into six-foot-wide stone channels through which flowed constant streams going in opposite directions, widening rapidly as they sped away from their source.

MacDougall drew a deep breath and stepped back. "Aptly named, the Well of Darkness. Never have I seen its like. Where do the streams flow?"

"The one to the left flows to Scathach's castle. It grows steadily wider until, by the time it reaches the sea, it divides in two, flowing around the Isle of the Tower. There it is almost a river. I know nothing about the stream to the right. It flows through—" Her voice sank to little more than a whisper. "—Amaruduk's land."

Brendah's manner was greatly subdued as she backed away from the wall. She spoke with a hint of horror. "Once in a fight, a guard was hurled into the well. I saw it happen. She was sucked down like a woodchip, disappearing at once. She never came up."

"What a place for you to wait!" MacDougall exclaimed. "What led you to do so?"

The Amazon did not answer and Alan did not press the point. Could she have considered suicide to escape Scathach's wrath? Was that the reason for her revulsion? If so, it helped him visualize a most unpleasant person. What had the Queen said at her first sight of him through her projection? "It has been so long, but at last you have returned to me."

He didn't at all like the idea her words suggested.

Brendah hesitated. "There are two ways we can go to the horses, directly through the woods or by following the stream to the edge of the forest and moving through the grass just beyond the trees. This is the longer but quicker way. Also more dangerous."

"More dangerous? Why?" MacDougall asked.

"There are things in the grass."

"Things?" Alan repeated.

The girl shook her head impatiently. "Things. And they seem never to look the same. But we shall go that way. You have your sword and I have mine."

Briskly she started out with MacDougall behind her and Taliesin, unseen, at his heels. They followed the stream to the end of the woods, then moved westward through the coarse grass, in some places reaching almost to their armpits. Alan could see how "things" of all sorts might hide in this thicket. Close to the trees, the growth tapered to near-normal height, enabling them to maintain a good pace.

They must have gone at least two miles before they sighted the horses. Brendah's fears had proved groundless; not a single "thing" had appeared. As they approached the animals a guard stepped forward and waved.

"Brendah, I see you found your prisoner. The pickers told me about him. But shouldn't you be following him?"

"He comes of his own accord."

They reached the horses, tethered by long ropes to ordinary hitching posts close to a narrow road through the woods, an open tank of water nearby. Two well-worn wheel tracks leading into the forest and cutting through the high grass showed the route the pickers followed.

"We are taking two horses," Brendah said. "One of you will have to ride double. Report to the Queen that we are coming in so that she can tell the others they can stop their searching."

"But didn't you—" the other began, then stopped as she noted the absence of Brendah's amulet.

"No I didn't," Brendah answered coldly.

As they selected mounts, MacDougall flashed a thought to the Bard: *"When she reports to Scathach she'll close her eyes. Your chance to make a horse disappear and follow."* Taliesin, Alan thought, would spend most of his time on Scath invisible or, through shapechanging, as a replica of someone else.

With Brendah leading they rode along the narrow road through the high grass. They had gone only a short distance when a thought came from the Bard: *"I am with you. No trouble—though I imagine we've left a very troubled and puzzled guard behind us."*

They started along the road at a gallop, riding on the shortened turf between the deep grooves worn by uncounted numbers of hand-drawn carts. This pace ate up the miles, but in time the horses began to tire, so they slowed to a canter. Initially there had been no conversation, but now MacDougall asked,

"Can you describe the Island of Scath to me? It might help me later if I had some idea of its makeup."

After some thought and slowing to a trot, Brendah answered, "It's oval in shape, divided into two parts by a broad band of woodland and orchards across the width. I believe the Well of Darkness rises close to the middle, the stream dividing Scath from end to end. On the left side of this half, where we are, but close to the sea lies the town of the warriors and beyond it the homes of the harvesters. To the right, on the other side of the stream, live the Druidesses. There, too, amid the rowan groves, rises the Temple. Only the Druidesses go there.

"The space we're crossing now is never entered except on these roads. It is not safe. Often it is not safe in the paths. So we cross as quickly as possible."

"Because of the things?"

"Because of the things. As for the other end of the island, I know little about it. I have never been there. And I know of no one who has been there. In the olden times, captives were taken, but they never came back."

Curious, Alan asked, "Is there no communication between the two groups—Scathach's and Amaruduk's? Any trade or other mingling?"

"None but fighting," Brendah said emphatically. "In earlier times we were constantly at war, with one or the other invading. Now there's a sort of armed truce, with only an occasional nuisance raid by them. For this reason we must always be on guard, for we never know if a raid may become a full-scale invasion." She hesitated, then blurted out, "You know, if—*he* learns of your being here and decides he wants you, there could be another war!" Her voice took on an injured note. "It's not fair. *We* die, and they never do, though they can be injured. If our numbers were not greater . . . But there are always replacements."

"Then there is on Scath a square white building—" Alan began. He went no further in his description of the Hall of the Dead where lay in eternal cold the new bodies, the replacements, for those who died. Brendah interrupted in obvious discomfort.

"There are two on the seashore on opposite sides of our half of the island. We do not talk about them." Strange, Alan thought; here, as on Ochren and Tartarus, reference to the Halls was taboo.

Conversation died; and a thought came from Taliesin: *"When we get to Scathach's castle, you obviously will be taken to the Queen and will be engaged as she decides. Forget me—unless there's real trouble, in which case I could be useful. An invisible aide could do surprising things. Otherwise I'll find a spot, a vacant room, probably near the food supply, where I can sleep, be out of the way, yet be available when needed. There are always such spaces in old castles."*

"Excellent," Alan responded. *"And we can always know what the other is doing and can plan accordingly."*

At length, after a tiresome ride, their destination loomed ahead, a tall, round tower rising from the plain, its top silhouetted against the aurora and its lower portion lightly veiled by the shifting curtain of mist. As they drew closer, Alan began to see details. It was wrought of roughly hewn gray stones, broad and massive in proportion to its height, not unlike the *broch* in the Highlands, except that this was as tall as a ten-storey building, tapering upward in a graceful curve from its broad base, its top the typical crenelated wall. Its sides were pierced by numerous narrow windows. Like a platform on which the tower rested, a two-storey structure encircled its base, the outer wall also topped by a crenelated barrier.

Great iron double doors, evenly spaced, gave entrance to the tower. Like armor, they were heavily studded with great cones and knobs. There were six doors, Alan learned later. Small windows, close to the roof, formed a pattern around this base.

To MacDougall's left, at least a hundred yards away, he saw an assemblage of low boxlike buildings, evenly spaced to form a large village; beyond them, barely visible, blocked by the first group, were numerous sheds and barracks. Between the three riders and the village were corrals and stables with scores of horses behind fences.

On the other side of the stream, Alan saw what appeared to be a series of round groves, too regularly shaped and spaced for the trees to be natural growths. He glimpsed a suggestion of buildings among the farthest trees, but they were too indistinct to be identified.

Brendah led the way to the corrals, where an attendant, clad in gray like the pickers, received their horses. The animals moved among the others, heading toward watering troughs, where a third one appearing out of nowhere moments later went unnoticed.

MacDougall saw a cart path east of the one that had brought them to Scath, a road angled to the southeast. From the girl he learned that it led to the stream a half mile to the south and to a bridge for the use of the harvesters and guards who worked the forests on the other side of the Well of Darkness.

On foot, with Brendah still leading, they moved across an expanse of turf toward the tower. As they approached it, Alan saw that the castle stood on an island in the middle of the stream, an island paved with hewn stones, flat and raised about a foot above water level. It was a symmetrical oval extending about thirty feet beyond the side walls, and double that at both ends. Narrow stone bridges, directly opposite each other and all of forty feet in length, arched from shore to island.

"The bridge is narrow," Brendah said quietly, "and

beyond it the maze is even narrower. It might be well if I led the way."

Narrow, indeed! Alan stared in unbelief at a wall no more than two feet wide, the top of which was the bridge. Its surface was rough, and there was no handrail to keep one on the track. Obviously this had not been built with ease of passage in mind; its purpose clearly was to make a mass attack impossible. He halted and surveyed the situation.

Now he noticed hazily through the mist Amazons on the roof of the base building, bows drawn and arrows aimed at him and Brendah. It gave him a decidedly uncomfortable feeling.

"Put away your arrows," he called. "This is not an invasion. I've been invited by the Queen." None of the warriors moved.

"Lead on," he said to his guide, and Brendah started over the bridge, with Alan a step or two behind her, his eyes fixed on the path. As they reached the highest point of the arch, a gas torch flared to life above the nearest doorway and the great double door swung outward. Only then did the Amazons lower their bows.

Alan halted and stared ahead at what he had thought to be an extension of the paved surface. Instead, a series of elliptical walls swept out in a wide half-circle, all on a level with the surrounding paving, with water at stream level between them! At most they were eight inches thick, nowhere less than five feet separating them, with eight-inch-wide bridges leading from wall to wall. The tops of the walls were rough and jagged. Since these bridges were randomly placed, a visitor having no lighted doorway to guide him literally threaded a maze. Of course, one could make his way to the central paving and try doors, except that there didn't appear to be any way to open them from the outside.

"Let's go," he said at last. With the main bridge successfully crossed, he tackled the eight-inch path. He was grateful for a good sense of balance and for the rubber soles on his hiking boots; but at best, the walk was disturbing. The tendrils of mist added to the interest, now and again making the footing even more hazardous. So did the glint of water between the walls and signs of life in the moats.

"Don't tell me," he said to the girl, "there are serpents in the water."

"Only in the first moat." Brendah chuckled. "There are crocodiles in the second and sharply beaked toads in the third. As for the rest—"

"Enough!" MacDougall exclaimed. "I get the picture."

"*How are you faring?*" he asked the Bard.

"*I can go where you go,*" the answer came.

At last, without mishap, they reached the open doorway. Alan had experienced several uncomfortable moments when he had slipped on the irregular surface and he breathed more easily with the smooth flagstones of a broad entryway underfoot.

Just inside the great arched opening stood two palace guards, or so he assumed they were. And above their heads, clear against a misty gray background, hovered the familiar face of Scathach. She was smiling faintly.

"Welcome," she said. "I trust your ego has been satisfied—though your joining me was inevitable. You—and Brendah—will follow the guards." The projection vanished.

The two women stepped to right and left and motioned for the visitors to enter, waiting expectantly, their gaze fixed on MacDougall. He halted as if to inspect them, taking ample time for the chore, really doing so to give Taliesin time to clear the gates.

Handsome, he thought, though he didn't care for the bluish shading around their eyes. Both were brown-haired, with tresses square-cut to slightly less than shoulder length. Unlike Brendah's very practical dress

for passage through the underbrush, the Castle Guards
were scantily clad. Above the waist, they were bare except for silver breastplates of delicate filagree; below
was a short kirtle, full-cut of a silky blue fabric; and they
were shod with silver-thonged sandals. Above their
waists were silver chain belts from which were suspended silver scabbards, holding slender rapiers. As the
doors closed behind them, one girl led the way and the
other fell to the rear.

And the Bard was on his own.

They moved along a wide, curving corridor, well
lighted by evenly spaced gas lamps and the high windows. The right-hand wall, of tremendous thickness, was
the foundation wall of the tower itself. They came to an
arched opening and turned into what appeared to be the
living quarters of the Tower Guard, scores of beds in
precise, barrackslike rows, spaced about a great central
pillar, filling the chamber. Some of them were occupied.
They crossed to and entered the pillar, which actually
was a stone stairwell, like a tower within a tower. It held
a spiral stairway, which they began to climb. As they
ascended, Alan counted the levels, small landings and
narrow doorways the indicators.

Here, for the first time since passing through the third
Gate, MacDougall was reminded of his injury. The climb
was tiring; at the fourth level, he halted to look into a
curving corridor, ostensibly out of curiosity but actually
to snatch a moment of rest. They halted finally at the
sixth level, the top of the stairway, solid stone overhead.
Beyond the doorway in a narrow corridor that girdled
the stairwell, they were met by another Guard.

She led them around the corridor past several doors in
a wall of well-fitted dark wood boards, halting before
another door. She knocked and called out, "Queen
Scathach, they have come."

The door opened of itself and the familiar voice of the
Sorceress announced, "Enter! Guards, wait for my call."

With Brendah following, MacDougall stepped into the room, the door closing behind him. Instantly the girl dropped to her knees, head bowed. Alan, after a quick step forward, remained standing, his steady gaze meeting that of the Queen. There was a long silence while the two appraised each other.

That, at any rate, was how it began for Alan. Appraisal. She was breathtakingly beautiful, he thought, seductive, the actuality far more impressive than her projected image. From her mass of raven-black hair with its gold tiara and the rose-tinted ivory of her face, she was perfection. A massive gold chain supported a pendant of lapis lazuli, larger than those of the guards but fashioned to match the same woman-feline model. Her lacy black robe with its delicate tracery of gold ornamentation barely concealed the voluptuous form; the gold breastplates and slippers added the final touch to create a picture of unnatural beauty.

Her intensely black eyes drew and held his, faint amusement, even a suggestion of mockery, in their depths. He tried to look away, tried to bring back that impression of evil which he had sensed at his first sight of her, but failed.

Finally she spoke, and the hypnotic spell was broken. And Alan, strangely shaken, mentally berated himself.

"You have not changed through all the centuries. Never did you bend the knee before man or god. And what did you say you are called in that land from whence you came?"

"I am Alan MacDougall—and I know nothing about those centuries of which you speak."

"Alan, Son of Dougall. A worthy name. As for your memory, that can be restored." She addressed Brendah. "Rise, girl."

As the Amazon stood up, the Queen continued with a frown, "You did well to capture him, but why did you fail to report as instructed?"

"Not capture," Alan interrupted firmly. "I was not captured. I came of my own free will. But she was so persistent in her search, clinging to my trail at every turn, that I decided she deserved to be my guide to your castle. And she could not report." He drew the girl's amulet from a pocket. "I relieved her of this." He returned it to the guard.

Scathach kept her gaze on Brendah.

"You should not have lost him in the first place; but with his resourcefulness and powers, none of you could have prevented his escape. Had you failed to find him— but you did not. So as reward you are promoted to the Castle Guard. You may leave."

The door opened, and the Queen spoke to one of the three remaining Guards. "Malveen, Brendah is now one of the Castle Corps. See to her dress and duties. Dismissed."

Bowing deeply, the four withdrew; the door closed; and MacDougall was alone with the Sorceress.

During the interchange with the Amazon he had glanced quickly about, gaining a picture of the room. It was triangular, like a blunted wedge, about ten yards wide at its broad end, with unusually high ceilings. Scathach was seated on a great, massively upholstered pale-blue chair, against a backdrop of heavy hangings of deep crimson. The floor was covered by a deep-pile, dark-blue rug. Several smaller blue chairs were scattered through the room; and there was a small carved table at her right hand. The walls to right and left were dark, of naturally finished wood, with a single door in each. Light came through two of the high, narrow windows and from two wall gas lamps.

The Queen motioned toward a chair facing her and MacDougall seated himself. As he waited, he told himself, Remember where you are and what she is. It would not be easy.

"You should know," she began, "you are the first man ever to set foot on Scath."

"So I have heard," Alan responded.

"You have met some of the—others—but they are not men, no matter what shape they take. We will speak of them later."

After a pause, she went on. "Tell me about this Other World from which Brendah said you come."

It was the obvious question; and he received the obvious response to his description of his world, and his assertion that fourteen centuries had passed since the days of the *Tuatha de Danann*—and her day, if she was of that time. She shook her head in unbelief, consternation on her face.

"It cannot be! I have not changed and Scath has not changed. I knew there must be weary years—but fourteen hundred! You must be jesting." After a long, thought-filled silence, she said somberly, "All dead—all the gods, the Druids." Then a startling thought widened her eyes. "Do you mean you have not come here as we have—through death? That you entered Scath some other way? And—perhaps can return?" She seemed to be holding her breath.

"I have not died and I can return."

A speculative look crossed Scathach's face as she considered this, and she smiled warmly. "The high hills of Alba, do they still stand? And the islands—they remain? Even the one in the north we called Dun Scaith?"

"All are there," Alan acknowledged, "though somewhat changed. But, unfortunately, none from this realm can enter mine and live. This is the third island I have visited in your world, and on the first one a Bard named Taliesin deciphered a scroll that he said was written by the one he called the Lord of Light or Lucifer. It told of a Gate about which the gods knew, knowledge that came with their new bodies, but it also declared that any dwellers in this world who passed through would crumble to dust, their spirits doomed to wander as ghosts forever."

The Sorceress frowned and bit her lip. "There are powers—" She left the thought unfinished. "This Gate— strangely, I have known of a Gate that leads out of Scath, though where it lies none can say. And Taliesin— there was a Bard of that name in my day. A man of wisdom, but a fierce warrior, as well. He lives, you say, on another island in this world. Are you certain that it is this world?"

"I am certain. The other two, as this one, are under the aurora." He paused, then continued, "Tell me, what leads you to think you once knew me? You spoke of my not changing through the centuries. And earlier, of my coming back to you!"

Instead of answering, the Sorceress picked up a small bronze bell from the table beside her chair. At its chime, one of the doors opened and an older woman in gray entered.

"Yes, your Highness."

"Serve the refreshments," Scathach directed. "We are ready." As the woman bowed and withdrew, she spoke to Alan. "In anticipation of your coming and aware that your experience in the forest might have wearied you, I had refreshments prepared. We will discuss matters further as we drink and eat. I find our conversation most interesting." She closed her eyes and leaned her head against the back of the chair.

MacDougall looked with admiration at the picture she made, a faint smile on his lips. The clichés "peace and tranquility" and "childish innocence" came to mind— both, he was sure, as inappropriate as phrases could be. Was she really meditating; was it an attempt to impress him; or was she providing an opportunity for him to feast lustful eyes on her loveliness? Or none of these? He, too, closed his eyes, seeking to free himself from the spell of her beauty.

He opened them at a bell chime in the next room, meeting the disapproving look of Scathach who stood above him. Whatever she intended, it did not include his wasting his opportunity.

"Follow," she said coldly, leading the way into a room the duplicate of the other in shape and size. Not quite the same, Alan noted for no particular reason. There were two doors in the facing wall, suggesting two rooms in the next section, one probably the servant's quarters or the pantry. They had entered a dining area, obviously, its furnishings appropriately luxurious. On a table made for two a sumptuous array of food and drink had been spread, the vessels entirely of gold. In memory, Alan saw the incalculable treasure store of the Trolls under the city of Findias on Tartarus. Precious metal was abundant in Lucifer's domain where there was nothing to buy.

At sight of the food, MacDougall realized he was hungry. This brought to mind the fact that much of Norah's lunch remained in some of his pockets. But this was neither the time nor place to produce it.

Scathach evidently had decided to hide her pique; with a great show of graciousness she said, "I suggest you remove your cape and sword. You will be more comfortable without them."

Promptly Alan complied. Whatever problems he faced in the stronghold of the Sorceress could not be solved with his uncertain swordsmanship. The servant sought to take them, but Alan objected, draping them over a nearby chair. The Queen watched, her face expressionless. As they seated themselves, she said to the maid, "You may leave, Isla. I will attend to my guest's needs."

She looked at MacDougall across the table, smiling faintly. "I wonder if you realize how unusual this is. Not only a man here, but our being alone. Only very rarely do I confer with a single person, and that with the leader of my Druidesses. Otherwise in my memory here in Scath, I cannot recall a similar situation. Why this singular privilege accorded you? I shall tell you." Her smile widened. "But first you must sample the wines of Scath."

She held a golden flagon aloft. "This is my favorite, a fruit wine of my own blending." She poured a generous portion into the goblet before him and, Alan noted, very little into her own. Raising hers, she said, "May we drink to the renewal of a friendship begun when time was young."

In silence MacDougall raised his goblet; they touched; and together they sipped. That was what Alan intended, but when he tasted the fragrant liquid, involuntarily he took a more generous draft. There was an incredible vaporous explosion in his mouth as he rolled the wine on his tongue, savoring it. Reluctantly he lowered the vessel.

"Fantastic! That is not mere wine; that's the nectar of the gods!"

Obviously pleased, the Sorceress admonished, "Drink it. I have an ample store. And there are others."

Alan took a second sip, then placed the goblet on the table. "With the permission of your Highness, I should like to sample the food. I have eaten little since entering this land, and much has happened. I have no idea how much time has passed—but these dishes send forth such delightful aromas—and frankly, I am hungry."

Scathach expressed contrition. "Of course! So thoughtless of me. I should have realized the situation. Enjoy the fare of Scath. We have only fruits and nuts but these in great variety, and we have learned to prepare them in many ways. While you eat, I shall answer your question about my recognizing you. Afterward you will tell me what happened in the forest."

Numerous exquisite small dishes held the food; evidently they were intended solely for him, for only he had the necessary tools, a two-tined fork and a spoon, of gold, of course. And the food was good—with strange exotic flavors, piquant aromas, and unusual consistencies, but good. As he ate the Sorceress talked.

"Apparently you have forgotten—and there are few who remember—that you have lived in other times, in other bodies. As have I. And in those times our paths have crossed, not once but time and again. And always in those lives we have been very close. Not always have we appeared the same, but in the last life I recall, you were very like you now appear."

MacDougall finished his wine and looked at the Queen curiously. "And all this you remember?" Boldly he added, "And perchance we were lovers?"

The dark eyes of the Sorceress burned into his. "I do. And we were."

Alan laughed lightly. "I have never believed in reincarnation, nor do I now. And even given the possibility of recurring lives, the likelihood of two personalities crossing again and again over centuries requires the wildest kind of coincidence. Why, if you have lived in other bodies, are you here? Why has the cycle stopped? In my world we have a saying, 'I'm from Missouri and I'll have to be shown.' It would require proof—much proof—to convince me."

"And proof you shall have in abundance," Scathach declared triumphantly, then sobered. "As to why the lives ended and I came to this place—who am I to question the decisions of the Son of the Morning?

"But your cup is empty." She raised another flagon. "Try this. It is the distilled essence of a berry that I believe exists only in Scath."

Obediently Alan tasted, another extraordinary flavor experience. Moments after swallowing the first draft he felt its impact. It began with a burst of suffusing warmth in the pit of his stomach, followed by a tingling from head to toe. That, he told himself, was dynamite. It could be habit-forming, but not a habit that appealed to him.

"A potent beverage, your highness, to be consumed in moderation, else one might say things that could lead to trouble later."

"It only seems so, Alan MacDougall," she said, a devilish twinkle in her eyes. "But as you wish."

She continued talking, telling of some of those past lives and of what Alan would see when she brought back his memories. When he drained his cup she refilled it promptly with the same potent brew. He heard himself chuckling and realized there was no reason for mirth. Slow anger rose within him. She was trying to get him drunk!

With the anger Alan sensed a recklessness, and an idea took shape. Gradually he permitted an apparent thickening of his tongue, the slightest slurring of his speech. When he saw sly amusement in her eyes he felt he was ready. She had made reference to their touring the tower, of seeing its treasures and its shrine, when he interrupted enthusiastically.

"You should see the Golden Tower of Ahriman! Do you know Ahriman? Beautiful man. Hmmm—mush more than a man. An' his Tower—beautiful. Saw him jus' a short time ago." He had been looking at her intently through narrowed eyes as he spoke; now he looked at her owlishly. "You sh'd meet him. What a pair you'd make." He looked down into his cup to hide any expression of triumph that might have shown on his face.

Very definitely the Sorceress knew, or knew of, Ahriman. His mention of the Persian had startled her. Had he detected a hint of fear or at least of uncertainty? Had she perhaps been told of his coming? He permitted his head to nod slowly, his shoulders to sag, then he snapped erect.

"Wha' did you say?" he asked.

Queen Scathach looked at him with barely concealed

annoyance and chagrin. Certainly she had not planned this development, his getting sleepy. She probably had wanted to rid him of any inhibitions he might have and to make him susceptible to whatever she had in mind. He thought he knew what that was. After all, she quite clearly was a woman who hadn't seen a man in fourteen centuries! But she was also a Queen and had to act like one. Or so it seemed.

"I didn't say anything. But I have decided that we will delay further conversation until you have rested. You appear overly tired." She stood up.

"Isla," she called; and the servant promptly reappeared. "My guest must have rest. Have the Guards conduct him to his room."

Alan arose. "Thank you for a lovely visit," he said solemnly, swaying slightly. "I enjoyed everything. I look forward to the proof you plan to show me. Should be inter-interesting. An' I mus' say you are far more hos-hospitable than King Arawn or Beli or even Manannan when I visited them on Ochren. G'night—or whatever." Picking up his cape and sword, he followed the servant out of the room into the stairwell where he was met by two Castle Guards. He could feel Scathach's eyes boring into his back until the door closed behind them.

Had he overplayed his little act? He didn't think so. Anyway, it had gotten him out of what might have been a sticky situation. Temporarily.

Without speaking, the Guards led him around the stairway to the second level below that of the Sorceress. Though they were silent, their eyes were busy, appraising this man, a head taller than either of them. Alan knew they would welcome any attention he might give them, unless fear of the Sorceress deterred them; but his thoughts were occupied with his visit.

They left the stairway, followed the corridor to the opposite side of the tower, and halted before one of the doors. To MacDougall they all looked alike. How did they know which was the correct room? He asked one of the Guards. Mutely she pointed to what appeared to be the ends of five half-inch pegs, flush with the door panel, just below the knob. "This is the fifth room on this level," she said shyly. "Yours while you are here."

They turned away and vanished around the curve of the stairwell. Like most of the doors in this world, it had no latch or lock. Apparently one locked it with a spell or not at all. MacDougall paused just inside the door and surveyed his quarters, a room the same shape as that of Scathach but narrower and with none of the luxuries, except perhaps for the heavy rug. As in hers there was a door in each side wall.

There were three single beds in a row, about a foot high, at the broad end of the wedge. In one of the corners parallel with the stone wall, an eight-foot-wide panel formed what he supposed was a closet. From the side walls, here and there projected heavy wooden pegs, about shoulder height—primitive clothes hangers probably. Nothing else.

Somewhat disappointed, MacDougall had expected better of Scathach than this. Fleetingly he wondered if he had displaced three women or if this was a spare room. Not that he really cared. Curious, he dropped his cape and sword on a bed and crossed to the closet. He looked into the open end and received one of the shocks of his life.

Plumbing! Copper pipes and running water!

Magic he could accept without question; invisibility, demons, new bodies supplied by Lucifer—none of these caused him problems. But a sort of bathroom on the fourth floor of a tower at least fourteen centuries old? That must mean some sort of pump to raise the water to the top of the tower. Impossible!

With his engineer's eye he examined the equipment. It was primitive to say the least. A broad copper basin set against the stone wall with a waste pipe that curved over to the wall and vanished through the floor. The water supply came through a smaller pipe from the floor above, ending in a large U; the open end was covered by a cup-shaped baffle that directed the water into the bowl. A similar arrangement supplied the necessary receptacle. Prodigal with their water—but it worked! There was even a mirror on the wall, a sheet of polished silver.

A sudden revolting picture formed of the sewage pouring into one side of the stream to be pumped back up on the other. Surely whoever had the ingenuity to plan this system would have provided for a safe way to dispose of the waste, probably a conduit running out to sea.

There remained the major mystery. How did the water get to the top of the tower? He had a sudden fanciful picture of an endless column of slaves carrying pails of water up one spiral stairway, emptying them into an open tank, and descending another. Around and around and around. Maybe he could find out.

Out in the hallway he called, "Guard!"

Instantly one of the girls appeared from the other side of the stair tower. "Yes, my lord." She was smiling eagerly, anticipation in her eyes.

"Tell me," MacDougall said, all business, "how does the water get to the top of the tower?"

She stared blankly at Alan. "The water—?"

MacDougall laughed. "I know it sounds crazy—but there's running water in my room, and I wonder how it is raised to the top of the tower."

The Guard gave a faint shrug, then glanced thoughtfully to right and left, as if trying to orient herself. "Yours is room five," she said to herself. "Why, you should be able to see from your window."

MacDougall held open the bedroom door. "Show me."

The girl glanced uncertainly at Alan, then slowly entered. "I fear I should not—"

"Oh, come now. Just take a moment, and this is business."

Hesitantly she led him to the narrow window and pointed out to her left. Crowding close, MacDougall saw a massive chain moving up at a forty-five-degree angle toward the top of the tower. Bronze pails filled with water appeared to be welded at intervals to the side of the chain. Nearer the wall at a lesser angle, the upended vessels descended. Never had he seen anything like it.

"The water goes up," she explained uncertainly, "empties into a big—dish, then comes straight down close to the side of the tower—no, the empty pails do— into the river where they fill up, and go back up again. I think that's the way."

"But what supplies the power?"

"Women—many women who pull and pull and pull. It is hard work. I am glad I am a Guard . . . But the Queen and those in the tower must have water."

Alan put an arm around her shoulders and squeezed. "Thank you for being so helpful. I shall remember you." On sudden impulse he stooped and gave her a fervent kiss. "But now you'd better leave."

The girl looked confused and her eyes sparkled. "Yes —I could be lashed." Hastily she crossed to the door and held it open, then turned and said, "My name is Sorcha, and if I can help—in *any* way—" Reluctantly she closed the door behind her.

MacDougall grinned broadly. That, he thought, was a dirty trick. Too much wine. He certainly need not lack company if he wanted it. But not fourteen-hundred-year-olds with bodies by Lucifer.

He moved back to the window, watching the endlessly moving chain, then glanced at the landscape across the river, a succession of rounded pillows of green foliage, the treetops of the rowan groves mentioned by Brendah. About midway, projecting well above the trees, a slender black spire pointed skyward, on its tip what appeared to be an Egyptian ankh. Evidently it was the Temple she had referred to.

Turning away, he hung his cape and sword on pegs in the wall, then sat on one of the beds. He noticed the absence of chairs; logical, he supposed, if Guards normally slept here. Only spartan necessities. One stood up or one lay down to sleep.

Sleep. That's what he planned to do. But first the Bard! Instantly he felt the familiar thought pattern.

"Taliesin, finally I am alone in my room. I've had a very interesting time with the Sorceress. She's the soul of hospitality—though her sincerity may be suspect. Not surprisingly, she's interested in the Gate and my ability to go through it. I told her it means death, but I'm certain she doesn't believe me. Oh—a first for your world. She tried to make me drunk. Not successfully.

"But what happened to you?"

"Very little," the Bard responded. *"I found ideal sleeping quarters. No chance whatever of being disturbed; and the kitchen is just a level below me. On the third level there are two rooms that from their appearance have not been used in a very long time."* Amusement was evident in Taliesin's thought. *"Two torture chambers."*

"Torture chambers?" The idea was incredible. *"You can't meant it!"*

"Indeed; and since they no longer seem to be in use, they are perfect for my purpose. After all, I can't maintain invisibility or a shape-change while I sleep. I have borrowed a few mats and covers from unoccupied rooms on the fourth level and, using one of the big tables or an oven for a bed, I'll be quite comfortable. When not using the bedding I will hide it in one of the chests which, I imagine, at one time held victims in very uncomfortable positions. Excellent quarters. Tomorrow, unless you have plans for me, I shall do some exploring." Again Alan felt the Bard's amusement. *"Tomorrow! You have me think-*

ing in your terms. Here we have perpetual today."

"*Enjoy your exploration*," Alan replied. "*I am certain the Queen has plans for me until and beyond the next sleep. So—sleep well amid your delightful surroundings.*"

"*And may your slumbers be undisturbed.*" With the words Taliesin severed mental connection.

Alan thought of the lockless doors and grasped his armlet. "Lord and Lady, I need uninterrupted sleep. Will you be alert and keep out intruders?"

"We are always alert. No one will disturb you. Sleep in peace—if you can."

He stood up and stretched, found a towel and a bar of motel soap in a compartment in his cape, as well as a toothbrush, and repaired to the "bathroom." Finishing there, he wondered if he should undress? Enough, he decided, to remove jacket and boots.

As MacDougall stretched out on the bed, his eyelids closed heavily and his body slumped. Only then did he realize how tired he was. He was exhausted. It had been a full day. One day? Enough had happened to fill three normal days. Starting with the nightmare attack in his bed on the Cameron farm, he had been in constant motion. He started reviewing all that had happened, but his thoughts became confused, occurrences merging in a dreamlike, disordered fashion. And out of the mental melange came a familiar voice. It was Danu, the Mother Goddess, for whom the *Tuatha de Danann* were named.

"*I advise caution*," she said quietly. "*I feel this trip should not be made. Although we know that Alan Mac-Dougall has returned to this world as Dagda has reported, we should remember that naught but grief has come of attempts to interfere with his movements. I say, let him alone.*"

Manannan, god of the sea, answered impatiently, "*I am sorry, Grandmother, but I have decided to visit this third island on the* Wave Sweeper. *Ignoring MacDou-*

gall, there is a new land to explore. No doubt we shall come to another imaginary edge of the world west of Ochren, but it, too, can be crossed.

"Nine others can go with me. Beli will go. So will Pryderi representing King Arawn. And so will Balor. The four of us have a score to settle with this trouble-maker. Then there will be two of my Druids and two of Beli's. I have room for two more."

"I should like to go," Nuada announced promptly. *"I want to see this island; and though I don't have the same compelling interest in MacDougall that the four of you have, I find him irritating and should like to send him back where he came from."*

"If I have my way," a deep voice commented, *"it will be for burial."* It was the voice of Beli, god of the Un-derworld.

"Very well," Manannan announced abruptly. *"Since Dagda is not interested in going with us, I will include as the tenth Mathonwy, Master Magician, who directs my Druids. Is there any further discussion concerning the coming journey?"*

As the full import of what MacDougall had heard dur-ing his uncanny and unwitting eavesdropping on the *Tuatha de Danann* fully registered, the voice faded and vanished. Alan was awake.

He lay with closed eyes, his thoughts dwelling on this new development. First the Sorceress Scathach; then the demon Amaruduk; and now his four worst enemies from Ochren and Tartarus—all converging on one lone Scot. He gave a sudden mirthless laugh and rolled over on his side. Let 'em come.

For the moment nothing mattered but sleep.

CHAPTER 4

Conducted Tour

Alan MacDougall's sleep was less than peaceful. Not visitors but dreams disturbed his slumbers—a confusion and profusion of dreams, spawned, it seemed, by all that had happened since his arrival in Scath. There was a weird order to his dream sequence, as if he were subconsciously reliving his adventures. He slashed his way through snakelike vines that grew faster than he could cut them. He ran through endless dark tunnels pursued by a black cloud that contained the bloated, twisted figure of Amaruduk. He gyrated madly around a bloodstone monolith hemmed in by a transparent, suffocating mass of the Daughters of Lilith. Hovering over all, smiling malevolently from a luminous cloud, shone a distorted image of Scathach clutching a flagon of wine. And in the distance, skimming across the sea, came the four who hated him—Manannan, Beli, Balor, and Pryderi—brandishing gleaming swords.

When a sharp rapping on the door awakened him, he felt as if he had not slept at all.

"Yes?" he called out.

"The Queen requests that you join her at breakfast." Evidently it was one of the Guards.

"Be ready as quickly as I can."

He arose, scowling, and glanced toward the window. Broad daylight, of course. It was always broad daylight here, with colorful variations. He stretched and stifled a groan. What a night! Night! Not night, but a nightmare, which he remembered all too vividly. He headed for the running water, fleetingly picturing the eternally pulling women raising an endless chain of buckets.

As he prepared for whatever lay ahead, he thought of the conference of the gods that had come to him through the fringes of sleep. Should he tell Scathach about her coming visitors, or let their arrival be a complete surprise? Telling would require an explanation—or would it? Let her speculate about his powers. He hadn't decided by the time he was ready to leave the room.

He hesitated before his cape, canteen, and sword, then strapped on the sword belt. The weapon went where he went. With a thought to Enki to secure the doors, he joined the waiting Guard. She held herself stiffly aloof.

"Not even a 'good morning'?" MacDougall exclaimed. "Anything wrong?"

"It is not allowed that I speak with you" came the subdued reply.

They reached the sixth level and halted before one of the doors. "Your Highness, the visitor is here."

"Enter, Alan MacDougall" came Scathach's voice.

In the same room from which he had retreated apparently "under the influence," he greeted the Sorceress, seated at the intimate little table. He removed his sword belt and draped it over a chair.

"No need for you to wear that here," she chided.

"It goes where I go."

As he seated himself across from her at her invitation, she said, "I trust you slept well."

"In truth, I slept poorly. I was much disturbed by dreams, a strange mixture of what happened in the forest and elsewhere, though quite distorted."

"Oh, you must tell me! I love dreams." Her face and voice expressed girlish enthusiasm. "They reveal so much. I am skilled at interpreting dreams." She became suddenly concerned. "But you have no food and you must be starved."

Instantly the woman Isla was at his elbow, placing before him unfamiliar food in a shallow golden bowl.

"Your cup," the Sorceress commented, "contains a hot beverage which you may enjoy—herbs and ground seeds blended—from the forest, of course."

Alan sipped the strange brew, slightly acrid and like nothing he had ever tasted, but quite refreshing. As he drank he thought, She's certainly playing the perfect hostess, all charm and consideration. This attitude continued during the small talk that followed, with her inserting occasional amusing anecdotes involving her subjects. Only once did she refer to any of her plans.

"When we have finished, we will visit the wonder of Scathach's Tower, a creation few eyes have ever beheld." A semireverent hush entered her voice. "There was nothing like this in the olden times. You shall see."

At the conclusion of the breakfast Scathach looked at MacDougall with an odd expression. "I hear," she said, "you had a visitor in your room after you left me."

For an instant Alan was puzzled, then understanding came. "You mean the Guard Sorcha? She wasn't a visitor. I called her in to explain the running water in my room, which I found amazing and, I quickly add, most gratifying. She explained and left. And that was that."

The Sorceress smiled. "So she told me, and I accept her story. But there will be no more visitors, no matter how innocent. I have issued orders."

MacDougall felt a flare of temper, instantly checked. It was not worth protesting. "If I really wanted company I would be very annoyed by your high-handed action, but since I don't—" He shrugged. He'd given her something to think about.

"Not all my vision was dream." MacDougall paused, holding her gaze with his own. "It was revealed to me that you will be receiving visitors from the other islands, four of them gods whom you may know. They will arrive in the copper coracle, the *Wave Sweeper*. The gods, of course, will include Manannan, Lord of the sea, master of the ship. There will be Nuada, King of the *Tuatha de Danann*; Beli, god of the Underworld; and Balor, god of the Fomorians. Also in the group will be Pryderi, jailer of Ochren, and Mathonwy, Master Magician. Four master Druids will complete the party."

As he spoke, wonder grew on the face of the Sorceress, wonder and unbelief. He continued talking.

"If you knew him long ago you would not recognize Balor. He still wears a golden eye patch, but his eye no longer slays, and he has a new body. He died a second time; and I suppose one would say I had something to do with it. And Beli—he has reason to remember me. He was once keeper of a fire-breathing dragon, until I released it. It should be an interesting visit."

When finally he halted she exclaimed, "How do you know all this? You say it was revealed to you. By whom? Or can you foresee things to come?"

Alan smiled inscrutably. Keep her guessing. "This may not be revealed."

"Why are they coming? Why *now*, after all these centuries? *When* are they coming? You have spoken before of these other islands. Do they really exist? You mention Manannan—I knew him well." Her dark eyes bored intensely into his. "Are you certain your revelation was not more dreaming?"

Under the barrage of questions, MacDougall merely

shrugged. "Believe me or not, as you wish. As to why they are coming—why now—I suppose I am the reason. Three of the four gods hate me and seek my death. They thought I had died, only recently learning I still live and have returned to their world. They would go to any lengths to destroy me. As to when, this was not revealed."

Still unconvinced, Scathach demanded, "How did they learn you are here? Or do they, too, receive revelations?" She shook her head impatiently. "If they come, they will receive a warm welcome from my Guards. You are my guest and, as my guest, you will receive my protection. I do know or know of the gods you name, and if they appear I shall recognize them. And truthfully, I shall be surprised."

Impatiently she stood up, seeming to brush aside a minor annoyance. Her expression changed to one of deep fervor. "And now you will see what I promised, something most important to you."

Alan stood up with her, thinking, So be it. In due time she would learn. But he'd not count on her protection. He knew his foes, and he'd look out for himself.

She drew aside a hanging in one corner to reveal a narrow stairway leading to the floor above, something he had not suspected was there. A seventh floor. Interesting. Accessible only through Scathach's apartment.

They climbed the stairs to a wide corridor that circled the outer stone wall, at its center a circular room with walls of carefully shaped black stones, fitted together with the precision of a skilled lapidary. Indeed, Alan could see no sign of mortar or cement, just a perfect meshing of every stone. Directly across from the head of the stairs, a narrow bronze door was set in the wall, the surface a maze of intricate symbols. Alan was reminded of the Gates in the Highland tower.

Scathach halted before the door and said softly, "May we enter?"

As if in response, the door swung open, and the Sorceress motioned for MacDougall to lead the way. She followed a step behind him, and the door closed.

Never since his initial passage through that unnatural Gate into Tartarus had Alan felt so strongly the weight of an evil personality; not even in the Temple of Lucifer in Falias, in Arawn's castle in Ochren, or in Annwn, when the cloud of eternally whispering souls had swept by their perch in the darkness, had the awareness of an evil presence been so strong. Evil had been there as an atmosphere. Here it was personified.

The room was a black cylinder, its upper end curving into a dome with a two-foot-wide aperture in the center. Beyond it was the sky, and the cold auroral light came through the opening, the only light in the chamber. The beam fell on an image in the middle of the room, squarely facing the doorway, standing at least two feet taller than Alan.

He stared at the image in fascination. The face was familiar, the model for the lapis lazuli pendants that Scathach and her guards wore. The features were a blend of the feline and human and somehow recognizably female. The eyes were two huge, glittering, faceted emeralds or, more likely according to their internal fire, matching green diamonds. Those eyes drew him; it required a conscious effort to tear his gaze away. Ivory-white fangs were bared in a half smile, half snarl, lips curled back.

The figure itself, a high-breasted female standing erect, was a grotesque merging of bird and beast. The arms, curving outward, were feathered and taloned; and clutched in the talons, wrapped and coiled about arms and body, was a great two-headed serpent of gold. The angular tips of folded wings thrust above rounded shoulders. A smooth torso and lean thighs, feathered lower limbs, and taloned feet completed the strange, exotic image.

The statue, mounted on a round gold base half a foot high, had been carved from a single massive block of blue lapis lazuli, shot through profusely with golden threads and veins and masses. It was the creation of a master, every minute detail skillfully wrought, reminding MacDougall of the exquisite workmanship of his armlet.

Ridiculous figure, Alan tried to tell himself; but the grotesque face held his gaze with hypnotic intensity. The shifting lights of the aurora did strange things to its features, creating the impression of movement, of changing expression. And that feeling of an evil presence persisted. Perhaps if he probed—

"Sit beside me." Scathach's hushed voice checked the thought. He glanced where she indicated and, for the first time, noticed a succession of black stone slabs projecting from the wall at a comfortable sitting height, circling the room. As the two seated themselves side by side, Alan noticed that she had chosen a spot directly facing the monstrous figure.

"That is Lamashtu," the Sorceress declared softly. "She appears to be mere stone and metal, but she is far more. The Lord of Light has given her vast powers upon which I as her priestess may draw. She will awaken and restore your memory of the lives you have lived. Not now; the Daughters of Calatin—"

Scathach stopped short as her great lapis lazuli pendant seemed suddenly to burst into life, glowing with internal fire. With a look of annoyance on her face she closed her eyes, seeming to listen.

MacDougall looked back at the image called Lamashtu; to mind came the serpent-gods. "Lady Inanna," he thought tensely, "can you tell me what, if anything, makes that thing tick?"

There followed a momentary delay; then a sudden mental exclamation exploded in Alan's mind: "Ereshkigal! Queen of the Nether World, Queen of the Great

Below! My self-sister whom I hate—who brought on all my woes—is imprisoned in that rock!"

Incredulous, MacDougall stared at the brilliant green eyes and he felt a sudden dread. No wonder he had sensed an evil personality when he entered this room. He remembered vividly the tale the Lady Inanna had told of her visit to the Nether World, of her shaming and death at the hands of her "self-sister," of her restoration by the Lord Enki, and all that followed. Ereshkigal, too, was imprisoned!

The Sorceress stood up suddenly, announcing, "That hellish horde of Amaruduk—but you would not be interested." She hastened toward the stairway. "I will have Isla escort you to my living room where you will await my joining you. She will serve you wine, which I suggest you drink in moderation."

As he followed Scathach down the stairs MacDougall grinned at her admonition. She wanted him to remain sober. He thought of her reference to "that hellish horde of Amaruduk." This must be one of the demon's nuisance raids that Brendah had mentioned. He watched the Sorceress hasten through the dining area and one of the doorways, going, Alan supposed, to wherever she kept the device she used for spying and image-projection.

Isla ushered him into the Queen's living room where, on a perverse impulse, he seated himself in the great chair. In moments the maid placed a flagon of wine and a goblet on the little table at his elbow, poured his first drink, and withdrew.

He leaned back and frowned as he realized he continued to follow Scathach's orders. What of his resolution to follow his own course? He took a sip of wine. Why not try a little rebellion? But first he wanted some answers. He addressed the serpent-gods.

"Lady Inanna and Lord Enki, what am I getting into? First Amaruduk from ancient Sumer, and now Ereshkigal. Dealing with the gods of old Britain as I did on Tartarus and Ochren—man-made gods, we might call them —was one thing. But these demons, I confess, disturb me. This self-sister of yours, my Lady, might be a very rough playmate."

"You forget," Lord Enki said ironically, "you have been dealing with two from Sumer from the moment you put on the armlet. I admit that Ereshkigal surprised me, the last of the ancients I expected to find here, though not really illogical."

"And of all places," Inanna exclaimed, "the proud one locked in a stone statue in a dark room! How appropriate. She always preferred darkness. And that lovely image, so very like her nature."

"I am puzzled," Enki observed, "by the two-headed serpent wrapped around the statue. Does it have significance for the Ereshkigal presence, hence reference to us; or is it part of Lamashtu? Interesting to speculate."

"Lamashtu," Alan commented. "Is that another of the Sumerian goddesses?"

"Not an important one," Enki answered, "though one of the most feared in the mountains and deserts where she lived. Utterly evil, she terrorized pregnant women and children. This was her delight. They called her the mountain devil."

Inanna added thoughtfully, "Ereshkigal might well have been given Lamashtu's form after our visit to the Nether World. We displeased the Bright One with the undoing of his dividing; but my darling self-sister made a major contribution to the trouble through her hatred of me. We were imprisoned in the armlet; and it would be logical for Ereshkigal to have received comparable treatment. If for a time she acted as Lamashtu, what a blow for the Queen of the Underworld with her countless subjects to become a she-devil wandering about alone frightening children. And afterward, a stone statue."

"But that would mean," Alan objected, "that this

tower was erected long before Scathach's day in Britain."

"Not strange at all, since Tartarus was created originally long before its present dwellers were sent there, as you know. Nor does any of this have bearing on the age of Lamashtu's image. Time means nothing where it is a variable and has no end."

Lord Enki's thought became pensive. "I well remember the first wearer of the armlet—Naram-Sin, grandson of Sargon of Akkad, King of Sumer and Akkad. He was a great general and ruler whose empire stretched from the mountains to the sea. He never knew the source of his skill and power. But like those that followed, he died."

Alan felt a sudden chill. Was death the only way to shed the armlet? He thought of the varied arms the twinned serpents had adorned, now crumbled to dust, and it gave him a strange feeling. Hastily he changed the subject.

"This is all very interesting, but my concern at the moment is whether or not I want to try whatever Scathach is suggesting, something concerning Lamashtu that is supposed to restore memory of former lives I reputedly lived. Since I know Ereshkigal occupies the statue, I find the idea unappealing, to say the least."

"We cannot advise you." Lord Enki's thought was solemn. "The decision must be yours. But we can guarantee one thing. Should you make this venture, Ereshkigal cannot possess you. This is not possible, else she would have left her prison long ago. As it is impossible for us. But beyond that we can give you no assurance."

Impatiently Inanna added, "We cannot make specific promises, but I personally will see that my self-sister's powers are limited. As yet, I believe, she has no knowledge of our presence. She will learn quickly enough as she feels our might."

At that moment a door opened and Scathach entered.

A look of annoyance, quickly masked, crossed her face.

"I trust you found the Queen's chair comfortable," she said with exaggerated politeness.

"Indeed, most comfortable." MacDougall stood up, a golden goblet in his hand. "I have been enjoying your wine—in moderation, of course." He bowed with a flourish. "Your chair, your Highness."

Scathach remained standing. "Come," she said briskly. "We return to the presence of Lamashtu to restore your memory. I will summon—"

"I don't think so," Alan interrupted. "I have lost all interest in your plan since seeing that ugly statue. Besides which, I don't really believe I lived any past lives. I've decided I want to see the rest of your castle. Remember, you promised a tour. And these rooms become quite confining." This was open defiance, and MacDougall knew it.

During the shocked silence that followed, he faced the Sorceress, smiling faintly, though his pulse quickened perceptibly. "Where shall we begin?"

For timeless moments, Scathach's luminous black eyes blazed into his; her jaws locked, lips stiffened; then the long-lashed eyelids lowered to hide her wrath, and briefly her face lost all expression.

"There is no need for haste, of course," she said, not quite convincingly. "Time means nothing on Scath. What matters it if our adventure follows one sleep or another? But surely you must be curious about your seeming to recognize me when you first saw my image. Do not deny it. I saw it on your face. Even as I knew you.

"But, I repeat, there is no need for haste. Just as there is no reason for you to be repelled by the strange form of Lamashtu. The outward shape, wrought by some ancient artist of great skill, is not important; the power within is all that matters. But enough of this. We will speak further about it after you have had time to reconsider.

"Now you shall see my castle."

As they passed through the rest of the sixth level—the dining room, Isla's quarters, the room of mirrors, and Scathach's bedroom, five rooms in all—the Queen gave an animated commentary. Alan made proper response, though, in fact, except for the room of mirrors, he had little interest in the tour, admitting to himself with chagrin that Scathach had won that round. He had wanted to precipitate some sort of crisis, and she had yielded without an argument. Stubbornly he thought she couldn't change his mind about the session with Lamashtu.

They descended to the fifth level, the Queen's personal Guards joining them, one leading the way, the other following. Before they entered the first room the Sorceress said, "Here are the rooms of the three Daughters of Calatin. They are my helpers in conducting the affairs of Scath. They, too, will play a part when finally you visit Lamashtu. Since they are in this room you shall meet them, and then we shall pass on."

Alan recalled Scathach's reference during the search to the Three Sisters who had indicated where he was to be found. These must be they.

She nodded to one of the Tower Guards who tapped on the door and announced: "Queen Scathach!"

The door opened, and they entered the room containing a bed, a single massive chair, and the familiar corner cubicle. There was also as ugly a woman as Alan had ever seen. Previously he had decided that all the bodies supplied by Lucifer for Scath had been designed with beauty in mind; now he changed his opinion. She was wizened, with a sharp, protruding chin, prominent hawk-beak nose, small, close-set green eyes, and long, stringy gray hair—a caricature of a conventional witch.

At their entry, the door to the next room opened and an exact copy of the first woman appeared. She said in a metallic voice, "Sister is busy in the workroom."

Introducing MacDougall, Scathach commented,

"These are two of the three Daughters of Calatin. Their names? So far as I know, they have none. They work as one, they appear as one, and none on Scath, except their Queen, has greater knowledge of the magic arts. Two of their five rooms are workshops; but we will not disturb their labors." They withdrew.

As they halted on the fourth level Scathach commented, "You slept in room five on this floor; and all the rooms are alike. These are rarely used except when, for some reason, a number of the Druidesses remain in the castle during a time of sleep."

They descended to the third, and again Scathach paused. "On this level we occasionally carry on activities that would hardly interest you. It would be unwise for you—"

"You mean the torture chambers," MacDougall said casually. "As you wish. I have little interest in such barbaric practices." In truth, he wanted to see Taliesin's strange quarters, the Bard being absent.

The eyes of the Sorceress widened. "How do you know—?" She stopped short. "You amaze me, Alan MacDougall. Maybe you *do* know about the coming of the *Wave Sweeper* and her passengers. On second thought it might be well for you to see these chambers. Nothing shall be concealed from you."

Which, MacDougall thought, was nonsense. There was much in Scath he would never see, if the Sorceress had her way.

Unlike the other floors, here there were only two doors on opposite sides of the stairwell giving entrance to the rooms. The one before them opened, apparently on mental command of the Sorceress. There were no lamps, only the narrow windows admitting the light of the aurora; hence the room was in semidarkness. It was large, like a half-slice of melon with a bite out of the straight edge. As his eyes adjusted to the lesser light,

Alan suddenly realized that a less appropriate comparison could hardly have been drawn.

A rack was the first instrument he recognized—not that he had ever seen one; remembered pictures helped him identify the long bed of planks, the bars at each end, the chains and pulleys. Nearby was a bed of sharp spikes, each fully four inches in length; suspended above it was another with downward projecting points, and beside it stacks of stone weights of various sizes. Here and there, chains dangled from the ceiling, some with loops at their ends, others terminating in great sharp-pointed hooks. He noticed stone grates where fires obviously had been built and near them soot-blackened iron boots. There were long tables, darkly stained, and beside them were cabinets filled with all manner of tools whose use Alan did not care to imagine. At the far end, beneath one of the windows, he saw what appeared to be two great ovens, with fire chambers dark and smoke-blackened, beneath them.

He turned from his inspection to stare askance at Scathach. She had been watching him with a grim smile.

"You understand, there is little occasion now for the use of such devices. There was a time when ambitions awakened, but we have few disciplinary problems now. Strict rules have been established, and justice is swift and sure."

"There is another room on the other side of the stairwell. Is that—?"

"Another room like this? Yes, but with different instruments." Smiling slyly, she asked, "Would you see more?"

"I have seen more than enough." With a touch of scorn he added, "I should think the exercise of a little magic would make this sort of physical effort unnecessary."

"There are some among us," she answered casually,

"who felt this was more effective as a deterrent for others."

The second level, like the third, was divided into two large rooms, the dining area for the tower staff and a kitchen, with a lounging room between them. The first, as Alan knew, was devoted entirely to sleeping quarters for the Tower Guard.

"There is another room underground," Scathach said. "It is a storage area for reserve arms, utensils, and the like. There are many bars of what we once considered precious metal, but of course they have no real value here. Beneath the storage chamber are dungeons, now rarely used. You may see these if you wish—"

Hastily Alan responded, "I have seen all I want to see."

As they started back up the spiral stairway, the Queen of Scath said firmly, "I have given you the tour I promised, so now I insist that you tell me of your experiences in the forest." There was a cold note in her voice. "I will not accept a refusal."

They were ascending to the third level as she spoke, and MacDougall pictured the tools of torture behind the walls. Better grant her wish, he thought; after all, he would only tell what he wanted to.

"Very well, your highness."

Seated comfortably in the Queen's living room with a goblet of wine at hand, he began his story. He spoke of his entry into the thicket, making only the barest reference to the Gate and saying nothing about the density of the undergrowth or the Gate's position despite her persistent questions. He followed with his first sight of the fruit pickers, his capture and subsequent escape.

When he came to the scene in the tunnel room and his meeting with Amaruduk, he omitted any mention of the attack of the demon, saying only that he guided him through the tunnel maze to thwart Scathach. The Queen pressed for more details, but Alan guilelessly insisted he had nothing more to add. He spoke of wandering through the forest, of several near misses by the searching Brendah.

He moved on to his wandering into the Grove of Spirits and his unwilling participation in the strange dance around the monolith. This held the full attention of the Sorceress, leading to numerous questions. It was evident that she and her subjects had little to do with the Ghosts, as they thought of them. He omitted all mention of Amaruduk.

He completed his recital with his joining Brendah at the Well of Darkness and his decision to accompany her to Scathach's Tower. He smiled brightly at the Sorceress.

"You may have noticed my failure to mention several very interesting appearances of a strikingly beautiful face set against a gray cloud that seemed to be earnestly seeking but only occasionally finding an elusive fugitive. You can have no idea how close you came to me, discovery prevented only by my invisibility. It was an interesting game until I became weary of the playing."

A dangerous glint appeared in Scathach's eyes. "If I had not been the soul of patience—"

She stopped short as the blue lapis pendant on her breast again burst into its lambent glow. She seemed to listen intently while the jewel pulsed rhythmically. Frowning, she looked strangely at MacDougall, then finally said in somber tones, "Put her in the dungeon until I have time to deal with her. Dismissed." The light in the pendant died.

"Well," she began, "that is interesting. Very interesting. My special Guards, stationed inside the rooms on either side of yours, heard a faint rapping on your door and came out into the hallway to find the Guard Brendah outside your room. She should have been sleeping, just having come off duty. Have you any explanation?"

Alan shook his head in amazement. "I find the whole

thing unbelievable. Her actions were utterly stupid, whatever her reason, in view of your orders making visitors off limits. Surely she must have known—"

"Evidently she did not know, and perhaps with reason. She had been on duty as relief, spending time at various posts, and it appears no one told her of the order when her rest period came." Suspiciously she added, "But why should she seek to see you?"

MacDougall shrugged. "It seems so senseless. I certainly can't explain it." It *was* stupid, he thought. He could see no logic in her actions.

"And now," Scathach said firmly, "it is time for us to go back to the tower room. Surely you are not afraid of a stone image." She arose and, taking his hands, drew him up to face her. Her lips formed her most alluring smile. "Or do you fear learning that we actually were lovers in past ages?"

MacDougall closed his eyes. No denying it, Scathach was beautiful and she could cast more than one kind of spell. He thought of Elspeth Cameron and opened his eyes; bringing the Queen's hands together, he released his own.

"I fear neither of these. And I have decided. I want some answers. So I'll let Lamashtu do her worst. I doubt that anything will make me believe I have lived earlier lives; but if I learn nothing else, at least I'll know whether or not I can be—" He halted, wanting to say "hypnotized," but there was no word with that meaning in this tongue. "Can be made to see things," he concluded. It was not Lamashtu he feared; it was Ereshkigal.

Visibly eager now, Scathach motioned for him to be seated, sank into her own chair, then briefly closed her eyes. Upon opening them she said, "I have summoned the Daughters of Calatin and seven of the Druidesses. All play a part in the ritual."

Hocus-pocus, Alan told himself. At least it should be interesting.

Scathach began to talk in an aimless fashion, apparently out of tension and repressed excitement. "It will be most gratifying when you, too, remember those days in the long ago. They were exciting times. Not like the eternal sameness of this place. In those days power meant something. Whatever is delaying those women? Especially the Three. They are only one level away—"

Sounds of commotion in the corridor filtered into the room. There were muffled voices, then silence.

"The Daughters of Calatin have come and are going directly to the shrine of Lamashtu. They know why they were summoned. And now we await the seven."

Shrine of Lamashtu! What was he getting into? Shrines! Behind Lamashtu was the one-time Queen of the Underworld, a powerful demon. Anyway, there was no turning back. He looked quizzically at Scathach.

"Seems to be a complicated process, this supposed restoration of my memory."

Somewhat stiffly Scathach answered, "All must be done properly and in order. One never questions the Powers. Why are you so skeptical? But you will learn."

Silence followed, broken finally by further commotion in the hallway. When this had subsided the Queen of Scath stood up, and MacDougall rose with her. Without speaking, she walked purposefully into the dining room, swept aside the curtain, and mounted the stairway. Mac-Dougall came behind her.

Now that the moment had come for this experience to begin, whatever it might be, he didn't feel at all confident or heroic. Damn it—he was scared! Sticking his neck out like an idiot, facing Ereshkigal!

"Here I go, Lady Inanna," he sent the thought. "I hope you two are equal to the occasion. I'm not."

The Lord Enki commented reprovingly, "Losing your courage is the worst thing that can happen. Where is that

Scots stubbornness of yours? Just remember—we are three, and there is only one Ereshkigal."

"And we have strong personal reasons," Inanna added, "for assuring not only your survival, but your victory."

With spirits rising, Alan climbed the stairs behind the Sorceress. Three! After all, together they had outwitted Balor and Morrigu, Manannan and Beli and all of his Druids. Except for an unpredictable madman, they had beaten them all—even Ahriman.

Side by side, MacDougall and Scathach entered the black chamber. As before, his gaze was drawn by the glittering green eyes of the grotesque idol; but with conscious effort, he looked away, scanning the room.

There were additions to the contents, other than the women. Directly before him, about midway between closed door and the image, stood a round, flat-topped pillar of black stone, seat high. To right and left, slightly taller, were triangular blocks of the same material. On them burned three tall candles. Beside each, facing the statue, knelt one of the three Daughters of Calatin. The other witch, he vaguely saw, was in an identical position behind Lamashtu. And in a half circle on the black slabs projecting from the wall sat the seven Druidesses in their black robes, faces alone eerily visible in the flickering flames of the candles, the auroral light doing little to reveal them.

The opening in the ceiling was much narrower now than during Alan's first visit, less than six inches across, giving an uncertain spotlight effect to the beam that shone down on the idol and casting strange shadows, but failing to dim the brilliance of the green eyes. Their fire seemed to come from an internal source.

MacDougall felt Scathach's hand on his arm. "Sit," she said softly, indicating the round pillar. With reluctance he did so, his eyes automatically turning to the green gems. As a tangible hush fell over the chamber, he sensed that the Sorceress stood directly behind him, only inches away. An attempt to shrug off the entire strange situation failed miserably.

The silence held interminably, the tension mounting. Alan realized he was holding his breath and forced himself to breathe normally.

When the stillness had become almost unbearable, the voice of Scathach intoned solemnly: "In the name of Lucifer, the Lord of Power, of Wisdom, and of Death."

MacDougall felt a sudden chill. This was not a game. He was not really religious, but Lucifer—Satan—existed; and he didn't belong here! Yet here he was. Whatever was going to happen, he hoped it would happen quickly.

He heard the nearest Druidess chant, an echo of Scathach's solemnity in her voice: "Lamashtu, Day of Life, born of Ur."

Immediately the next one followed: "Day of Bright Face, Nursling of Kish." And the next: "Day of Delight, Grown up in Eridu." And on around the half circle: Day of Plenty, Gracious One of Nippur; Day of Good Fortune, Exalted Judge of Lagash; Day that has given life to him who is smitten, Protector of Shuruppak.

The last Druidess chanted: "Oh, Lamashtu, be conjured by Enlil; be conjured by Ea, by Nergal, Nusku, and Lutarak—may this one remember."

As they ceased their chanting one of the Three Witches spoke, a voice old and rasping. "We adjure you by the Son of the Morning"; the second continued, "We beseech you by the One Who Excels in Strength"; the third, "We entreat you by the Master of the Flame"; and again the first, "We adjure you by the Master of All Waters"; the second, "We beseech you by the Overthrower"; the third, "We entreat you by the Lord of all Wisdom"; and finally the seventh conjuring, "Lamashtu, we adjure you by the Sevenfold One—may this man remember!"

In a hushed voice the Sorceress Scathach added, "May he return to the times when the lands were young, when we walked in them together. Lamashtu, I command you!"

Now from the seven Druidesses and the three Daughters of Calatin came a low chorus, doleful, little more than a monotone. Fascinated, Alan listened, trying to catch the words. There were syllables, but none that he could identify as any language he had ever heard. There was much repetition and frequent use of labials; and as the chorus grew louder and faster, filled with frenzy, MacDougall thought of it as an unintelligible cacophony, plain gibberish—a babble. It rose in a wild crescendo, then slowly faded until it was little more than an echo, but with its rhythm persisting and having an almost hypnotic effect.

During all of this, his gaze never left the glittering green eyes of Lamashtu. Futilely he tried to look away and failed even in an attempt to blink. His eyes grew dry and began to smart. He felt motion about his head and heard the faint words of the Sorceress: "Rest, rest your eyes. They burn, burn, and must be rested."

He tried again to close his eyes, then concentrated on his peripheral vision; he saw fingers moving at right and left like sentient things, long and white and graceful. Their movements were rhythmic, seeming to be echoed in the swaying of the candle flames at the edge of his sight. And the voice droned on. "Rest, rest" became "Sleep, sleep."

Strange, strange—a weaving of sound and motion and green, green orbs that grew and grew, becoming a misty haze. Out of it came a sound, a voice, harsh and cold and domineering. . . .

CHAPTER 5

Spell of the Sorceress

"...*March, you ill-begotten sons of Nergal, march!* Mighty warriors you call yourselves because you slew a few of the sheep of Shuruppak, a city without a wall. Yet you cringe before a little rain. March!"

Ziusudra glared in hatred at the broad back of King Etana of Kish, riding in triumph on his four-wheeled chariot while he howled at his men because they moved too slowly through the knee-deep flood. Sheep, were they, the dwellers in Shuruppak? Sheep with fangs and claws! Not cheaply had victory come to the raiders who attacked without warning in the sodden gray of a stormy dawn. A full half of the marauders had fallen, to be swept away in the rushing waters. But—bitterly he berated himself for the hundredth time—he was their prize! He, Ziusudra, son of King Shuruppak of the city that bore his name, locked in a massive square neck stock, the corners chained to the back of the chariot, and hands chained behind his back. Wearily he slogged along in the flood, like the two score prisoners plodding behind him. They were chained together, hemmed in by spear-men—stalwart warriors of his city, destined for slavery.

King Etana turned and looked gloatingly down at his prize prisoner. The driving rain poured from his polished gold helmet, streams washing his dark and heavily whis-kered face.

"Ziusudra, King's son—what a lovely picture! I think for ransom I shall demand thrice your weight in gold. Or perchance the gods who dwell in the great Tower of Kish may desire a royal sacrifice. The Oracles will decide." King Etana cocked his head to one side. "Has the Prince of Shuruppak nothing to say?"

With hatred and loathing obvious in his glare, and with the torrent beating on his uptilted face, for answer Ziusudra noisily cleared his throat and spat into the churning waters.

For an instant Etana's spear hand rose menacingly; but a sudden lurch of the chariot sent him sprawling as one of the wheels sank into a deep rut. Struggling erect, he vented his anger on the driver who was fighting to control the team of four asses. Then even the King seemed to weary of speech as the rain intensified, the blinding sheet of water driving slantingly down, making breathing difficult.

Every man was drenched to the skin; the heavy felt kilts were soaked to capacity, weighing like lead. Fortu-nate were the foot soldiers, bare to the waist, unlike the King with a heavy felt shawl, and his protective armor, which must be a wearying burden, draped over one shoulder and crossing under the other arm.

Staring into the downpour and slogging ahead dog-gedly through the racing current, a stream where a road had been, Ziusudra sought for a glimpse of the Tower of Kish. This, the wonder of the world, would be his first sight of the walled city. There, perhaps, would be shelter and warmth, even dryness if there was dryness any-where. Never had he seen a rain like this; now was the second day of unending downpour. Which of the gods had been angered? Mayhap Inanna, goddess of storm!

At last he saw the square Tower rising dimly in the mist, its top lost among the glowering clouds, step upon tapering step, each smaller than the one beneath it, a wonder to behold. Could Etana have been the builder of so great a *ziggurat*? Grudgingly admiration awakened, but his hatred did not wane.

The tale was told that King Etana, who had no son, had caused the Tower to be built to reach to heaven where he might persuade the gods to give his wife Nanshe offspring; but that was absurd. Shuruppak, his father, a man of great wisdom, had spoken of the real purpose of the Tower; on its top in the heavens were the symbols of the holy stars, where the readers of signs and omens divined the times and seasons. There, too, close to the gods, the holy men fasted, returning after many days with no hunger or thirst but with the wisdom of the gods. Or so it was said.

At last, through the curtain of rain, Ziusudra saw the wall of Kish looming ahead, with its bedraggled guards on the great barrier of fired brick and bitumen. As the marauders approached, the high-held banner of King Etana was recognized and the double gate swung open. Instantly the flood swirled into the city where the water level was substantially lower.

"Inside fast!" King Etana bellowed; and with all possible haste, struggling to maintain footing in the treacherous currents, soldiers and prisoners crowded the opening. The last ones inside joined the guards in forcing shut the massive wood and copper barrier.

The King shouted another directive: "Lumma, see to the prisoners." An officer led the captives away with a salute, the soldiers, except for Etana's personal guard, driving them on with prodding lances. To the charioteer the King exclaimed, "The Temple!"

As they wound their way past the one-storey, boxlike

dwellings, people, cowering on some of the rooftops under improvised shelter, waved, but with little enthusiasm. At length the little group reached the great oval wall, also of fired brick, which surrounded the Temple area and the Tower itself. Here Ziusudra was released from the chariot, two soldiers taking the chains and leading him through the gate.

The Tower, the Prince saw, rose in seven square, sloping tiers, with massive outside stairways visible on first and fifth levels, indicating the probable placement of others, circling the Tower on successive levels. They crossed a second great brick-paved courtyard, deep in flood water, and came to a second curving wall and arched doorway that led to a long flight of stairs, probably a hundred steps high, which they mounted. Because of the neck stock, Ziusudra could not see the steps, which made climbing awkward and increased his anger. By the time they reached its top and crossed the terrace to the first level of the temple, he was seething.

In his fury he paid scant attention to his surroundings, barely noticing the ornate interior of the room they entered. Scores of lamps with steady yellow flames, high up on the blue walls, lighted the windowless chamber. They had nothing its equal in Shuruppak, Ziusudra thought grudgingly. And it was dry. He blinked to free his eyes of the water that persisted in trickling in tiny rivulets from his mass of black hair.

King Etana was greeted by three blue-robed priests. "Dry garments," he said briskly, and followed one of them into another room. As an afterthought he glanced at Ziusudra. "Dry his hair and beard and give him a dry kirtle. After all, he is a valuable slave, worth his weight in Shuruppak gold."

Stoically, the captive Prince submitted to the ministrations of the priests, though inwardly boiling. There would come a time of reckoning!

With the King's return, Ziusudra's humiliation began.

All of the priests and their acolytes on that level were summoned, and he was paraded before them while Etana boasted of his success during the raid on Shuruppak and of the value of his hostage, King Shuruppak's son. He spoke of the possibility of a sacrifice to Enlil, Father of the gods, or to Inanna, goddess of heavens and storm, who perhaps had sent the rain; but Ziusudra stared stonily ahead, refusing to react visibly to anything that was said.

Finally seeming to tire of his sport, King Etana directed the High Priest: "Lock him in one of the stalls reserved for sacrifices and post a guard. Tomorrow the Council will discuss our future actions. If only this accursed rain would end." He scowled and faced the High Priest. "Have you been petitioning all the gods for their favor? Prayer should be made without ceasing."

The High Priest responded in a voice too low for Ziusudra to hear, but the King's response was quite audible.

"She is? Bring her to me."

Immediately one of the priests was sent from the room to return minutes later with a lovely woman, young, of surpassing beauty in her dark splendor, the ornate gold and begemmed headdress on her full black hair, and her leopard-skin garments suggesting royalty. This impression was confirmed by King Etana's first words:

"Nanshe, why are you here? Enmerkar tells me you have not permitted the priests of Enlil, the *ishib* and the *gala*, to enter the Place of Libation and petition, nor the Place of Sacrifice. What is the meaning of this?"

The Queen Nanshe, who had entered with bowed head as befitted a woman, even though a Queen, now looked steadily at King Etana.

"I came to cry to all the gods for a son that my reproach may be lifted, and here I will remain until one of the great ones answers. Thrice seven hours have I prayed to Enlil, Father of the gods; now I will ascend to the Temple of Enki, god of wisdom. And then higher to Nintu, the Mother Goddess; and to Ninurta, god of the south wind; and to Martu the Wanderer in all the lands; and to Nanna-Sin, the moon god; and last to Inanna, Queen of the World Above. To each I will cry thrice seven hours before I leave the Mountain of the gods. Perchance one will look with favor upon me and answer my cry."

Queen Nanshe lowered her eyes and turned away. "But I am troubled. I did not sleep, yet awake I saw a vision, I dreamed a dream. I who have interpreted dreams for others dreamed a dream. And I know not—" She raised her eyes, and her gaze fell on Ziusudra for the first time. Slowly, in startled unbelief, her eyes widened, and she seemed to lose color. Her voice trailed into silence. Quickly she recovered, turned back to the King, and spoke hurriedly. "But my waking dream can have no meaning since I, the interpreter, can see no meaning in it." She bowed deeply. "If my lord permits, I will withdraw from your presence and ascend to the Temple of Enki to continue my praying."

"Your dream—" King Etana began, then seemed to change his mind. "You do well to cry to the gods. You may go; and since the god Enki is also god of the waters, ask him to withdraw the rain."

As Queen Nanshe left, the King waved toward Ziusudra. "Take him away. Remove his bonds—after you have summoned a well-armed guard; feed him, give him a mat for sleeping, and, above all, guard him well." There was more, but Ziusudra heard none of it as two priests led him away. One thought shut out every other —that startled expression on the face of the Queen, like sudden unbelieving recognition, a look, he was sure, the King had not seen. What could it mean? Could he have been part of that dream?

The room to which they led him contained no lamps, only faint light from the hallway coming through the inch-wide spaces between the heavy planks of the forward wall. Indeed, it was more of a stall than a room, logically enough since it was actually a holding pen for animals awaiting their turn at the altar of sacrifice. But it was strongly made, its door of massive planks secured with a heavy copper bolt on the outside. He could see no way of escaping. Along the back wall, a deep trough extended beneath adjoining walls, evidently the means of flushing the floor after removal of selected goats, sheep, or cattle. As nearly as he could see, his stall was clean.

Rid of the galling neck yoke and with hands freed, he began pacing about, chafing his wrists to restore circulation. He could hear the measured stride of the guard pacing back and forth before his cell. After a time, Temple acolytes brought food and water. After he had eaten, he stretched out on the felt mat and, despite his mental unrest, fell asleep.

He was awakened by the sound of voices, one a woman's. He had no idea how long he had slept, but he felt refreshed. Soundlessly he arose and moved to the wall, placing an ear at one of the cracks.

"Go!" the woman said imperiously; and Ziusudra recognized the voice of Queen Nanshe. "I was praying in the Temple of Enki and I heard footsteps behind the altar. When I investigated there was no one there, only footfalls hasting away. Again I prayed, and again I heard someone. You must investigate and find the intruder."

"But, your Highness, I dare not leave my post!"

"Go! Go! Give me your sword or even a dagger and I will remain on guard. I looked. All the priests of Enki are asleep. It must be an intruder; and if I am harmed you will answer."

"Very well." Reluctantly the soldier agreed. "Here is my sword. My mace and lance should be arms enough for me. And there can be no danger to you from the prisoner."

His retreating footfalls faded and finally vanished.

Breathless moments passed until finally the Queen spoke softly through one of the spaces, a tremor of excitement in her words.

"Ziusudra, can you hear me?"

Inches away, the Prince answered as softly. "Yes. I am awake and listening."

"I have come—" She hesitated uncertainly, then plunged on. "When I saw you with the King, I knew you. You were in my vision—you and no other! I cannot be mistaken. And in the vision you and I alone were on the top of the Tower, the Mountain of the gods. And the water—the water had risen to hide all of the city, reaching almost to the top of the Tower itself. We alone escaped!" She had become breathless with excitement.

"It was a true vision. This gift of sight has been given me, and I am never wrong. The priests have decided that you should be sacrificed to the gods of water and storm to appease their anger and thus end the flood. If I release you, will you climb to the priests' place of fasting and the holy stars, and there await my coming after the water rises higher? None will think to look for you there, nor will any expect the flood to continue rising. It is night and the rain is a river from the sky. None would see you climb."

"But," Ziusudra objected, "if I were up there several days I should starve. And the rain—"

Impatiently Nanshe interrupted. "Shelters are built into the walls, and there is food for the fasting priests. At the far end of this stall is a space for feed for the animals. You can safely hide there in this dim light, and when the guard returns I will give him his sword just in front of that opening. You will have my dagger—and he must not be able to speak of my being here. Will you do it? Quickly!"

Ziusudra did not hesitate. What had he to lose? And if her visions were correct, he had everything to gain.

"I will do it."

Even as she slid back the bolt, the Queen said hurriedly, "Do you swear it by Enlil?"

"By Enlil and all the gods in the World Above and on earth and in the Nether World I swear it."

Moments later Ziusudra had slid into the niche between the stalls, a small dagger, needle sharp, held in readiness; and the Queen Nanshe paced the hallway before his empty bolted cell. The Prince of Shuruppak now noticed she was wet, her jewels and hair awry. She had had to go outside without protection to descend from the Temple of Enki to that of Enlil. He thought of what lay ahead. It was not his preference, a blade driven from ambush; but as he thought of the men of his city—and women and children—slaughtered as they slept, all compunctions vanished. As for the Queen's vision, through all Sumer she was known for her powers of divination.

At last the heavy footfalls of the returning guard echoed through the corridor. As he approached he said almost condescendingly, "I searched everywhere, your Highness. I found no one and saw no one, which is just as well. You may return to your crying to the gods with complete safety."

As she returned his sword, Nanshe put one hand on his shoulder, turning his back toward Ziusudra. "A kiss for your faithful service," she said; and as she drew his face down to hers, the Prince of Shuruppak struck.

The soldier died with scarcely a sound; as he tottered, Ziusudra caught him under his arms. Harshly he rasped, "Quick, the bolt!"

Swiftly he dragged the still-twitching body into the stall and eased it to the floor. After removing the belt with its weapons, he strapped it around his own waist. Now armed with a dagger, a sword, and a mace, he felt more like a man. He retrieved the weapon from the soldier's back, wiped it free of blood on the man's garments, and returned it to the Queen. With the door bolted behind them, they hastened down the corridor. She led the way to the exit. Without meeting a soul, they reached the outside.

The blackness of the pit greeted them, and with it a downpour heavier than any either had ever seen. Certainly with the torrents descending in solid sheets, the idea of water rising to engulf even this great Tower no longer seemed impossible. On the terrace itself the water was knee-deep. There was no chance that they would meet anyone, nor did they. Their only difficulty lay in finding the stairway; they did so by walking into it. After groping to the top, not an easy task, Nanshe indicated the way Ziusudra should go, then vanished into the darkness.

Splashing through the black and blinding torrents, he had a momentary stab of uneasiness. What if he should walk off the edge? But the depth of water reassured him. There had to be retaining walls to dam the flood.

Following the Tower wall, he passed around a corner and, despite the slowness of his progress, reached the next stairway. Counting, he climbed it. In due course came the next, the fourth, and another, and still another, and finally the one that must lead to the very top of this man-made mountain.

The last stairway, he found, was almost impossible to ascend. In fact, before he realized the danger, he was almost swept from his feet by the powerful flow. Torrents of water poured down its face like the rapids in a mountain stream. Only by placing hands on the steps ahead and literally crawling did he manage the climb.

At the top he realized why. Moving out step by slow step, arm outstretched and hands groping, he became aware that the wall enclosing the roof was all of five feet thick, shoulder high; and the surface of the roof itself, apparently slightly pitched, poured its water as down a chute onto the stairs. This ensured a relatively dry surface no matter how heavy the downpour.

He remembered the Queen's reference to shelter, and the thickness of the walls provided the explanation. They must be hollow. He had merely to find the openings and he could get out of the rain. To verify his idea he began a slow circling of the wall, facing it, hands on the surface and moving with slow care. He knew of only one danger, that of falling down the stairway, but in this pitchy blackness he could be certain of nothing.

He found an opening in the wall; with careful touch he estimated its size—large enough for him to crawl into. He groped within and found dry covers on what seemed to be a bed; by touch, concluded it would accommodate his tall frame. Further exploration would await daylight.

Swiftly he removed his weapons and thrust them into the opening. The heavy kirtle followed; after wringing out all possible moisture, he thrust it into the dryness. Sliding into the opening, he used the garment's absorbent felt to mop head and body. After further wringing, he struggled out of his footgear and rolled onto the covers. Wrapping himself in their damp but dry comfort, for the first time in what seemed to be ages he began to feel warm.

He lay in the darkness, listening to the roar of the rain, reliving all that had happened since his rude awakening by the marauders. His last thoughts were of Queen Nanshe, her dark loveliness, and her strange waking dream. Finally he slept.

When he awakened, a gray day greeted him, speaking in the voice of ceaseless rain. He looked out through the opening into the deluge, trying to find the energy to get up. He knew he should determine what, if anything, was happening below. He looked around the shelter and saw huge covered clay vessels set in niches in the wall. Reluctantly he left the warmth of the covers to investigate; he found the jars contained dried fruit and roasted grain, salted meat and fish—enough to provide "fasting" priests food for a long time.

He reached for his kirtle, still cold and wet. Better

nothing than this. He crawled out of the shelter as he was, birth-naked.

The downpour removed any trace of sleepiness. Briskly he rubbed himself, looking skyward. There was no sign of a break in the leaden gray blanket of clouds, nor any letup in the volume of rain. He glanced around the tower top, the "place of fasting, of the holy stars." He saw a square, slightly sloping expanse of mosaic, finely wrought, with figures of the gods, the seven stars, and strange symbols, meaningless to him. The wall was as he had pictured it, with a single oblong opening centered at the end and another in the wall facing him. At his left lay the stairway.

He moved cautiously to the head of the stairs, staying close to the wall to be less visible—needless caution; below he saw only water. He caught his breath and stared in unbelief. The city of Kish was no more! Even its great wall had vanished in the deluge. He saw objects floating past: some, crude rafts with huddled figures on them; others, odd objects with people clinging to them; still others, bodies floating inertly. He moved closer to the edge of the stairs to see the lower levels of the *ziggurat*; then as he felt the current swirling about his legs, strongly tugging, he drew back. Better to look from the top of the wall.

Moving back to the opening, he used it to climb up on the flat top of the wall and, on hands and knees, looked over the edge. Endlessly he stared. Already the three lower Temples of the Tower were under water—those of Enlil, Enki, and Nintu—and already the waves were lapping at the top of the terrace wall on the fourth level.

Grimly he stared, the extent of the disaster starting to register on his consciousness. Shuruppak, farther down the valley, must certainly be covered. The other cities, Ur, Lagash, Nippur, Eridu, and all Sumer, were under the flood of water. He felt numbed, his mind refusing to accept what his eyes saw. Slowly out of the numbness grew anger, anger at the gods who had destroyed the world. The world? He thought of the great mountains to the east, rising far higher than the Tower of Kish. Not the world, only the land of the twin rivers. Their world. Why? What had they done to bring the curse of the gods upon them?

He caught a glimpse of motion on the terrace of the fourth level and saw priests lifting a giant raft of heavy planks, balancing it on the wall. Apparently it was a part of a stall like that in which he had been held. A crude seat had somehow been fastened to its center. Heavy cords were lashed around it: holding tightly to these, the sodden white-robed figures lowered the raft into the water. Watching, Ziusudra saw King Etana climb over the wall and seat himself on the raft. One by one, the priests, each carrying an improvised oar, climbed aboard. The priest, holding the cord, finally stepped from the wall into the water to be hauled up by his fellows even as the cumbersome craft was swept away by the current.

Ziusudra climbed down and returned to the shelter. Half drying himself with the soggy felt, he crawled between the covers, his thoughts on what he had seen. It was too devastating to grasp. Shuruppak, his family, his people—maybe they, too, had found ways of escape. There had been some boats. . . . He tried to think of other things. Nanshe—what of the lovely Queen? Still praying to the gods? She had not left with the King, which was not really surprising. Women were not that important. Her vision—was she still depending on its truth?

Slowly the hours passed, the sound of the ceaseless downpour dulling the senses. He ate, thinking cynically of the priest who came down from the Tower after many days of "fasting" with no loss of strength to impress the unsuspecting worshipers. He ventured out into the wet to explore the other shelters and found them identical with the one he had chosen. In one of them, he found white priestly robes; these, with the covers, he rolled into a tight bundle and dashed back into his shelter.

At long last darkness came, and with it Prince Ziusudra became alert. This was the fifth night of the flood; surely Nanshe must join him tonight. He felt a growing eagerness, a certainty that she would come. He put on one of the priests' robes, though he knew it would be soaked in moments after he ventured out. Over it he strapped the belt of weapons, then waited. Several times his muscles tightened as he thought he heard sounds other than the rain. When nothing followed he decided he must be mistaken.

Finally his impatience demanded action. He stepped out into the black torrents and groped along the wall to the stairway. He thought of his own struggle up the steps and wondered if the Queen would think of crawling as he had done. His own actions had been instinctive; hers should be, too.

Time dragged by, and he heard a voice—a man's, then a woman's in answer. He could not distinguish words over the drumming of the downpour. There was anger in the voices coming, he believed, from the foot of the stairway. Ziusudra peered down into the darkness, instinctively drawing his sword, but he saw nothing. He ground his teeth helplessly; there was nothing he could do. Or—perhaps one thing.

"Nanshe!" he shouted at the top of his voice. "Crawl!"

Would she hear and, hearing, understand?

Tensely he waited, bracing himself against the pressure of the water buffeting his legs.

He heard a shrill scream just below him, and dropped to his knees, reaching down, moving his extended arm and outstretched fingers back and forth. "Here, Nanshe!" he cried. He felt her fingers clutching his, locking in desperation. With a lunge he drew back, dragging the Queen. Her grip tightened; then unaccountably she shouted, "Let go! Let go!"

Startled, Ziusudra momentarily ceased pulling, then realized the truth as her other hand grasped his wrist, and he felt her body twisting as she kicked out. Apparently someone had seized her ankle. Suddenly the male voice cursed in pain; and Ziusudra dragged the woman the rest of the way, backing up. Standing erect, he drew her with him and stood her on her feet. He felt the wall on his left and pressed the Queen's hand against it.

With his mouth close to her ear he directed, "Move back out of the way. Who follows?"

"The High Priest and three others." She released his hand and moved into the darkness.

Admirable woman, the Prince thought as he switched his sword for the mace and groped back to the stairway. As he reached the edge of the wall, he again sank to his knees, bracing himself on his haunches, his weapon gripped in both hands, sweeping with all his power back and forth in the opening.

He felt it strike; heard a howl of anguish, fading swiftly, as a climber was swept away into the blackness. Then came a shout: "Enmerkar—what happened?"

Ziusudra continued his flailing and struck a second climber. This one evidently tumbled backward, taking another with him, for two shrieks followed, ending in a great splash. Another voice cried in desperation, "Nergal, have mercy!"

Ziusudra waited, again swinging his mace close to the crest of the streaming flood. Suddenly with blinding intensity, lightning unexpectedly flashed and thunder rolled mightily, the first of the storm. In the glare the Prince saw as an afterimage the last of the priests, his face just above the flood. Down swept the weapon and Ziusudra felt the blow land; he heard a groan and moments later another great splash.

As a second lance of lightning pierced the clouds, he drew back, stood up, and reached for the wall. He followed it with sure steps, catching up with Nanshe, putting an arm around her waist. Quickly, helped by another flash, they reached the shelter.

With all the intensity of the rain, the electric storm broke, flash following flash and thunder rolling in a crackling and roaring that shook the massive tower. By its light, the Queen looked around the little chamber, stared intently at the Prince, then flung her arms around his neck.

"Safe at last," she cried. She drew back, her hands on his shoulders. "I have never been so wet. As are you. Get out of that robe." With the words she struggled with her own clinging garments. "Use one of those covers to get us dry." In due time they slid under the remaining covers.

"There are two other shelters," Ziusudra began.

"We will be warmer this way," she interrupted. "*Much* warmer." Later she said, close to his ear, "The King blamed me for not giving him a son. He never spoke of his concubines who somehow never became with child."

All that night and the following day, the seventh, the storm continued in all its fury. When they wakened on the morning of the eighth day, the sky was blue, a gentle breeze was blowing, and the waters had stopped rising, level with the top of the stairway. The sun in the east, a great ball of fire, shone blindingly above the rippling surface of a vast inland sea.

Alan MacDougall hovered in the airy realm between waking and sleep, not quite aware of his surroundings, but fully conscious that he had been dreaming. And what a dream! So vivid, so incredibly real. Almost he could feel the pelting of the rain...Ziusudra—he had been Ziusudra. And that woman, Nanshe—what a woman! She reminded him of someone. An equally strange reality struggled into his consciousness. He remembered—

the Island of Scath. And that Queen—Scathach. Another Scathach!

He opened his eyes to stare into an expanse of emerald radiance almost blinding in its brilliance. Vainly he tried to turn his head away, to lower his eyelids. Power poured from something—someone—within that light. He must raise his hands to shut out the glare; he could not: he had no strength to move his arms, which suddenly had become unbelievably heavy.

He felt a strange probing, a questing, a sifting of his thoughts, a most uncomfortable intrusion of another mind. Instinctively he tried to block out the invading intellect, tried to set up a barrier against its trespass; he felt relief as it withdrew.

Dimly then he heard a whispered chant, rhythmic, wordless, yet strangely arresting. With it he sensed rather than heard a feminine voice intoning: "Back—back—back to forgotten times, awakening now in your memory. Back—back . . . back . . ."

Stubbornly Alan MacDougall resisted the voice, clinging desperately to awareness, and to a degree succeeding. Even as deep sleep engulfed him and he began to dream he knew he was dreaming. Inexplicably he became both participant and spectator. It was as if he were viewing a film of himself, a film as real as life.

He was Naramu, marauder, preying upon merchantmen at night in the Gulf of Dilmun; and he watched while Naramu led six of his crewmen, clad only in black loincloths, as they stealthily boarded a Babylonian trader, moored for the night in a small cove, a wooden vessel bound for the Port of Ur. He both joined in and watched the seizing of the Hittite Princess, Beltu, who was aboard. As they plunged over the rail, and the black waters of the Gulf closed over them, he felt another dark wave, mental and frightening, flood his mind.

Again the faintly droning voices and the emerald glow penetrated the darkness. And again he felt himself part of the contradictory combination of observer and actor.

He was in the Temple of Ma'at in Denderah in Egypt. He was King Nectanebus seeking an oracle from the Priestess, Thanatha, known for her powers through all Egypt. After an impressive display of the insight of the goddess Ma'at, he received the word he sought, but left the temple more impressed with the dark beauty and witchery of the Priestess than with the goddess she served.

As King Nectanebus left the Temple, the gathering dusk deepened into total blackness; a faint high humming sounded in his ears, and again that emerald glow swelled and grew. Dimly as from an infinite distance he heard again a rhythmic chanting; then it was gone.

Voices, excited and raucous, surrounded him as he saw in bright sunlight a throng of a hundred or more robed Romans gathered before a raised platform of planks and timbers, sheltered by a broad awning. On the marble pavement sat or stood two score nearly naked slaves, women and men, awaiting their turn to be sold.

On the platform, the center of attention, stood a powerful, yellow-haired giant, deeply tanned, with only a loincloth around his middle. And, realization came, he was that giant. Beside him stood the brightly robed auctioneer, extolling his virtues, cajoling the potential buyers.

"Zamergan of Sarmatia in the north," he cried. "A powerful man as you can see, valiant in battle, a gladiator born. Am I offered ten thousand sesterces?"

Some in the crowd laughed as someone cried, "One hundred sesterces for the barbarian."

From the rear, where stood a royal hooded carriage, ornate with gold and gems, came a woman's imperious voice. "May we see *all* of the slave?"

A slave master standing at an end of the platform with a coiled whip in one hand sprang forward and stripped away the loincloth. Zamergan of Sarmatia whirled and with a single motion seized and flung the offender high into the air. Even as he landed with a dull thud on head and shoulders on the marble floor, the same voice said, "One hundred thousand sesterces. I like his spirit."

The crowd was hushed as the auctioneer announced, "Sold to the House of Herod Agrippa, the Empress Herodias the buyer."

Zamergan caught a glimpse of a darkly beautiful face as the woman said, "Send him to the castle. And see that no harm befalls him." The carriage drove away as six guardsmen, shortswords drawn, came from behind the platform and converged on the Samartian. He fought valiantly until the world came crashing down on his head and darkness fell.

. . . Struggling endlessly upward as out of vast depths, against incredible pressure, Alan MacDougall sought to return to consciousness. Somewhere, infinitely distant at the edge of sound, he could hear voices, a slow wordless chant that soothed and that bade him sleep, to live again a life that had once been his. But he had had enough of dreaming, he thought with weak stubbornness, enough of floods and goddesses, of darkness and death. Not quite, not quite, came a faint low voice. Voice? Rather, a thought, feminine, persuasive, insinuating itself in his mind.

Out of the depths from which he had been seeking escape welled up sleep, deep, engulfing, overwhelming. . . .

. . . Waking from a restless, troubled sleep, Vollmar flung aside the coarse wool cover and sprang erect. Dousing his face with cold water from a wooden pail in a corner by the dead fireplace, he half noted with approval the stubble of yellow beard. A man—it was time! He was a man now that his mother had died. A black scowl settled on his craggy features and remained there as he broke fast with cold mutton left from the previous evening.

Eight days had passed since his mother's death and serf's burial—and it seemed forever. As she lay dying, she had told him the grim secret that had weighed upon her through all the years of his growing, all the years of her labor as a drudge in the household of King Vortigern —the years of his serving and taking the abuse of Prince Vortimer.

King Vortigern was his father. Prince Vortimer was his half brother; Princess Inge his half sister. And he was the dust under their feet!

Vollmar stared without seeing into the gray ashes of the fireplace. His birth was not the fruit of a passing love. His mother, Hille, young, fresh, yellow-haired, and newly come across the water with her father and the other Saxons, had been desired by Vortigern, not yet King. She had scorned him; and in his drunken anger he had seized her, beaten her, and forced her, not once but many times before letting her go.

The hump in her nose and her twisted mouth—they had come from Vortigern's beating and they had so changed her face that she could live in the King's household unrecognized.

All this she had told him in the black night by the light of the fireplace—and more. Always she had reminded him he must be strong, must master weapons, must be best. By watching, he had learned from the teachers of Vortimer, and later had been used by the Prince for practice, always letting himself be beaten, though his own skill was far greater with sword and axe or with spear and bow. Now he knew why. She had lived for revenge. Now he knew why she had seldom smiled, and why the lines deepened on her face with the passing years.

He must be the avenger. No seed of Vortigern must reign in Britain, unless it be *his* seed. He had sworn it would be so. And someday, someday—the sight had been upon her and her eyes gleamed in the dark—a son of Vollmar's line would rule!

Vortigern the Usurper, as he had been called, had escaped his hand. The King, too, had died after a twelve-year reign; and Aurelius Ambrosius, a son of the Romans, had made himself King. But this very day the son, Vortimer, was to lead a rebellion against Uther Pendragon, general of Aurelius' army. The once-Prince had made common cause with Gilloman, the young King of Ireland; and during the night the rebel forces had assembled near the Prescelly Mountain for a march toward St. David's.

Only the Prince and his lowly servant, his guard and slave, had yet to leave for battle. Vortimer had demanded his sleep; and the two traveling together would attract no attention. Even now, Vollmar was expecting a shout from the Prince. There would be harsh words, for he should be waiting with the horses. He had better start.

He strapped on his sword belt, threw a heavy wool cape over his shoulders, and left the hut. As he walked through the gray of dawn, he relived an experience never far from his thoughts. Two nights after his mother's burial, he had wandered aimlessly into the silent dark, with only the infrequent barking of dogs or the howling of wolves heard in the stillness.

He had come upon the Circle of Standing Stones, which all men shunned. The dark gods were said to appear there with the coming of the new moon. When he saw the thin sliver of moon appear from behind a cloud, he felt a stab of fear; and even as he thought of it, that fear returned. Yet as one under orders, he had entered the Circle.

The great central stone drew him, and as he slowly approached it, he thought of his mother's last words and of his oath. He thought again of her never-forgotten mis-

ery, reflected in her last gasping words, and he cried out
suddenly:

"Whatever god dwells here, I call for you to help me.
I have made a vow. Grant me the power to do what I
have said, and I will serve you with my life." Heart racing, he waited anxiously in the shadow of the great
stone. And waited. Then, with eyes drawn upward, he
saw the tip of the new moon appear above the topmost
edge of the stone. As if at a signal, he sensed an over-
powering Presence, and a voice seemed to speak in his
mind.

"Vollmar, it is a wish easily granted. It shall be as you
ask. Your hand shall cut off the seed of Vortigern."

Somehow Vollmar gained the impression that the god
lingered, waiting. A sudden bold thought burst from him.
"My mother spoke of a day when one born of my seed or
seed of my seed will rule. May this also be true—not
only of Britain but of the whole world!" Fearfully he
listened for the response.

There was vast amusement in the thought that formed
in his mind. "You appear to value your service very
highly. But since it pleases my will, since it fits into a
plan I foresee, this, too, will be granted. And yes, when
it happens you will know." The thought seemed to fade.
"You will know." And again it came even more faintly.
"You will know."

Alone, Vollmar had run from the Circle.

"Vollmar, where are you?" The querulous cry came
from the stables. Almost there, the object of Vortimer's
annoyance quickened his pace.

"Coming!" He closed his ears to the abusive words
that followed, telling himself it was the last time. Minutes later, with the Prince still complaining, they
mounted and started away, Vollmar behind his master.
He smiled grimly. Not behind for long.

He knew the way they followed, and he had in mind a
clear area within a small wood where none might see. As

they drew near the chosen spot, now in the full light of morning, Vollmar's pulse began to race. He had little stomach for what he planned. But with thought of his mother's twisted mouth and drunken Vortigern, whose blows he also had felt, there was no weakening of his resolution. The time drew near and he sent his mount level with Vortimer's.

Now!

He thrust out his strong left arm, encircling the waist of the smaller man and lifting him out of the saddle. A startled cry burst from the Prince.

As Vollmar swung to the ground he shouted, "Are you mad? You will pay for this!"

With a single motion Vollmar set the other on his feet, whipped out his sword, and set the point against Vortimer's throat.

"Not so, my brother."

Suddenly paling, the Prince gasped wildly. "Brother? You *are* mad. What has happened to you?"

"Brother, indeed. Your father was my father, so my mother told me as she lay dying. But not by her wish. You remember her, her crooked nose and twisted mouth. They, like me, are his work. And you shall collect the reward in his stead, since he is dead. Like this!"

In a flash Vollmar flicked his sword point across the Prince's lower lip. As the blood spurted, Vortimer screamed, "No—brother—no! You shall share all I have—"

"Even your blade," Vollmar cried. "Draw—and fight so that I need not kill you like a dog."

With sudden wild eagerness, Vortimer sprang back, tearing his blade from its sheath, desperation turning to triumph. "Now you will pay," he screamed. "You know I always won when we dueled."

"Because the slave never dared beat the master. Now, fool, fight!"

Furiously Vortimer attacked, seeking speedy victory;

but in moments he knew the truth as Vollmar parried every lunge and thrust—then ended the play with a single sweep across the Prince's throat. Half-sickened by the spectacle of the gushing blood, Vollmar averted his gaze, wiping his blade clean on Vortimer's garments. Then mounting his horse, he sent the animal galloping back toward the stables.

His morning's work was not yet finished.

He tried not to think of what lay ahead—a task he loathed that cried out against his every instinct. Not so had he been taught. But his vow was that "no seed of Vortigern shall reign in Britain." And a daughter could continue the bloodline. As the great home of the one-time King came into view, he steeled himself for what he must do.

Spurring his horse cruelly, he raced into the grounds, shouting as he drew near, "Princess Inge! Princess Inge! Call the Princess. Vortimer needs her. Hurry!"

At his shouts, a few servants came running, older men and women who had not gone off to battle; and moments later the Princess also appeared, still in garments she wore for sleeping. Fear marked her dark, lovely face.

"Vollmar, what happened? Where is Vortimer?"

"He fell from his horse and is injured. He kept asking for you, though I know not why. Hurry! The servants can follow."

"Like this?" Doubtfully she indicated her night-clothes.

"Yes! There's no time to spare. This horse can easily carry two." To the startled servants he said, "Beyond the ridge, you take the road to the left, the one going by the Circle. Better bring a cart to carry him."

He leaped to the ground and turned to Inge. "You are light. I can carry you easily." And before she could object, with a quick easy motion he swept her into his arms, lifted her to the saddle, and swiftly mounted behind her. Holding her with one arm, he sent his mount dashing away.

It had been so easy, he thought with mingled jubilation and self-disgust. The warmth of her body against his made the rest of the task easier—and more difficult. When they came to the fork beyond the ridge and Vollmar veered to the right, she objected, but he quieted her fears. "We go a shorter way, impossible for a cart."

They came to the grove and Vollmar halted. As he stepped to the ground, holding the girl, Inge caught her first glimpse of the body. Her breath rasped into her lungs; then she screamed and screamed and screamed. She turned wildly on Vollmar.

"You—you killed him!" Still screaming, she beat with all her strength on his chest, repeating her cry again and again. "You killed him! Why—why?"

Releasing her, Vollmar stepped back and with open hands slapped her face violently, one side then the other. Sheer terror choked off her cry as she saw the menace in his eyes.

"Yes, my sister," he said hoarsely. "I killed him, as I would kill your father—and mine—were he alive. As I must—" He left the sentence unfinished.

"Sister." She gasped numbly.

"Sister, indeed. Your father was my father—but not by my mother's choosing." In a dull monotone he repeated the story of his mother's ordeal as he had told it to Vortimer. Then as Inge bit her lip, her body rigid in a frenzy of terror, he thrust her down into the deep grass and, with a single vicious lunge, ripped her single garment from her, staring with racing heart and panting breath at her nakedness. . . .

"*. . . Alan MacDougall—Alan MacDougall—this is Taliesin. What is wrong? Can you hear me?*" Faintly, insistently, the anxious thought of the Bard of Tartarus registered on his conciousness, piercing through a red haze of fury, passion, and confusion, touching a mind struggling to awaken from a revolting nightmare.

Mechanically he responded to the silent thought. *"I hear you, Taliesin. I have been under a spell. Give me a few moments and I'll get back to you."*

It took conscious effort for Alan to open his eyes. Succeeding at last, he stared stupidly at a flimsy fragment of black cloth clutched in one hand. And below him, stretched out on her own bed, lay the near-nude form of Scathach the Sorceress.

Alan thought of that last remembered moment of his nightmare, and the two black-haired women merged into one. But in the eyes of this one there was no fear, no terror, only eagerness, and on her lips was a smile of anticipation. For an uncomprehending moment, Mac-Dougall stared; then with a furious oath, he sprang erect and flung the cloth at the recumbent woman.

"You damned witch," he exclaimed furiously. "Pick on someone your own age!" And turning swiftly, he swept up his sword and stalked out of the room.

CHAPTER 6

Visit of the Wave Sweeper

Outside of Scathach's chambers, Alan MacDougall halted and tried to think rationally. His thoughts were in turmoil, but one thing was clear. He was in trouble—not that he regretted what he had done; but the cliché about a woman scorned still held true. And she *was* a sorceress.

First step, invisibility! Then as soundlessly as possible, he made his way to the stairway, passed the Guards undetected, and went to his room. There he hastily strapped on his sword belt, clipped on his canteen, and flung his cape over his shoulders. He clasped the armlet.

"Lord and Lady, as you probably observed, I have insulted Queen Scathach, and without a doubt she will respond, I believe unpleasantly. Will you give me warning if she moves against me? I'm getting out of here. What's she doing now?"

"We did indeed observe," Inanna responded dryly. "And we will watch her Highness. At the moment she is being ministered to by her maid, Isla."

"Then I have a few spare moments." The thoughts came pouring forth. "I am concerned, greatly concerned about this whole experience in Lamashtu's shrine, especially about my leaving that room with Scathach without my knowledge, and about a distinct recollection I have of her probing my mind. What did she learn? How deeply did she go? Mind control and the power of suggestion could account for my recollections of supposed past lives, though I don't see how Scathach could have known of ancient Sumer, nor of any part of my dreaming except for the time of Vollmar in Roman Britain. But my leaving that room without my knowing—"

"Not Scathach" came Enki's solemn thought, "but Ereshkigal would know of all the older times. As for what Scathach learned, we cannot be certain, but we think not too much. We sought to block her delving, but met resistance from Ereshkigal, who gave her power. The matter of your leaving the shrine—remember, she *is* a sorceress."

"But those dreams, those visions were so real! I could swear—"

"*Alan,*" the thought of Taliesin touched his mind. "*Forgive my interrupting, but I really have important news.*"

"*No problem,*" Alan responded. "*I am myself again. During the time you were trying to reach me, I seemed to be living several lives under a kind of spell; and I ended by greatly angering the Sorceress. She made a fool of me, and I insulted her. There is no time now to go into details. I will be leaving here in moments, probably to get out of the Castle. But you have news—*"

"*The Wave Sweeper is offshore, cautiously approaching the mouth of the river. I can see it now from my post on a rock in the Grove of the Druidesses. Manannan could reach land in moments if he wanted to. Maybe he wishes to be seen. I am in hiding. Not from the women, since invisibility conceals me from them, but*" *from demon spies of Amaruduk. They are here unde-tected; and they can see through my vanishing spells, as I can see through theirs. Regarding the coming of Man-annan and the others, I thought you should know as quickly as possible, since you are part of the reason for their visit."*

"Indeed," Alan answered thoughtfully. *"And that changes what I'll do. My intention was to put as much distance as possible as fast as possible between me and Scathach. But with Beli and the others here, I had better be on the scene. Besides, I'm not inclined to turn tail and run from any of them."* The rest of Taliesin's state-ment registered. *"Spies of Amaruduk? Interesting. Per-haps they are here in the castle as well. We'll have to be on the lookout."* He paused, then continued. *"I think I'll move to the torture rooms, your excellent idea. Will you join me there? We have a lot to talk about."*

"As quickly as I can. My spying on the spies can wait."

"Until then." And Alan ended the thought exchange.

"What of Scathach?" He asked the serpent-gods.

"She has just received word of the sighting of the *Wave Sweeper*, and there's a lot of excitement. She is rushing to her room of mirrors."

Hastily MacDougall left the room, again invisible, and moved to the stairway, passing the Guards unobserved. In moments, the stillness and gloom of the torture chamber closed about him. He felt inclined to cringe as he sensed the aura of pain that seemed to linger in the place. Ignoring the momentary revulsion, he sat on an iron chest and addressed Lord Enki.

"May I see what Scathach is doing?"

Instantly a mental image formed of a three-sided room, its walls completely hidden by gray hangings, with a gray rug on the floor, two wall lamps and a single win-dow providing the light. The room was filled by a strange and complex arrangement of what appeared to be numerous round mirrors or one-way windows; in their heart was a broad, pillarlike seat; before it was a great disk of the reflective material rising to the ceiling, and behind it another much smaller. All of it was faintly aglow.

In the space between the larger mirror and the pillar rose a slender, silvery rod, supporting a glittering green sphere, its surface made up of countless fine facets, each flashing with internal fire. The very heart of this device, it almost seemed alive.

Scathach was seated on the pillar, facing the main mirror on which appeared a brilliant view of the river mouth and the open sea beyond it. It was a breathtaking spectacle of the restlessly dancing aurora with its red and white undulations and the vagrant waves of pastel blues, lavenders, and yellows, reflected in a perfect mirror-image by the placid water.

Silhouetted against this backdrop, slowly approaching Scath, came the burnished copper vessel. MacDougall's heartbeat quickened at sight of the gleaming coracle, her backward-curving prow sending gem-tipped waves to right and left over the quiet sea. In a breath, he relived the excitement of his wild ride on the coracle when he, in the likeness of Manannan, had "borrowed" it for his and Taliesin's escape from Ochren. And now it was bringing his deadly enemies to Scath.

Others of the mirrors reflected views of the guards on the lower rooftop, bows in hand and arrows nocked, of rapidly assembling warriors on the left riverbank, of the Castle Guard on the tip of the island, swords in hand, and of more slowly gathering black-cowled Druidesses on the right bank.

Suddenly the *Wave Sweeper* sprang to life, racing over the water toward the shore, her prow sending twin billows of white foam sweeping along the bows. A picture of grace and speed with her figurehead a lifelike image of a spirited horse, neck arched, with back-swept mane and forehoofs cleaving the air, she bore down on the island tip with breakneck speed, only to swing broadside at the last moment and stop dead.

Except for Manannan, the occupants of the *Wave Sweeper* were not prepared for the maneuver; had it not been for the starboard rail, some might have pitched overboard. It was a startling display of Manannan's showmanship. For moments it had seemed as if the coracle would leap out of the mirror.

As the ten visitors scrambled to regain footing and assumed what appeared to be prearranged positions, the projection of the Sorceress, thrice normal size, appeared in midair against its gray background, looking down at the visitors. It was a far sharper image than any television picture, three-dimensional and living. Watching, MacDougall thought of his own first impression of Scathach's dark beauty, strength, power, and evil.

Finally she spoke, her voice hostile and cold. "Who comes uninvited to Scath? And why have you come?"

Manannan, god of the sea, who stood in the middle of the five gods, advanced a step, impressive with his leonine, blue-white mane and carefully groomed mustache and beard. He wore a dark-green cape and kilt and a white tunic. He held out his hands, palms up, a yard apart.

"Scathach! Surely you remember me, Manannan, and my *Wave Sweeper*! We were friends in the Olden Times. And you must have known Nuada, King of the *Tuatha de Danann*. We learned only recently of the existence of your island; and even then, we knew nothing of your being here. Had we known we dwelt in the same world, we would have visited you ages ago. So have your bowmen put up their weapons. An arrow might slip."

The Sorceress ignored the request. "How did you learn about Scath after all the centuries?"

Nuada answered, "A report came to us indirectly through a visitor who came to your island from the Other

World where once we all lived. His name is Alan Mac-Dougall."

"And you are his friends, I suppose?"

The red-haired giant chuckled mirthlessly. "I am Beli, god of the Underworld. We have never met, though of course I knew of the gifted Sorceress and Master Warrior, Scathach of Dun Scaith. As for MacDougall, let us say we owe him much and would repay."

Smoothly Manannan added, "So that you may know all of us, the two others in the front row are, in order, Balor, god of the Fomorians, and Pryderi, jailer of Ochren. In the rear are Mathonwy, Master Magician, and four of our Druids."

Scathach had looked stolidly at the ten during the introductions, then she spoke. "Is is not true that you seek to take the life of Alan MacDougall? I had been told of your coming. Be warned, if I permit you to land, MacDougall is my guest and is under my protection. He is not available now, but when he is, I will determine if you are to see him.

"I am Queen Scathach, the supreme authority on Scath, a land where, until the coming of my guest, no man has walked. And if I permit you to come ashore, it will be on the condition that you leave all your weapons in the coracle."

Instant protest arose from Beli, Nuada, and Balor. The Sorceress remained unmoved, her face expressionless. Finally Manannan called for silence.

"A brief conference, your Majesty, with your permission." For moments all faced the god of the sea, their heads together, then turning, Manannan announced, "We agree."

And as MacDougall watched in unbelief, they unbuckled their sword belts and dropped them to the deck.

Or so it appeared. "Lord Enki, can I really be seeing them disarm?"

The serpent-god responded, "You do well to doubt.

With Mathonwy and four Druids, this illusion was no problem whatever. Their problem will be its maintenance over a period of time, but at least it will get them ashore."

MacDougall thought wryly that had they been denied here, with the long, unguarded shoreline, they would have landed in any event. This just made their quest more convenient.

During this interchange, Alan had lost the view of the mirrors; but through the armlet he continued watching while the *Wave Sweeper* moved up to the tip of the island, and the guards separated into two columns. After the visitors left the coracle, Manannan faced it briefly and it moved, seemingly of its own volition, far out on the water, just remaining in sight. The sea god apparently remembered a time when Alan had absconded with it. Mental control was sending it beyond any possible unauthorized boarding. So, he suddenly thought, must Scathach control her maze of mirrors.

He watched with amusement as the visitors carefully threaded their way over the narrow top of the walls. Beli's large boots, especially, found the going difficult.

The projection of the Sorceress followed the ten as they were escorted by members of the Castle Guard into the tower and to a lounge area on the second level; then it vanished. The group was followed by two score of the warriors, who ranged themselves around the walls of the room, bows and arrows in hand.

Rather awkwardly the visitors found seats, trying to appear at ease. Tension built until Scathach herself appeared, after which wine and food were served, and the Sorceress became a semigracious hostess. Evidently they were drinking liquid dynamite, for in a very short time the visitors' tongues were loosened and reminiscences about the Olden Times were on every lip.

Alan MacDougall turned his attention to his surroundings. It was time he thought about where he would sleep. If Taliesin returned, as he logically would, the problem would be compounded. This was hardly a bedroom. As he started exploring, hunting for the Bard's bedding, the oppressive gloom of the poorly lighted chamber became disturbing, and finally he drew out his flashlight. Its warm beam was a welcome relief. And since he aimed the beam toward the floor, and the buzz of conversation continued filtering from the second level, he felt there was little chance of detection.

He found the blankets in one of the iron chests; he'd take one to lie on, using his cape for a cover. There were two great ovens, large enough to hold even his tall frame; one would provide an adequate bed. With the door almost closed, if invisibility failed while he slept, as it probably would, even Scathach's floating projection would not see him.

What next? He wouldn't spend any more time than necessary in this morgue. The sounds from below drew him. And there was food on the second level; he was hungry, not having eaten anything since breakfast. He still had a bit of Norah's lunch, but, if possible, he'd keep that in reserve.

About to leave, he sensed Taliesin's thought: *"Alan— I can't get in! I've tried the seven doorways, and all are heavily guarded. My banging led to their opening only wide enough for a Guard to peer out, so there's no chance of my slipping through. I'm not built for narrow openings. I'm invisible, of course, so they see nothing outside. I suppose they think I'm one of the demons. I tried to open a door from the outside, but they're apparently bolted from within. So I'm returning to the village of the Druidesses. There's a gathering in the Temple I'd like to investigate. How do you fare?"*

"I'm in the torture room," MacDougall responded, *"but I'm about to leave. The visitors are being entertained by Scathach in a lounge on the second level."* He told of the faked shedding of the weapons. *"I'd like to*

find a way to expose their deceit." He told Taliesin about finding the blankets and the bed he had chosen, learning that the Bard had used the same macabre resting place. He mentioned his need for food; and the Bard told of his finding the larder of the Druidesses and helping himself. On this note they broke contact.

After checking his invisibility, MacDougall slipped out into the corridor. No guards were in sight; probably all were on duty on the floor below. Stealthily he descended the steps, though any sound he might have made would have been covered by the voices from the lounge. He found the kitchen. Though girls were entering and leaving, he had no trouble in avoiding them and in helping himself to all the food he wanted.

He moved through the dining area with its long tables and benches and slipped into the lounge. Scathach was the center of the group of gods, all of whom had goblets of wine in their hands, their tongues wagging busily. Nuada and Manannan were obviously fascinated by the Queen, and Beli and Balor seemed especially boisterous. Even the Sorceress seemed to be enjoying herself. The Druids sat quietly with Mathonwy, each with his goblet of wine. Only Pryderi, seated alone and staring morosely into his cup appeared out of harmony with the spirit of the group.

Alan MacDougall watched unseen for quite a while, then grinned mischievously. Maybe he could liven the party.

"Lord Enki and Lady Inanna, do you think the creators of illusion have imbibed enough wine to weaken their concentration? Or to put it more baldly, can you counter their spell and make the weapons appear?"

Inanna answered, "We wondered when you would raise the question. Watch for the answer. Especially watch Scathach."

With that thought, the five gods suddenly wore visible weapons, ornate sword belts and scabbards gleaming in all their splendor, two on Manannan, two on Beli, and one on each of the others. Only Mathonwy and the Druids were unarmed.

The change did not instantly register on the mind of the Sorceress; but when it did, she sprang erect, dark eyes glaring, one arm waving and cried, "Liars! You deceived me! Guards, your bows!"

Instant response came. In the sudden shocked silence, the sighing of bowstrings was audible all around the chamber. The ten visitors froze as realization awakened. Quietly MacDougall slipped out of the room. He didn't want to be in range if arrows flew. Through the doorway he watched as Scathach's fingers closed on her lapis pendant.

"Guards—at once!"

Recovering, Manannan tried to protest, "We but sought—"

"Quiet!" she rasped, backing away from the gods. "No one makes a fool of Scathach. If any of you move, you die."

Alan heard the sound of racing feet in the stairwell and moved far to one side. It was well he did so, for in seconds twenty warriors poured into the lounge, swords in hand.

"Disarm them," the Sorceress directed curtly, waving at the five. To the gods she added, "Remember, there are metal-tipped arrows on every side in the hands of skilled archers."

Frustration and fury showed on five faces, both at the failure of their trick and the loss of their swords. Beli's face was as red as his beard. But no one moved as warriors went to the offenders and removed their weapons. As they did so, Alan thought, the hornets lost their stings. Scathach motioned for one of the Guards and whispered in her ear; she led the way from the lounge.

"Lord Enki," MacDougall requested, "will you check where they hide the swords? It might be useful information."

The answer came as an amused question. "What would you do without us?"

"Without you I would never have heard of Tartarus or Ochren or Scath, and would be leading a normal life in my own world."

The Sorceress was speaking. "I trust you have learned that my word is law. I know you had to make the attempt. But remember, you are far from replacement bodies that would be to your liking. This is an island of women."

She addressed Mathonwy. "Master Magician you may be, but you will do well to remember there are only five of you and many of us. If you value freedom, attempt no more spells. Every moment while you remain on Scath you will be watched."

She stared piercingly at Manannan. "I may regret it, but for the memories of the Olden Times I will grant you one mistake." As the god of the sea tried to protest, she cut him off. "Say nothing now. You will be shown to rooms for a time of sleep. You will be summoned to this level for breakfast. Your weapons will be returned when I decide you may be trusted with them."

With regal tread, the Queen of Scath left the room, followed by her personal Guards, passing within three yards of MacDougall on her way to the stairwell. Moments later, Alan headed for the stairs, debating on his course of action—to return to the third level or to leave the tower. If he *could* leave! After Taliesin's report about the well-guarded doors, maybe leaving was out of the question. He had to know.

After descending to ground level, he crossed the deserted sleeping quarters to the circular hallway and the main door. Yards away he grinned ruefully and turned back. The way was barred by a double wall of Guards, swords in hand. Scathach intended to keep him in the castle.

As he reached the second level, he saw the column of

Guards approaching with the visitors and raced by, two steps at a time, grateful again for rubber soles. He was safely inside his chosen retreat by the time he heard the passing of the visitors and their escorts. He seated himself on the iron chest to think things over.

What would happen next? There could be only one answer. At Scathach's orders, a search would be made for him. The arrival of the *Wave Sweeper* had been a diversion; but assuredly the Sorceress had not forgotten nor forgiven his insult and his dropping out of sight. One didn't do these things to the Queen.

In this contest he probably had a slight edge. Scathach knew he could become invisible, but she did not know of the serpent-gods and the abilities they gave him, including that of watching what she did. There was the problem of sleep when spells failed. He could ask Enki to maintain the spell, but he'd rather stay awake. Who needed sleep anyway?

It was important that he should know when the search started. He grasped the armlet. "Lord and Lady, inevitably Scathach will begin searching for me. Will you keep me informed?"

"We shall, indeed. And since she is already in her room of mirrors it appears it will not be long delayed."

Now it was a matter of waiting. Too bad he couldn't sit on the covers! A startling thought struck him. During a physical search the Guards would certainly look inside closed chests and they'd find the covers! Where could he hide them?

"You are not thinking," the Lady Inanna chided. "Wrap them around yourself as clothing and they will vanish."

"Thank you," Alan responded sheepishly. "That should have occurred to me. Certainly it's worth trying."

It was the work of moments to follow the suggestion; and the bedding disappeared. It was fortunate that he had remembered. Awkwardly he seated himself on the now-empty chest and waited. At last word came.

"The search has begun, two levels at a time. They are in the dungeons and the storage area, about fifteen searchers to each level. We see the girl Brendah is alone in the dungeons while she awaits trial, which is punishment in itself."

MacDougall cursed silently. In the press of other things he had forgotten her, the victim of Scathach's stupid order. Nothing he could do would help, but he felt guilty nonetheless. "Is she all right?"

"Not comfortable, nor cheerful, but she is being adequately fed, and there is a bed of sorts in her cell. She is a tough person." After a pause came the added thought, "A projection of the Sorceress is carefully observing all that is done. This is a thorough search."

Alan thought of asking to watch the search, but decided against doing so. He did not want to see the Sorceress at work. He still burned at the thought of her trickery. After a time, word came that the lower levels had been declared clean, and four Guards had been posted to solidly block the stairway downward. The first and second levels followed, taking longer and requiring greater attention; but in time these, too, produced no results and were closed off.

In preparation for the searchers' entry into the torture rooms, MacDougall chose a wide stretch of bare wall as the least likely spot for anyone to investigate. They came and searched; and though the covers interfered with his mobility, there was no occasion for him to move. It was a strange experience, watching the Guards delving into every possible nook and corner, and seeing the floating image of Scathach watching all they did. Finally they evidently determined he was not there, and two more levels were sealed off.

On the fourth level every room save those occupied by the visitors was thoroughly searched, Scathach alone sending her projection, unseen, into the occupied rooms.

The Sorceress evidently felt that, with the gods feeling as they did about MacDougall, it was most unlikely that he would hide in their bedchambers.

The Daughters of Calatin protested vehemently against a search of their quarters, but Scathach insisted; and for the first time in memory their sacrosanct rooms were invaded. Her own quarters followed, as did the shrine of Lamashtu and the roof of the tower, all without results. At last the weary searchers were dismissed, and quiet prevailed in the castle.

Before MacDougall crawled into the oven to get some sleep, he hunted for the local equivalent of a bathroom; to his surprise, he found one. He took advantage of the opportunity to fill his canteen. When at length he stretched out on the covers, he made a final check on Scathach. Enki reported that through her mirrors she had called the Daughters of Calatin, demanding if they still felt that Alan was inside the tower. After consultation they insisted he was, and they could not be in error. On this note the Sorceress sought rest.

All too soon an urgent thought from the serpent-gods awakened MacDougall.

"You are about to receive a visitor. The five from the other islands have sobered up and have left their rooms, invisible, of course. Mathonwy and the Druids have a twofold task—to maintain the images of the gods in their beds, and to screen the eyes of the Guards throughout the tower. Because of their earlier failure they are devoting their total power to their assignments and should be equal to the tasks."

Eyes still heavy, Alan left the oven and mechanically checked his invisiblity. Realization that he could be seen jarred him fully awake, and instinctively he set the spell in motion.

"Your visitor will be Pryderi," the thought continued, "and even now he approaches."

Thanks a lot for your timely warning, Alan thought sarcastically as he saw the door slowly move, swing open, and then silently close.

Pryderi was supposedly invisible—but not to Alan. He could see through the concealment—and though somewhat tenuous, the stocky figure of the jailer of Ochren stood there, his bald pate and great black beard making his identity unmistakable, even across the width of the room.

Secure in the belief that he could not be seen, the visitor stood motionless, peering about, letting his eyes adjust to the dim light. Cautiously he began moving; and as his seeing improved, he peered around the larger instruments of torture, lifted the lids of chests, and in general repeated what the Guards had done earlier. Gradually he drew closer to MacDougall, and suddenly stopped short, staring fixedly ahead, then hastened toward the oven.

Alan held his breath. Could he, too, see the invisible?

With sudden disgust, MacDougall knew the answer. The whiteness of the covers in the oven was a dead giveaway. If only he had closed the door—though that would merely have delayed the inevitable. And there hadn't been time enough to wrap them around himself.

Pryderi reached the oven and pulled out the bedding. Alan heard him mutter, "Warm! He is here!" The jailer dropped the covers and stepped back hastily, his head moving jerkily as he stared from side to side.

Alan's thoughts raced. He could not stay here, and there was no time for hesitation. What should he do? Lead in a cat-and-mouse chase; fake going through the doorway, actually leave the room, or gain time by knocking Pryderi out? Deciding, he stepped up to the jailer and swung his fist with all his power squarely against the bearded jaw, then sprang back, his knuckles aching.

His retreat was fortunate; though his victim staggered, Pryderi did not fall. He growled angrily, shook his head like a bear, and his massive arms groped bearlike for his assailant.

A tactical error, MacDougall thought. He had overestimated his own strength and underestimated the other's resistance. Reluctantly he drew his sword. He had started something he should finish, but he couldn't. He pictured the man as he had first seen him holding his whip with its metal-tipped thongs, and knew him for the brute he was; but what Alan had to do still went against the grain. With a shrug he crept up behind the jailer, grasped the sword with both hands, and swung the flat of the blade down on the bald head. Pryderi dropped with a thud, blood oozing through the lacerated scalp.

About to reach down to check his pulse, MacDougall hesitated. It wasn't likely, but the man could be faking. "Lord Enki," he asked, "can you tell me Pryderi's state?"

After a moment the answer came. "As you would say, he is out like a light. I see no permanent damage."

Alan looked around, scowling. He needed all the time he could gain; he had to find a way to keep Pryderi out of circulation as long as possible. No cords were available, and to tear a blanket into strips seemed impractical. To put him in one of the chests might do if he could manage it physically, but it didn't seem too feasible.

His gaze fell on the bed of nails with its reverse counterpart suspended above it. His eyes narrowed. It was inches above the floor; he should be able to drag the jailer to it and roll him on its spikes. Gagged, and with the upper half lowered just enough to snag his clothes, he should be held until the other gods found him.

Quickly Alan tackled his task. He was puffing by the time he dragged the dead weight to the torture machine; and rolling him onto it was even more difficult, requiring turning him on his face beside the bed, then gradually lifting him over on his back on the spikes. A strip torn from a blanket provided the gag, and the remainder placed under his head served as a pillow. Cranking down the upper part was easy; and Pryderi's rounded middle kept the points away from his face. As MacDougall surveyed his handiwork somewhat guiltily, he hoped the heavy garments would prevent damage from the spikes.

An impression of light caught the corner of Alan's eye and he turned to see the door opening. Balor's hushed voice, asked, "Problems, Pryderi?"

"No," Alan growled, grateful for the semidarkness. "Just finishing. The devil's own place to search." With a flash of inspiration he changed to Pryderi's form and assumed visibility as he strode toward the exit. "The swords are not here," he concluded, again invisible, "nor is MacDougall, so far as I can tell."

"Up to our rooms," Balor breathed. "We can't get into the fifth and sixth levels, so that is where the weapons and probably MacDougall must be."

MacDougall sent a thought to the serpent-gods. "Which is Pryderi's room? I have to go there."

"Number five, your former room. Balor is in four and Mathonwy in six. It's a logical arrangement. Nuada is in one, Manannan in two, Beli in three, and the Druids in seven to ten."

Interesting coincidence, Alan thought as he stretched out on one of the beds and, retaining his Pryderi change, became visible. He assumed Mathonwy had removed the illusion. For the first time since being awakened, he relaxed to a degree. That had been a close thing. If Balor had come a few minutes earlier—but he hadn't. And as Alan thought over the situation and his present position, he realized it couldn't have worked better if he had planned it. He had a safe hideout until the jailer was able to make his plight known, which might be a long time. Had Balor not appeared, he wouldn't have thought of taking Pryderi's place. He had merely to remain awake though simulating sleep and maintain the shape-change to be well hidden.

He had a question for the serpent-gods. "Lord and Lady, why has Scathach returned to her normal number of guards with the visitors in the tower, and with me missing?"

"A good question, but we think it is a quite logical move. The guards at the exits on ground level have not been reduced at all. We think the Sorceress believes the ten will do nothing to jeopardize the recovery of their arms. Perhaps she foresaw this search. And perhaps the apparent relaxing will draw you out of hiding. You are still her chief concern."

That was not a comforting idea, but then nothing about the Sorceress was comforting. He thought about his experience in Lamashtu's shrine and its startling conclusion. The induced visions or memories, implanted experiences, or whatever they were remained in his mind with startling clarity. At will, he could recall every detail of the nighttime attack of King Etana of Kish, of the flood, of the great *ziggurat*, of Prince Ziusudra who seemed to be himself, and of the lovely Queen Nanshe, the likeness of the Sorceress.

Equally clear were the other scenes and adventures that strangely, seemed to be his own—his and Scathach's. Mentally he reviewed the visions, marveling at his recalling every detail, more vividly real than his memory of what had happened in the Witch Wood, his adventures on Ochren and Tartarus, or his wanderings in the Highlands of Scotland.

He thought of the women in his visions—Nanshe of Sumer, Beltu the Hittite, Thanatha the Priestess of Egypt, the Roman Empress Herodias, and Princess Inge of Britain—all Scathach in those earlier lives.

He centered his thoughts on his last "dream," his supposed reincarnation as Vollmar, bastard son of King Vortigern. He tried to remember earlier incidents in that life, images other than those in his dream. There were none. He pictured the last visualized moments in his Egyptian "adventure" when, as King Nectanebus, he had sought an oracle from the Priestess of Ma'at; he tried to recall happenings before and after the experience. Again he drew a blank!

So it was with each of the visions. It was as if on the screen of his mind there had been projected segments of carefully enacted scenes, inventions created by some intellect, some master craftsman manipulating the very cells of his brain. Hypnotism? Or something far beyond mere mental suggestion?

Was it the work of Ereshkigal, as Enki had suggested, or behind her Ahriman, who had planted in his mind a false message from Taliesin before Alan's entry into Ochren? Or—he felt a sudden chill—Lucifer himself?

Alan's pulse quickened, and the palms of his hands became moist. His thoughts flashed back to the Temple of Crystal in Falias and the strangely eerie cry of the Stone of Fal as he sat upon it, proclaiming his royal descent. The Prophecy of the Scroll supposedly applied to him, supported by the repetition of his royalty in the "memories" from Lamashtu's shrine: Prince Ziusudra of Sumer; King Nectanebus of Egypt; and Vollmar, illegitimate son of King Vortigern of ancient Britain. Repeatedly, he was shown his reincarnation as Prince or King. With the coincidental appearance of one like Scathach in each life. Were the nonroyal sequences inserted to make the total picture more convincing? MacDougall gave a short, soundless, derisive laugh. Absurd! This was spreading it on too thickly.

He felt better now. Ahriman—or whoever—had overplayed his hand. Annoyance awakened slowly, became indignation, then cold Scots anger. It centered on Scathach, the instigator of the charade. Sorceress she was and probably the greatest power on Scath, unless that of Amaruduk was greater; but from now on he'd really play the game his way.

He thought of his abrupt departure from her bed and

of what must have preceded it—his acting out the violence of his "dream," being there through her leading, her power. Her control of his movement while under her spell was a sobering thought. What a shock his sudden awakening must have been to her, as it was to him. That had been through Taliesin's timely call—

Taliesin, now locked out of the tower! And Scathach had not yet learned of his presence. Certainly, sooner or later, one of the gods would mention him as the means of their learning about Scath. How was the Bard faring? He sought the mind of his friend and made instant contact.

"Alan—I lie here wondering about you and wishing I were part of whatever you were doing. Not that I have been idle. I've discovered that these demons either come out of tunnels under this very grove, exit at the most unlikely places, or suddenly appear. Their numbers seem to be increasing.

"Nor is that all. These Druidesses are involved in something that concerns you, though I have not been able to determine what it is. It goes on without ceasing and it requires groups huddling in this Temple repeating something almost inaudible, to me a meaningless drone. Each grasps a lapis lazuli pendant like the one Brendah wore; and a few times I know I heard your name in the incantation."

MacDougall felt a faint prickling of his skin, but he tried to keep his comment light. *"Such popularity must be deserved. I'm receiving a fair share of attention here in the Castle."*

"Is there time to tell me about it? I know little of what has happened to you since your first visit with Scathach."

"At least I can start. I don't expect an interruption for quite a while. I told you I was going to the lounge. I did so." He described the gathering and his revealing, through the armlet, the weapons of the visitors.

"Scathach was furious and, under threat of her corps

of archers, really disarmed them. Then she sent them to their rooms like disobedient children." He told of his being awakened by the visit of Pryderi and its aftermath.

"*So here I lie as a replica of the jailer of Ochren, forced to stay awake. Yes, there should be time to bring you up-to-date. I told you Scathach had made a fool of me.*"

In a flash Alan saw again the supine form of the Sorceress with her dress torn from her, the cloth clutched in his hand. At Taliesin's mental gasp, he realized that he had sent the Bard the vision!

Grimly he commented, "*I did not intend letting you see that, but perhaps it's just as well that you received the picture. Your call brought me out of a trance, a spell in which I had relived—I can think of no other term— what supposedly was part of an earlier life of mine. The life of a sixteen-year-old serf named Vollmar, illegitimate son of Vortigern, the King in Roman Britain. I had just killed my half brother and was about to rape and kill my half sister when I awakened to the scene you saw. Better I attempt to show you as best I can in pictures these preincarnations, if that's a word, instead of trying to tell you.*"

Taliesin's response was genuinely startled. "*Vortigern the Usurper, your ancestor? It is hard to believe. And your killing—but show me. You appear to have had a most interesting experience. I outlived Vortigern in the Other World; not one I would have chosen as an ancestor. Show me,*" he repeated. "*Skip nothing. Except for the group huddled in the Temple, all activity here seems to have ended for their sleep time.*"

Beginning with the gathering in the shrine of Lamashtu and his entry into a dreamlike state, he pictured each of his experiences. Everything remained so clearly in his mind that he was able to transmit each bit of action, each alien setting, and each character in the dreams, even conversations with full fidelity.

He began with the flood on the road to Kish as he had seen it through the eyes of Ziusudra and went through each adventure, ending with Vollmar, bastard son of King Vortigern.

In vivid pictures, Alan relived and revealed the grim experiences of that day in Roman Britain, climaxing with his awakening in the bed of Scathach, led there while under the spell of the Sorceress.

As he concluded the long revelation, MacDougall could feel the excitement of the Bard.

"Do you realize, Alan, what this experience means? What its real significance is?"

Alan was incredulous. *"You mean you think I—my soul, or whatever—have lived these past lives, and Scathach was there with me?"*

"No, no!" Impatiently Taliesin's thought rushed on. *"Nor do I mean that Scathach planted all this in your mind through her sorcery. Rather, I mean that someone or something involved in that session had accurate, even living knowledge of those times and their people. Sumer, Babylon, Egypt. Any of those present could have supplied the sequence on Britain, but not on the other three. There was a great Tower as you saw it in Kish; and Ziusudra existed, as did King Etana and his childless Queen. There was a flood in which Ziusudra figured. So with King Nectanebus of Egypt and Thanatha, Priestess of the Goddess Ma'at. I know—"*

"You know?" Alan interrupted. *"How do you know?"*

Momentarily Taliesin seemed at a loss for words. Then he answered lightly, *"Let us say that I have knowledge of the truth of these things. And whatever the source of your visions, they were born out of knowledge —and knowledge which neither Scathach, the Daughters of Calatin, nor the seven Druidesses could possess.*

"So Lamashtu must be more than a stone image! The real power in that chamber is a god and not a god like Nuada, Beli, or Balor. Rather it must be one like this

Ahriman of whom you speak, like Amaruduk, or like whatever gods are imprisoned in your armlet."

The final reference caught MacDougall up short. He could not recall having told the Bard about his constant companions. Had he forgotten—?

As if sensing his thought, Taliesin volunteered, *"Alan, do not be concerned about the little I have learned. The power of your armlet could only come from a personality or intelligence within it. The twin heads suggests two; and you have not always blocked me out as completely as you might have wished when directing a question to them after our own dialogue. But you know you can trust me."*

"Of course." MacDougall came to a decision. *"It is time you knew all the facts."* In a series of vivid mental pictures he drew from his memory the experiences of the Lady Inanna and the Lord Enki as they had revealed them to him in his room in the Red Bull of Ballydhu before his entry into Ochren.

"And now," he concluded, *"you know the source of the power of my armlet."*

"Thank you, Alan." The Bard's response was solemn. *"This explains much and increases my confidence in your ability to cope with whatever arises."*

After a long pause MacDougall returned to the subject of their discussion. *"What about the possibility of my having lived other lives in the past?"*

The Bard answered hesitantly. *"I confess I have never been able to decide definitely on this, though I think my being here with all these other dwellers in Tartarus and Ochren and Scath would negate the idea. Why here and why us? Why not a continuation in other bodies in later times in the Other World?*

"For us, at least, things appear to have come to a halt in this world of Lucifer's creation." The Bard seemed to be groping for a thought. *"There was something else . . . and now I remember. When you were telling me of your*

last interview with Ahriman, you mentioned his saying you might be in the line of an illegitimate son of an ancient King of Britain—'born on the wrong side of the blanket' was his phrase. And he said something like, 'Who knows what kind of a pact may have been entered into—or what promises made?' This lad Vollmar son of Vortigern, and his going to the Circle of Standing Stones—the visitation, his promise—"

"I know," Alan interrupted testily. *"I've thought of it—and it is so perfect a fulfillment it helps to convince me that Ahriman was controlling the entire experience. But—"*

His thought was cut off by a frantic, deeply pitched bellow echoing through the stairwell. It sounded repeatedly, increasing in volume and rising in pitch. Pryderi!

At the first note, MacDougall returned to his own form and vanished, then sprang from the bed and dashed into the corridor. He was the first one there, though moments later doors on the right and left swung open, and the gods and Druids burst forth looking wildly around. Somewhere a guard shouted, "Level three! At once!"

Manannan made the first move, dashing toward the stairway; as one, the others followed. There was no thought of concealment in their race down one flight. More slowly, Alan moved along the hallway and, entering the stairwell, started upward stealthily, clinging to the outer edge. Two Guards darted past, following the inner, shorter way.

At the sixth level, MacDougall emerged, just in time to see Scathach in flimsy blue sleepwear appear at a doorway, calling "Guards!" The cries from below continued unabated, now becoming words but quite unintelligible.

"What happened?" she cried as the Castle Guards came running.

"We have no idea, your Highness, though it sounds like one of the visitors."

At that instant, another door opened, and Isla the maid appeared. From level five came the metallic voice of one of the Sisters. "What madness is this? Is someone being tortured?"

"MacDougall!" Scathach exclaimed, moving out into the hallway. Alan, holding his breath, slipped past her into the bedroom. This was the chance he had been hoping for. Swiftly he moved to the far side and into the dining area. As he closed the door behind him, he heard the Sorceress say, "I'll know in moments through the mirrors and I'll let you know."

As he passed into the curtained corner and mounted the hidden stairs to the shrine of Lamashtu, he breathed again. It was a place to hide and perhaps to get some answers.

He halted before the bronze door with its strange hieroglyphs, hesitating. When he had entered with the Sorceress, she had asked permission. Should he follow the same procedure?

With the thought, the door slowly opened as Alan stared, and a voice spoke within his mind:

"Enter, Alan MacDougall, and welcome. I have been expecting you, you and your servants, the Lord Enki and the Lady Inanna, my sister in the Olden Times."

CHAPTER 7

Trial and Trickery

Slowly, like an automaton, MacDougall moved into the
black chamber. Had he really sensed the words of Ereshkigal, goddess of the Nether World? He knew he had,
and the implication of her thought had a jarring impact.
Not only was his presence known but his coming antici-
pated, with knowledge of the serpent-gods as his companions. He sank to a seat against the wall, staring up at
the grotesque image, his gaze held by the green gem
eyes, which began to glow. He groped for a comment,
but needed none as the Lady Inanna responded, her
thought fairly bristling with indignation.

"Servants, indeed! Rather counselors, teachers, and
helpers. And it cannot be said of us that we once indwelt
the Mountain Devil, Lamashtu, delighting in frightening
children. Nor have we been imprisoned in a stone statue
in a small room for millennia."

"An added indignity." Ereshkigal moaned. "I receive
credit for nothing. Lamashtu, always Lamashtu. And I
am barred from identifying myself." Sharply she added,

"But wherein is a golden armlet superior to a statue? How uncomfortable! Two of you in that small space."

"Wherein? We move about. We have had different hosts during the centuries. We have been involved in the great events of many ages. We have been called by the Lord of Light to serve in other times and places, even while imprisoned."

"You mean other than serving your host? How unfair. But then you always were the favorite—and I can't see why."

There was a brief break in the dialogue, and Alan MacDougall, again master of himself, interjected, "Hold everything! You call yourselves gods, and the three of you are acting like children. You bow to one master, the one you call the Lord of Light, the one better called the Power of Darkness. The three of you are under restraint because you have displeased your Master and because you fit into some plan of his.

"As do I, apparently," he added in deep disgust, "according to a prophetic Scroll ascribed to Lucifer, which the Bard Taliesin deciphered. Why not forget the things that happened thousands of years ago and face the here and now?"

"Out of the mouths of babes," Ereshkigal responded.

Inanna added, "I agree there is nothing to be gained by looking back, though I cannot help feeling resentment."

"Mine is the greater punishment," the dark goddess observed. "This was brought home to me again when, Alan MacDougall, I had to draw up memories of the ancient times." There was a mental sigh.

"Lady Ereshkigal," Alan asked anxiously, "those memories of ancient times—what was their source? It would mean much for me to know."

After a moment she responded, "It is not permitted that I answer. You must decide for yourself."

Enki inquired, "Was it during that 'drawing up' that you learned about us?"

"That and much more, though you sought to block me." Grudgingly she added, "And in part you succeeded."

"And I suppose," MacDougall interjected, "you passed your findings on to Scathach."

Ereshkigal's answer held derision. "That arrogant one! I tell her only what she asks. At least now she has given up the idea of returning to your world. *She* knows it would mean death with no release, eternally wandering as the thinnest of ghosts." She was warming to her subject. "Her arrogance! Rarely does she consult me. *She* is the Queen. *She* decides." The goddess spoke directly to Alan. "She has two purposes regarding you—to keep you here and to bend your will to hers. Your hiding from her has annoyed her greatly but instead of consulting me, she depends on the three Witches. So I tell her only what she asks, all I am bound to do. I may not deceive her, but I am not required to advise her, except at her request."

"You have not changed during the ages." Inanna's thought was honeyed. "You are still the sweet, accommodating, helpful soul you always were." Her words became bitter. "If it had not been for your hellish disposition, none of us would be where we are today. All this is your fault."

The green eyes flared with sudden wrath. "I have become utterly bored with this conversation." And Alan felt the abrupt cutting off of Ereshkigal's thought, and the light in the emerald eyes died. Moments later Enki and Inanna also withdrew, and Alan was alone.

He sat in the quiet of the round room and looked through the circular opening in the roof at the aurora. The waves of rainbow light were forming a rippling curtain of unusual brilliance and he watched in fascination. He became aware of a peculiar feeling of detachment, as if there were two of him. One sat quite calmly in the shrine of Lamashtu, observing the sky of Scath. The other, strangely, felt as if he had just been left alone after a four-way conversation. And the first, considering the matter, felt an urge to burst into wild laughter.

This was the stuff of madness.

MacDougall shook his head as if to dislodge cobwebs from his brain. Mac, he told himself, you're here and it's very real. It's this world, not you, that's crazy. So make the best of it.

He sat watching the play of the aurora, in memory reliving some of the wilder adventures that had followed his first entry into this world: trapped in the frigid Hall of the Dead; his first exposure to shape-changing and his involvement with the hag Morrigu; the invisible Golden Tower, and Ahriman, its master; his escape from Tartarus, despite a blacked-out aurora; the castle of King Arawn and its rooms of suffering; the clouds of whispering spirits in the depths of the abyss; Beli's dragon; the revolving castle, *Caer Pedryvan*, and the empty undersea city, Lochlann; the wild ride on the *Wave Sweeper*; the fantastic land of Einurr and his Trolls; the Crystal Temple in Falias and the Stone of Fal with its unearthly cry; the knife of the mad Druid, Semias.

Unreal! Yet he had lived through all of it and more. So why be disturbed by a few ancient gods, whether of the man-made variety or the demonic kind? He was ready for whatever lay ahead.

He addressed the serpent-gods. "Lord and Lady, is private communication possible here, or will Inanna's friendly sister overhear?"

"There is no problem," Enki answered. "We have been a bit careless about concealment in the past, but that will not happen again. She is blocked out."

"Very well. Let me observe Scathach."

Instantly he saw the Queen of Scath seated in the heart of her mirrors, the faceted emerald sphere alive before her. Her projected image hovered over several Druidesses seated around a table in a shadowed room.

"Lucradh, there will be a trial of the Guard, Brendah. Assemble the judges in the Circle of Justice. I will supervise in person."

Without waiting for a response, the Sorceress changed the scene, and her image now appeared before one of the Daughters of Calatin. "We will proceed with the trial as planned. You have arranged for the visitors to be present, as well as the witnesses and the accused, of course?"

"We have, your Highness. All has been prepared."

"Very well. I will appear when the judges are seated."

MacDougall arched his eyebrows as he cut off the scene. It seemed surprising for Scathach to be acting as judge at Brendah's trial. He was sure this was not normal procedure, and certainly not Brendah's importance that had brought it about. More likely it was intended to impress the visitors with the justice of Scath. He closed his eyes.

"Lord Enki, may I now see Manannan and the others?"

In his mind's eye he saw the ten in the lounge. Pryderi was there, a white cloth wrapped around his head like a tight turban. Otherwise he seemed none the worse for wear, though his expression was more grim and savage than usual. He was on the outer edge of a tight group centered around Beli, who was speaking in a low voice.

"We will attend the trial and continue to cooperate until we get our swords." The fury in his voice intensified. "There are things we could do with magic, but none would produce our weapons. So our hands are tied. But find MacDougall we will, and when we do—"

A formless growl came from the throat of the jailer of Ochren as a column of Guards entered the room.

The leader announced, "We go now to the Circle of Justice."

"Lord Enki," Alan thought, "back to Scathach."

The Sorceress sat watching a scene on the large central mirror. She seemed to be hovering high above a round grove of rowan trees, closely planted and growing with unusual symmetry. The smooth gray bark and graceful branches and leaves made a fitting setting for the clusters of crimson berries. As she zoomed down, Alan saw, almost as if looking over her shoulder, that the trees were a thick border for a circle of standing stones, a smaller Stonehenge, but with long, slender, flat rocks completely bridging the monoliths, forming a roofed outer circle. Within this circle stood a second row of substantially shorter stones without covering slabs; within this row was a third, low and squat like a circle of great seats, slightly higher than normal stools. In the center of the circle lay a round, flat slab raised on smaller stones about a foot above the ground. On opposite sides of the platform were waist-high, three-sided enclosures. Beyond all this lay a flat-topped stone wall, gently curving to conform with the general contour of the circle. The open ground between the rocks was the usual pale-green turf.

A column of black-robed women filed through the trees, their pale faces half hidden by peaked black hoods. One behind another, they moved solemnly into the circle and seated themselves in order on the pillars. Alan counted; there were twenty in all. One pillar, which remained empty, he noticed, rose about a foot above the others, with stone steps at its base.

As if on signal, from the opposite side of the circle came a smaller group, five of the Guards, the central one Brendah. They led the prisoner to the platform. Head proudly erect, she stepped up and moved to the center. The others then entered one of the enclosures, which, Alan thought, must be a witness box. MacDougall recognized one of the four as Sorcha, the girl who had told him about the tower's water supply, the one he had kissed.

There was a buzz of voices, quickly hushed, as the visitors were escorted into the circle. They were led to seats on the stone wall, facing the judges' pillars. A Guard stood behind each one.

The scene vanished, the mirrors lost their glow, and the green sphere died as Scathach stood up and left the room. Mentally MacDougall followed as, with her personal Guards, the Sorceress wound her way downward through the stairwell and across the room on ground level to a rear exit where a double row of Guards opened a way for her passing. Outside, a two-foot-wide strip of metal had been laid across the maze of walls, leading to the bridge. Of course, Alan thought, the Queen would not be expected to thread the maze; bad enough that she had to cross the rough bridge.

Watching, MacDougall contrasted his mental view with the life-sized image in the mirror, the difference between a small television screen and the wide screen in a theater. So why not use the mirrors? He found perverse amusement in the idea of watching Scathach with her own private equipment, if he could.

"Lord and Lady," he asked excitedly, "do you think you can operate Scathach's mirrors?"

"Of course we can; they are mentally controlled. But do you think it wise to—?"

"Of course, there's the matter of her maid, Isla. You could put her to sleep, couldn't you?"

"That would present no problem, but—"

"Then do so. With me invisible and with Scathach gone and the mirrors so close—why not?"

Springing to his feet, Alan moved swiftly to the corridor, down the stairs, and into the room of mirrors. Seated on the pedestal, he demanded, "Now show me."

"As we said, it's entirely mental," came the reply. "Think into the green globe, as once you thought into the armlet before you knew we were here. Will it to life. Then picture the Sorceress."

Fantastically, the sphere began to glow, intensifying in seconds to its maximum brilliance; and on the mirror appeared a view of the Circle of Justice. The Sorceress had just entered the circle, her guards behind her. At her entry, the Druidesses and the visitors, the only ones seated, stood up, the ten tardily and reluctantly. As she mounted the steps and seated herself on the pillar of the Chief Justice, the Guards stationed themselves behind her at right and left, and those standing resumed their seats.

Scathach's voice rang solemnly through the grove. "Let the trial begin."

The judge at her right arose and asked, "Who is the accused?"

"I am," Brendah answered. "Brendah of the Castle Guard."

"What is the nature of the offense?"

The judge at Scathach's left stood up. "She attempted to visit our Queen's guest, Alan MacDougall, after the Queen specifically forbade it."

"But I did not know," Brendah cried. "No one told me—"

"Silence," Scathach interrupted. "You will present your defense in due time."

The first judge asked, "Who speaks as accuser?"

One of the Guards in the witness box answered, "I do. I, with Gerdah, was assigned to stop visitors who might seek to visit Alan MacDougall." She went on to describe how they had caught the accused at Alan's bedroom door. Her companion corroborated her statement.

As this went on, MacDougall felt his temper rise. This was the silliest nonsense, childish to say the least.

Sorcha was speaking. "Brendah had just come off relief on level five, and she asked me if I knew which room had been given to the visitor. I knew because I was on duty on level four when he came and I was one of those who escorted him to his room. A bit later he called me to ask about his water supply, which I thought was strange. So I told her which was his room. But I felt her asking was suspicious, so I also told her he had just gone to his room." Triumphantly she added, "I was right. It *was* suspicious."

The little witch, Alan thought angrily, deliberately setting a trap for Brendah to walk into!

Now Scathach spoke. "Why, Brendah, were you so anxious to see my guest?"

The girl flushed and hesitated. "I—I merely wanted to thank him for letting me bring him from the forest. As you know, he had escaped while he was my prisoner. Had I failed to find him, I would not have dared to return. I had even considered jumping into the Well of Darkness."

There had to be more than that, Alan thought. She *had* thanked him. It must be something she could not speak of.

Scathach frowned. "Am I so fearsome? Are you sure your interest in my guest is not deeper than you have said?"

Brendah's color deepened. "Your Highness must know that he would not look twice at one such as I."

The Sorceress scowled. "Justice must prevail. My edicts are law, and ignorance can be no excuse. What say you?" She spoke to the judges.

In unison they answered, "Your word is law. Ignorance can be no excuse."

"I am fair," Scathach declared. "Since this is a first offense, I order ten lashes. Lucradh, let the sentence be carried out."

Back in the room of mirrors, Alan MacDougall mentally cursed. He felt so helpless. This was his fault, and there was nothing he could do about it.

The Druidess Lucradh called out, "Treen! Your duty."

From the grove of rowan trees came three huge women. Immediately Alan thought of Japanese heavy-weight wrestlers, masses of fat hiding bulging muscles. And these three women wore little more than the wrestlers, sandals in addition to a loincloth. One carried a long black whip. These grotesques crossed the circle to the platform where Brendah waited, her face set in defiance. One of the monsters removed the girl's breastplates and flung them aside. Then two of them grasped her wrists and stretched her arms straight out, the strain visible in the taut muscles and tendons. Standing well to one side, the whip wielder lashed the air with a trial swing, the tip of the whip snapping like a pistol shot.

"Now!"

Alan was startled by the single word that burst from the Sorceress. It revealed an eagerness, a gloating savagery utterly revolting.

The whip rose and fell in a vicious arc, the weighted tip burning itself in the bare back and drawing blood. A single shrill scream burst from the girl, and her head sank forward.

From Lucradh came a sharp "One!"

Again the whip cut its red stripe into Brendah's back; she quivered, but made no sound. And so it went through the ten slow, merciless blows. At last the sickening spectacle ended and the ungainly trio waddled back into the grove. Slowly Brendah turned and stared up at Scathach, hatred on her ashen face, a trickle of blood coming from a corner of her mouth, drawn from lacerated lips.

The Queen of Scath said tonelessly, "Justice has been done. Take her to the barracks in the warriors' village. She is no longer in the Tower Guard."

She paused, then spoke again in an altered voice, every word emphasized. "Before you leave—all of you —mark well this word, and tell it to all in Scath. Alan MacDougall is mine. None may communicate with him except at my instruction or with my permission." She glanced across the circle at the visitors. "You are no exceptions. If any harm befalls him at your hands, you will answer to me. He is mine."

Livid with rage, MacDougall leaped erect. If only he were there, facing her! He spoke aloud.

"What in hell do you mean by making so stupid a statement? I am not yours!" Dimly he was aware of a gasp rising from all in the circle and of Scathach staring at something directly before her.

"Whether or not you like it, I will come and go as I please. Not you or anyone else can stop me."

Startled, he realized his projected image hung in mid-air facing the Sorceress. Mental control of the mirrors, his wish, had become a fact. Good!

"After the disgusting spectacle I've just seen, I'm about fed up with Scath and everything in it. And that includes you, Scathach. Especially you." Nostrils flaring, jaws clamped tight, his glaring image met the Sorceress' startled gaze. Savagely he continued. "You are venting your anger on this girl because I rejected you. You offered yourself to me and I refused you, and I want all of Scath to know it."

Sharply the Sorceress drew in her breath and her face lost all color, a murderous light in her eyes. Alan halted. Had he gone too far?

At that moment in the room itself he sensed movement and heard sounds of commotion. He whirled to meet the triumphant leer of one of the Daughters of Calatin. Behind her were a dozen Guards with ready swords, filling the doorway. For an uncomprehending instant he stared; then, at a faint cackle from behind him, he glanced over his shoulder. There, at the other doorway, stood a second Daughter with her Guards.

Trapped! In a flash he saw it. Scathach was conducting the trial, leaving the mirrors unguarded, to bring him out of hiding. As it had done, idiot that he was.

"There is no way out of this room," the grating voice of the Witch exclaimed. "And the three of us can counter any one man's invisibility spell, as you will learn. So you had better yield."

"Brilliant, aren't you?" Alan commented as he drew his sword. "What would you do if I were to start swinging among the mirrors? Scathach would be most unhappy, I fear. Stay back, all of you, or I swing."

Alarm appeared on the ugly face. "You would not dare—even you!"

Alan backed against the main mirror so he could see both doorways, stalling for time. "I am thinking," he said. "Do not disturb me."

To the serpent-gods he asked, "Lord and Lady, *can* she block my vanishing?"

The answer was encouraging. "Your power alone, perhaps, but not ours."

"Good. Then let us repeat a bit of the illusion of Lochlann. As I disappear, have another MacDougall appear, darting out, sword raised, apparently attacking the group on my left. Leave my back exposed so the other group will attack from the rear. I'm in your hands."

"Ready." Enki flashed the thought. "Go!"

As MacDougall crouched and slid invisibly out of the mirrors' protection, he saw the amazing spectacle of another MacDougall leap with a shout toward the shocked women. Stealthily, he slid to the far wall and waited, but not for long, as a very noisy attacker seemed to weave a wall of steel before the Guards, impaired by an ugly harridan who had fallen to her knees and crouched there. The second group, motioned on by the second gray Witch, crept up from behind. As they left the doorway, Alan darted through.

He was in the dining room. And in the corner hung the curtain concealing the stairway to the shrine. Swiftly he swept it aside and ran up the steps, two at a stride, onto the roof. He wanted no more of Ereshkigal.

"Lord and Lady," he directed, "keep them occupied as long as possible while I explore."

Enki answered with enthusiasm. "I'm enjoying this. A chance for me to brush up on my swordsmanship. Inanna is working on the Sisters, keeping them deceived."

MacDougall made a rapid tour of the roof. There was little to see beside the dome over the shrine with its adjustable opening and the great open water tank, plus, of course, the endlessly arriving bronze containers of water.

This, he told himself grimly, was the end of the line. There was no place to hide and no way out but the way he had come. It was a blind alley, a cul-de-sac. Perhaps he could shape-change to match one of the searchers and get through; at least it might be worth a try. He saw again the face of Scathach as he told her world of his rejecting her. At the moment, he definitely did not want to face her fury. She needed time to cool off. And then there were Pryderi, Beli, Balor, and Manannan—especially Pryderi. Alan *was* in a spot.

While he dwelt on these thoughts, his eyes idly followed the perpetually moving chain, arriving with upright pails, more or less filled with water, passing over a huge sprocket wheel, and, after pouring their contents into the tank, passing bottoms up to another sprocket wheel about two feet beyond the edge of the roof and descending to the river. As he watched he had a sudden wild idea.

A momentary distraction came with a thought from Taliesin. *"Alan, are you free for a few moments? Or are your hands full after the explosion?"*

"So you were there for the blow-up," MacDougall answered. *"I wondered. I'm still steaming—and I guess you'd say my hands are full—but I'm free at the moment, though probably not for long."*

"I was at the trial and now I'm with Manannan and the rest—of course without their knowledge. There was pandemonium after you appeared. Though the Sorceress was badly shaken by what happened, she remained in

control and for some reason kept everyone there until things had calmed down. We're on our way back now, and I am certain I can get into the Castle—".

"*Don't!*" MacDougall interrupted. "*Stay out. I've just slipped out of a trap of Scathach's setting. Her delay was to make sure the mouse had been caught. My stupidity—but I'll tell you later. Go to the west side of the Castle, outside the moat, opposite the door we entered, and wait. I'm on the roof of the tower, but I've just had a wild idea; if it works, we'll be out of here. If it doesn't, I may die. Enough! I hear them coming.*"

There were voices in the stairway, those of the Daughters of Calatin and the Guards. They stopped at the shrine, and Alan heard a harsh voice asking Lamashtu for permission to enter.

The thought of the serpent-gods came through: "We're sorry, but they finally saw through the deception. There are limits, you know."

"It sufficed, I think. Now I have some calculating to do."

He moved swiftly to the chain of pails, looking over the crenelated wall, following the descending containers. At a quick count, there were about thirty pails per side —thirty empty, thirty full, with probably three gallons per pail. Roughly ninety gallons at a time—seven hundred pounds of water. He looked down at the stone landing where twenty women dragged in unison on the heavy chain. Thirty-odd pounds per puller; his two hundred pounds shouldn't cause a problem. It would probably mean nothing but an easier pull on one cycle.

He was going to ride the chain down to ground level!

He heard the searchers mounting to the roof and saw them spread out, apparently trying to cover every inch of its surface. Invisibility was no defense against this tactic. He climbed to the top of the wall and looked down, trying to quell the queasy feeling in his stomach. Ten storeys! The women looked awfully small down there, some of them almost ghostly in the shifting mist. What if something gave way! Off to one side he could see the stream of people flowing from the grove into the castle, but he ignored them.

He tried also to ignore the searchers and the dizzying height, watching the chain and pails passing overhead, the heavy links meshing with the sprockets. Solid enough, but so very old. What about the wear of many centuries? One weak link... Again he looked down. There must be another means of escape; and an idea came, born of the tightness of his stomach.

When the rooftop was crowded with searchers, he'd have an illusory MacDougall appear, standing on the wall; after a defiant shout to get everyone's attention, he'd leap out into space, arms and legs outspread, and plummet to the rock floor below, his cry following him all the way down. All of the Guards would rush down through the tower, leaving him free to descend as he wished.

It was a good idea, except that it wouldn't work, not after a fake MacDougall in Scathach's quarters. Some would believe the illusion, but others wouldn't.

Time to go, Mac, he told himself, inhaling deeply. He tensed his muscles, then reached far out to the side and grasped the chain. He caught it cleanly and swung free, wrapping his legs around one of the pails and clinging with all his strength. He waited for a pickup of speed. When it didn't come, he blew out a great breath of relief.

Grinning, he looked down, watching the stone paving slowly approaching. That had been easy. His grin widened as he thought of the frustration of the Daughters of Calatin and, more important, Scathach, when they finally decided he had slid through their fingers. Only one problem remained—getting off the chain. He passed within a few feet of one of the Guards on the roof of the two-storey base; then, suddenly clear in the veil of fog, he saw another shaft and sprocket wheel below him.

When about three feet above it, he swung vigorously out, away from the pullers, and let go. Knees bent, he landed with scarcely a jar.

Well done, Mac, he thought. After a single glance at the dull, fatigued faces of the women, and a longer look at the bridge and covered maze with the last stragglers from the trial passing over them, he walked briskly around the Castle. He looked for what he thought of as the main entrance, the one closest to the bridge. He passed two doorways, each with its pair of Guards, and at the third, he faced the moat.

On this side of the Castle there was little activity. He saw several warriors in the distance, walking toward their village, one of them probably Brendah. Thought of the girl brought back the question of why she had tried to see him. With it came a twinge of conscience; again his visit to this world had created trouble for another. He'd have to see her. But there were more immediate concerns.

"*Taliesin,*" he sent the thought. "*Where are you?*"

"*Where you told me to be—outside the moat, opposite the main entrance.*"

Then Alan saw him, faintly ghostlike. "*Good. I'm starting across the maze.*"

"*I see you.*"

Alan took two steps on the narrow way and came to a jarring halt. If felt as if he had stepped into a heavy surf and a powerful undertow were forcing him back. He tried a third step, and the resistance intensified. Into his mind poured a feeling of negation, a concerted chorus telling him to go back, that there was a barrier that he could not pass. Incredulous, he thrust stubbornly against the force but to no avail.

"Lord and Lady, what's happening?" he asked in exasperation. "Something is preventing my crossing the moat."

After a momentary delay the answer came. "Interesting. We sense the same sort of mental interference, of

tides of power, we experienced after your escape from
King Arawn when we could not guide you out of the fog
the Druids created. A weaker manifestation, but effective, obviously the doing of the Druidesses. We can
counter this to a degree."

Alan felt the resistance weaken, but progress remained slow, and the effort was exhausting.

"*What's amiss?*" the Bard asked. "*You move so
slowly.*"

In a few terse thoughts MacDougall told him; and as
he did so he thought of the Bard's reporting the gather-
ings of Druidesses in the Temple and their incantations
that included Alan's name. This would be a real problem,
he added, if it persisted.

"*I may be able to do something about this,*" Taliesin
responded and ended communication.

MacDougall continued his labored effort until he
reached the bridge, then abruptly all resistance ended.
He halted for a startled instant, then hastened across. He
met the Bard at the end of the arch.

"*What did you do?*" he demanded. "*It has stopped.*"

"*I gained the help of an unlikely ally.*" Taliesin's
thought was amused. "*I called on a demon named Kindazi who had spoken to me while I was in the village of
the Druidesses. He had approached me out of curiosity
when he realized I could see him. I invited communication, all of which was mental. When I realized what was
causing your problem, I managed to reach him and suggested that he and others of his kind interfere with the
group in the Temple as a means of annoying Scathach,
their main purpose in life. They responded immediately,
disrupting their concentration by materializing in their
midst.*"

MacDougall started toward the guards' village, the
Bard at his side. "*We'll want horses; but before we leave,
I want to visit Brendah. I owe her that, and I'd like to*

learn why she wanted to see me." He spoke to the serpent-gods: "Will you guide us?"

Past the corral, they entered a narrow lane between rows of one-room, boxlike frame buildings of rough-hewn boards, flat-roofed, with a single window and doorway. As they proceeded Alan asked,

"Why didn't you interfere with the Druidesses before this?"

"Because I had hoped to learn what they were up to. Now we know."

They were guided to one of the frame huts, and as they halted outside it they heard Brendah's voice.

"Thank you, Veenah. That feels much better," she was saying.

Hesitantly Alan led the way into a room containing a single bed and chair and with wooden pegs in one wall, some holding garments and weapons. Brendah lay face-down on the bed, her head resting on folded arms, while another guard applied an ointment to the raw and swollen welts on her back. As the two invisible men entered she turned her face to one side, exposing a badly swollen lower lip. "I could kill the bitch," she whispered.

"Careful," Veenah said hastily. "Sometimes walls have ears. You are not the first to be lashed, nor will you be the last." She moved toward the door. "Call me if you need me. I will bring food when it is ready."

"Bring me food!" the Amazon exclaimed indignantly. "I can make it on my own after a bit of rest. If nothing else, I can manage soup in spite of this mouth."

As Veenah left, MacDougall asked the serpent-gods, "Is Scathach at her mirrors, or is it safe for me to reveal myself?"

"Not at her mirrors," the answer came, "but very busy with her visitors. During all the confusion they got into the apartment of the Three Sisters and have recovered their weapons." There was a brief pause. "They are furious. They can't get the swords out of the sca-bards; a spell, it would appear. There is complete confusion in the Castle."

"Wonderful," MacDougall responded. "No more than Scathach deserves."

Knocking on the wall beside the door, he said softly, "Brendah, this is Alan MacDougall. I am here in your room."

Instantly she turned, starting to sit up, then winced and dropped back. "Alan—sire! Let me see you! But how did you leave the Castle?"

Letting himself be seen, MacDougall said, "I came to tell you how very sorry I am. Your being lashed was all my fault and I know it. How I left is a long story. But tell me, why, why did you try to see me?"

"Because I had heard something I thought you should know. I had been assigned as relief Guard, going from station to station to permit regulars to leave their posts for short periods, and had just come to the fifth level. When passing a door of the Three, I heard Scathach's voice, so I—I listened. It must have been her image. I heard her instruct the Three to have the Druidesses set up a spell to stop you from leaving the Castle, and to keep this in force until she gave other instructions. I thought you should know. Then Sorcha lied, and they caught me.

"As for the lashes, give them no thought. My back will heal."

"I am glad you feel that way, but I still feel guilty. What you heard was worth telling me, and I thank you. I learned about the spell as I crossed the moat, but was able to leave in spite of it. We will be leaving here—"

"We!" Brendah cried, sitting up, ignoring the pain. "You mean I can go with you? Oh, take me—even into the Other World."

"I am sorry," MacDougall said gently, "but that is impossible. Anyone from this world going to mine will die in a very short time, and there will be no other bodies and no other land, even like Scath, to go to. By 'we' I meant—" Suddenly he decided. "—I meant the Bard of Bards from Tartarus, Taliesin, my very best friend in this world, who has joined me."

Instantly the Bard appeared with his warm smile and twinkling eyes. "It is good to meet you, Brendah. As friend of the MacDougall, you are my friend. Who knows, in this small world perhaps we will meet again."

The girl stood up in confusion. "Gods and Druids and Bards—and Alan MacDougall! Scath was never like this during all the ages."

"And now," Alan concluded, "we must leave. Sooner or later Scathach will learn of the canceled spell and will realize I've escaped." Stooping, he kissed the girl. "Good-bye, Brendah. Be careful." And the two vanished.

Outside they hastened toward the corral. There were several Guards in the stables but none outside among the horses. They halted at the rail fence.

"Simple enough to make a couple of horses disappear," MacDougall observed, *"but we need saddled animals. Any ideas?"*

"Easy," the Bard answered airily. *"An illusion. Scathach and, say, one of the Daughters of Calatin rushing out of the Castle and ordering up a pair of noble steeds. Then we shape-change to match, get on the animals, and ride away."*

Enthusiastically MacDougall commented, *"Except that they're women and we're men. Is it possible?"*

"No problem at all," Taliesin responded. *"What made you think gender was a barrier?"*

"I don't know. I just assumed it couldn't be done. I like your idea, but with some changes. It wouldn't be logical for the Sorceress to leave her Castle with all that's happening, and she wouldn't have only one attendant. Instead, suppose her projection appears above the corral and directs the Guards to prepare horses for two

of her messengers, already on their way. They may wonder where messengers could be going, but they'd obey without question. And as they approach, we shape-change and take their place. It should work." To the serpent-gods he added, "What think you, Lord and Lady?"

Inanna answered, "You are ingenious. Of course it can be done."

Alan watched the illusion develop, marveling at its perfection. The pseudoprojection of the Sorceress appeared above the corral and gave orders in Scathach's voice. Then the illusion of two approaching members of the Castle Guard followed. Alan and the Bard shape-changed to blend smoothly into the picture. In a short time the two very feminine riders headed their mounts toward the narrow cart road leading out of Scathach's domain.

CHAPTER 8

The Anunnaki

With only the top of the tower visible behind them, Mac-
Dougall drew rein.

"So far, so good," he exclaimed, returning to his own
form, "but now we need to do some planning."

"Agreed," Taliesin said, again his rotund self. "May I
suggest we visit Amaruduk? I really am quite anxious to
meet him."

MacDougall looked quizzically at the Bard. "I don't
profess to understand why you want this, but you
usually have a sound reason for whatever you do. And
since we're either in Scathach's area or that of Amaruduk, we have no choice. So we'll head for the other half
of the island. However, to make pursuit more difficult I
suggest we leave the worn paths and cut across country
to the seacoast and follow the shoreline. Who knows,"
he added with a grin, "we might even meet some of the
'things' Brendah talked about. Let's go."

"A moment, Alan." Taliesin gazed out over the undulating expanse of waist-high grass that was like an enor-

mous hayfield. "Have you forgotten so soon how the real projection of Scathach can scan the countryside? If we rode through that growth, we would leave a trail a blind man could follow. There has to be a better way."

MacDougall frowned. "You're right, of course. We could ride back through the village to the seashore—"

"A better idea," the Bard exclaimed. "When you asked Brendah about the building where replacement bodies were stored, did she not very hastily say there was one on the east and one on the west shores of this half of the island?"

"She did, indeed. And there must be a path for the replacements to follow as they walk to their future home. Brilliant idea. Scathach would never look for us riding toward the Hall of the Dead.

"So we vanish, we and our horses, and go around the nearer end of the village until we find that path, logically at the western end. Then we ride into the sunset." He grimaced at the aurora. "Except here there is no sun to set."

As they rode back to the warriors' village under a cloak of invisibility, Taliesin commented, "Our starting out on this road in the sight of the corral Guard should misdirect the Sorceress; and she may be puzzled at there being two riders. I wonder how they are faring at the Castle."

"I'll find out." Alan directed the question to the serpent-gods.

After a short delay the answer came. "Bedlam still prevails. Scathach is back at her mirrors, delving everywhere, both inside and outside the tower. Her Guards are searching frantically, the torture rooms receiving extra attention. To add to the confusion, the visitors, too, are searching—and still struggling to draw their swords, still unable to counter the spell. Nuada is in his room lying with eyes closed, but I am certain not asleep.

I should say he is trying to establish contact with Taliesin."

MacDougall repeated the essence of Enki's words to the Bard, concluding, "It would be well for you to be on your guard. In Manannan's Castle when we were seeking to escape, you were able to look through Nuada's eyes. Can he do the same with you?"

"Only if I permit it. I can close my mind to any outside approach, or I can be selective, as I am now while exchanging ideas with you."

They reached the edge of the village and turned left to follow the open area where ordinary turf bordered the first row of houses. The grass cushioned the horses' hoofs, and, though they passed numerous guards, their presence went unnoticed. They crossed four cart paths, each slanting more obliquely toward the west than the one before, once seeing a small caravan of hand-drawn carts approaching, with mounted guards leading and riding in the rear, but they crossed the road well in advance of the caravan's arrival.

They were aware when the guards' huts ended and the harvesters' began, the boxes of the latter being even smaller. All were strictly utilitarian.

Between the groups of cabins lay a succession of long windowless structures that evidently were the warehouses for storing the produce of the orchards. In their midst rose a larger building from which came the mixed aromas of food being processed. Built against the side of the last warehouse was an open shed filled with empty carts.

Finally they came upon what they sought, a narrow path opening through the tall grass, just wide enough for two horses to walk side by side; the growth crowded close, indicating the infrequent use of the path. This lay well beyond the western edge of the village; no one was in sight when Alan led the way into the path, setting out at a brisk canter.

After several minutes MacDougall glanced over his shoulder, past the Bard, at the path behind them. The wind of their passing stirred the grass briefly, a suspicious sign if Scathach were scanning, but they left no permanent trail to be followed. And with all of Scath to search, there was little chance of her picking on this spot.

The village was well behind them when they encountered their first "thing." They had gone over a slight rise and were descending into a little valley when Alan noticed a stirring ahead in the grass beside the road. Just before he reached the place, a grotesque, headless creature with numerous spiderlike limbs and a bulbous red body all of two feet high leaped into the path. Alan's startled horse reared up wildly, almost unseating his rider. A second leap carried the monstrous thing into the field, barely in time to escape the descending hoofs.

It took Alan's utmost skill to quiet his mount; when he had done so he exclaimed aloud, "What was that? One of Brendah's things? If so, it was well named."

Taliesin, who had had some problems of his own, said quietly, "I believe you've missed something, Alan. Either that was an amazing coincidence or that creature could see us! The timing was perfect. Yet we are supposedly invisible."

The implication was suddenly clear. "You mean—a demon, shape-changing? You said they could see you, though the Druidesses could not. It might well be. It's a lot more plausible than a thing like that existing without a head. But let's not decide on the basis of one appearance. There may well be a repeat performance."

They started on their way, the horses' gait slowed to little more than a fast walk. They had not long to wait for a second manifestation.

As before, they had gone over a hillock and were riding downhill when another nightmare creature leaped onto the path. It bore no resemblance to the first one. A four-legged reptile with bright-green scales, it reared up all of five feet on a long serpentine tail, opening a gaping, crocodilian mouth to emit a loud and prolonged hiss. Then it leaped into the grass and disappeared. The horse, already skittish, sprang to one side and stood high on his rear legs, kicking defensively. Again with difficulty, MacDougall managed to calm the stallion.

"I was right," Taliesin exclaimed aloud. "I was ready, and I saw through the shape-change. It was a twisted human form, like all of those in the groves. They're not as malformed as the Fomorians, but just slightly askew —shoulders sloping to one side or the other, limbs of uneven length, and so on. And they have very unpleasant faces, perpetually resentful. They call themselves the Anunnaki, the sons of Anu in the Sumerian pantheon."

"Lord Enki and Lady Inanna, were you following the Bard's statement?" MacDougall opened his query to Taliesin, as he did the answer.

"Indeed we were," Inanna responded. "And their claim is absurd. A few may be Anunnaki—definitely those who shape-change; but most of them are of the Igigi, the lowest level of gods, the common, serving demons who have not these abilities. But here, what matters it? Call them as you wish."

"The Anunnaki," Taliesin added, "as you recently told me, were the judges of the Nether World, who could destroy with a word or condemn with a look."

"You remember?" Alan asked aloud, recalling Inanna's being judged by the Anunnaki and condemned without a word being spoken. "You refer to the judges who sentenced Queen Inanna to death in the realm of darkness." Still speaking aloud he added, "We now know what the 'things' are; but what about the horses? If these imaginary creatures continue to appear, as well they may, we'll never make it to the seashore.

"Lord Enki, can we possibly control them—the horses, I mean—mentally?"

The serpent-god answered with annoyance in his thought. "Possible, I suppose. But wouldn't a simple blindfold serve the same purpose?"

Taliesin laughed aloud and MacDougall grunted rue-fully. "Sweet simplicity; and I seek to make things complicated. Now we need merely find cloth for blindfolds."

"No great problem," the Bard responded. "A strip or two torn from the bottom of my cape should do the trick."

Shortly thereafter they were again on their way. And although the fantastic array of chimeras appeared at regular intervals, the horses continued their flight into darkness undisturbed. After a few of the Anunnaki barely escaped the flying hoofs they confined their cavorting to the roadside. But their numbers remained unchanged, about two appearing in every mile, MacDougall estimated.

"I'm getting tired of this." He addressed the serpent-gods. "Is there no way to stop them?"

"Why didn't you ask us before this?" Enki demanded. "Of course there is."

Magically the interruptions stopped.

As time passed with no further appearances, Taliesin asked aloud, "What happened? No more Anunnaki."

"I don't know. I simply asked the Lord Enki if he could stop them, and he did." Mechanically he removed the blindfold from his horse, as did Taliesin.

There was a long silence, then the Bard said wonder-ingly, "Do you mean they could have done this after the first manifestation?"

Enki and Inanna answered as one through MacDougall's mind. "Obviously we could have. Think you an Anunnaki would dare to disobey two of the Powers? We did not take action earlier in order to teach you to stop your muddy thinking. We should not have suggested the blindfold for the horses, but not to do so was too painful." The thought became deadly serious. "During the times that lie ahead of you, your decisions, your actions will have significance beyond anything you can conceive. So, Alan MacDougall, think!"

They rode on in silence while Alan considered the serpent-gods' statement. Then he said to no one in particular, "And I was only hunting for Malcolm in the Highlands."

He was glad when the white, angular Hall of the Dead appeared on the horizon, silhouetted against a colorful curtain of waves and streamers of the aurora. After the flat expanse of sea with its near-perfect mirror image of the sky came into view, he was struck by the incongruity of the boxlike structure.

He heard the voice of Taliesin from behind him. "I'm sorry, Alan," he said apologetically, "but I prefer not to go any closer. I'll be riding through the grass toward the shore."

As MacDougall looked back, the Bard sent his mount to the left in a wide sweep around the taboo building. Quickly Alan left the path to follow.

"I should have remembered," he responded, recalling the dread of these places implanted in all those with bodies by Lucifer. "I certainly have no wish to get any closer than this. One visit was more than enough." The Bard had left the road at the crest of one of the numerous small hills; and as he reached its base, he suddenly drew rein.

"Look at this," he exclaimed.

Drawing up beside him, MacDougall saw through the screening grass an opening in the hillside; and scurrying into its depth was one of the Anunnaki. This explained the regular appearance of the fantastic creatures along the way, always at the base of an undulation in the landscape. Probably regularly spaced branches of a larger tunnel ran parallel with the path.

"And they are stationed here," the Bard added, having followed MacDougall's thought, "thoroughly to frighten all the replacements before they are fully awake to what has happened. No wonder they fear the 'things.'"

Their ride ended at a stretch of beach, if one called pebbles of assorted sizes a beach. There was no sand here, only pebbles. As the hoofs of the horses crunched over the rounded stones, Alan decided it was another anomaly. Pebbles were formed by the action of water in motion. This sea was as placid as the proverbial millpond. And the stones were white quartz; with tunnels driven through solid clay, there was no sign of quartz in the structure of the island. On the other hand, what about the deposits of metal ore in the rock crust of Tartarus, segregated for the convenient mining of the Trolls? Lucifer made his own laws.

Taliesin interrupted his thought with a question. "What happened in Scathach's tower? With the diversions created by the Anunnaki we failed to talk about it."

Switching to mental exchange, Alan told him all that had happened, starting with the bellowing of Pryderi, caught in the bed of spikes. He omitted nothing, including the conference in the shrine of Lamashtu and his blundering into Scathach's trap. His projection appearing at the trial and his furious statement had not been in her plans. He told of his escape to the roof with the help of the serpent-gods' illusion, concluding with his descent down the outside of the tower, clinging to the chain. Though he made light of it all, he thoroughly enjoyed the Bard's reaction, especially his praise of his ingenuity in the final adventure.

Taliesin in turn told of his stay among the Druidesses and the Anunnaki observers. It was MacDougall's first clear idea of that part of Scath. Indeed, Taliesin's telepathic visualization enabled him almost to see things as the Bard had seen them.

There were three circular groves of rowan trees, one against another, all carefully planted, of uniform shape and size and of great age. The first held the Circle of Justice in which Brendah had been tried, a symmetrical mixture of trees and rocks that MacDougall had seen in Scathach's mirrors. The second, also symmetrically arranged, was a solid stand of trees with individual rock seats under each tree. At its center stood a surrealistic pillar carved of bloodstone, reminding Alan of the monolith in the forest of the spirits. This area was used by the Druidesses for meditation. The third circle enclosed the Temple, a black, cone-shaped structure with a lancelike black spire at its peak, topped by a looped cross. It was formed of perfectly fitted black rock, smooth and polished, like that of the wall around the shrine of Lamashtu. Seven narrow windows, close to the top of the cone, and a slit of a doorway admitted the faint light that alone dispelled total darkness. A polished black floor completed the Temple.

It was here on their knees that the Druidesses had maintained their unbroken chanting, which was to have compelled MacDougall to remain in the Castle.

Beyond these three groves stretched a great parklike oval, also of rowan trees; and regularly spaced between them were small igloolike domes of natural wood, each with a single window and doorway, which housed the Druidesses. Finally there was a fourth grove in which stood a single larger dome devoted to food storage and preparation. To east and south stretched an expanse of the inevitable grass.

"I moved unseen anywhere I wished," the Bard concluded, "watching and listening to the Druidesses until I became aware of the twisted demons. They, too, were invisible to the women and moved with equal freedom, until they realized that I could see them. Then it became a game, each trying to observe without being seen, until at last one demon approached me, wanting to know who I was. I told him in part and learned he and his were of the forces of Amaruduk, God of gods. From him I learned they called themselves the Anunnaki; and they, too, he said, were gods. This was Kindazi, who helped you to escape from the Castle."

During this interchange, the horses, left to their own devices, had slowed to a walk, heads hanging in weariness. MacDougall looked at their surroundings. On one side lay the width of pebble beach and ocean, and on the other the endless grass. He halted, shedding his and his mount's invisibility.

"My friend," he said as if he had made a discovery, "I'm tired. Tired and hungry and thirsty. You must be in the same state. And so are the horses." He swung out of the saddle and took a few awkward steps. "This is as good a place to stop as anywhere. I judge we're about halfway to the woods, and there is no real reason for our driving ourselves. And in an isolated spot like this, there's little chance of Scathach finding us."

"Agreed on all counts." The Bard dismounted. "Grass and water for the horses—"

"Water?" MacDougall demanded. "You mean the sea?"

"Watch." Taliesin removed the animal's harness, and immediately it waded knee-deep into the sea and began drinking. Alan shook his head.

"For no real reason, I assumed the sea was salt." He thought of the Great Lakes; there was more fresh water there, probably, than in all of this world. Minutes later his own stallion was satisfying his thirst.

"My canteen is full," MacDougall said, "though I suppose we could also drink from the sea, and I still have some food I brought from the Other World."

The Bard chuckled. "Surprisingly, I had enough forethought to borrow a morsel or two from the Druidesses; and my cape now, thanks to your example, has acquired pockets."

Seated on their saddles, they ate a mixture of oatcakes, shortbread, and assorted dried fruit and nuts and drank to repletion. The horses were busily feeding on the grass, evidently familiar fare. Afterward Alan stretched and yawned.

"I think sleep is next. I haven't enjoyed a really good sleep in ages. This grass should make a soft bed; and the serpent-gods will protect us from the Anunnaki. As for the horses, a mental suggestion should keep them nearby. It worked in Ochren when I slept by the lakeside near the Hall of the Dead; and the serpent-gods will warn us of any disturbance."

MacDougall's last words to Taliesin as sleep closed over him were: "Don't call me for breakfast. Just let me sleep."

Alan opened his eyes to stare into a fantastic auroral display directly above him. He lay on his back, aware of the silence and the faint aroma of crushed grass. He felt more rested than at any time since coming through the third Gate. He sat up and stretched, glancing toward Taliesin, lying a dozen feet away. The Bard had stirred, then settled deeper into the grass, and Alan heard his deep, regular breathing.

Carefully, grinning broadly, MacDougall got to his feet and moved along the edge of the grass until he was out of earshot. He'd prepare for the day, including a dip in the sea, before he disturbed the Bard.

When he finally returned, he found Taliesin on his feet, a troubled look on his face. "You thought you'd get started before me. I went up the beach in the other direction." He paused. "But we have problems. I can't find the horses."

"Oh, they can't have gone far. Where would they go?"

"There are signs they went into the grass. There wasn't much of a trail, but I followed what I could. It ended quickly, as if they had gone into thin air. And I haven't found the harnesses!" He halted.

Then the thought struck both at once: "The Anunnaki!"

MacDougall clutched the armlet. "Lord and Lady, what happened to the horses?"

After a brief delay, Inanna answered apologetically, "It appears we confined our concern too strictly to your instructions. At no time while you slept were you menaced in any way. We sensed the Anunnaki in the area but they never came close to you. Unfortunately, they made away with your horses, and the animals are now in a tunnel built to carry mounted riders."

"And what are we to do?" Alan was thoroughly annoyed. "A fine fix we're in. How are we to get them back?"

"Alan!" the Bard exclaimed. "I'm in touch with one of the Anunnaki. Hold." He closed his eyes.

Intently MacDougall watched his face and saw the features suddenly relax.

The Bard met Alan's gaze. "They want us to go with them through the tunnel under the forest into Marduk, which is what they call the section ruled by Amaruduk. They want to take us to the God of gods. They know we have great powers and that two of the gods speak through us; but they are many and we are few. They do not want to attempt to use force, so they have taken our horses."

MacDougall shook his head in disgust. "Here we go again! First I am brought to Scathach's Castle; and now the opposition wants me." He shrugged resignedly. "Why not? That's where we are headed; and this way we'll be escorted in style. I agree." To himself he said, Mac, just remember they're demons, and don't trust them too far.

Moments later, the Anunnaki stood up, thirty or more of them, rising well above the tallest growths, forming a great half circle around MacDougall and Taliesin about fifty feet away. They began closing in on the two, halting just out of reach. No grotesque chimeras now, all were the twisted, slightly distorted shape that evidently was their natural form. About five feet six inches tall, all were dressed alike in coarsely woven brown robes, gathered about the waist by a heavy silver chain from which was suspended a medium-length scabbard and sword.

One of the Anunnaki approached the two and spoke, uncertainty and apprehension in his voice.

"I am Ashak and I speak for Amaruduk. Who are you who cannot be of this island?"

Briefly Taliesin introduced himself and Alan, giving a minimum of information, to which he added, "It is our wish to visit your master, so we will greatly appreciate your guiding us to him."

With obvious relief, Ashak answered, "We will do so."

They followed the demon deeper into the heavy growth, five of the Anunnaki joining them; three demons took the lead, and three walked behind them. They had gone about a half mile when, at the top of one of the little hills, Alan looked back. The rest of the Anunnaki had vanished; and the resilient grasses were springing back to hide their tracks.

In one of the little valleys, they halted; and before them, as if by magic, two sections of the valley floor, each about five feet wide and ten feet long, opened like double trapdoors. A long ramp led down into a tunnel, deep and wide, cut through the solid clay. In the mouth of the tunnel stood another of the Anunnaki, above him floating a fuzzy green globe of luminescence like that which had accompanied Amaruduk. Behind him, Mac-Dougall glimpsed a number of horses, moving restlessly.

As the Anunnaki led the way down the ramp, Alan's engineer's curiosity cast a probing gaze at the structure of the trapdoors. They were flat metal plates, with long, heavy rods running along their center, and weights and counterweights explained how one man—or demon—

could move them. After the eight had entered the tunnel, the demon who had opened the passage pulled on a chain to close the doors behind them, then vanished. Alan was watching him when he disappeared, not becoming invisible, but transferring elsewhere.

There were eight horses, among them the two Alan and Taliesin had "borrowed" from Scathach. At a word from Ashak, all mounted and they set out, with the green glow floating before them and lighting the way. The clatter of hoofs echoed through the tunnel. They passed several intersecting passageways, and the way wound and twisted; but their leader seemed certain of his course, never hesitating or slowing.

With his riding mechanical, MacDougall asked the serpent-gods. "What is Scathach doing now?"

A vision appeared in his mind, the projection of the Sorceress hovering over a gathering in the lounge. Present were the usual complement of Guards; but of the visitors, only Manannan, Mathonwy, and the four Druids were there. Scathach was speaking, frustration and anger in her voice.

"Where are the others? I directed that all should be here."

The sea god answered with exaggerated earnestness. "Truthfully, your Majesty, I have no idea. I saw Nuada speaking with Beli and Pryderi, and suddenly they were gone. Balor, who had been standing nearby, disappeared a few moments later. I feel certain that their going had to do with MacDougall, but I have no way of knowing." A trace of mockery entered his voice. "Surely your three advisors can tell you."

"But how could they leave?" the Sorceress protested.

"Perhaps you have forgotten that the gods have the power to transfer themselves instantly to distant places. Some of us have lost that power, but some still have it."

Hastily MacDougall cut off sight of the lounge. "Lord Enki, where are Beli and the others?"

There was amusement in the serpent-god's answer. "They are having problems. Here they are."

The three, Nuada, Beli, and Pryderi, were standing in the midst of the tall grass staring around in frustration. Beli was berating the King of the *Tuatha de Danann*.

"You said you knew where MacDougall and Taliesin were. You said you had learned it from the Bard's unguarded thoughts while they slept, that they had taken the road to the Hall of the Dead and then gone along the beach. You said you could transport two of us to the spot. So here we are—and where are they?"

"We should have followed on horses," Pryderi growled, "as they did. And as I suggested."

"We found where they slept," Nuada said defensively, "and we've followed their trail to this spot."

Beli snorted. "But where are they now? Horses don't vanish into thin air. And where is Balor? He was to have followed."

"A bungler," Nuada exclaimed. "It may well be that he lost some of the power when he took over an unauthorized body, though that doesn't seem logical since the ability is mental. However, I am not concerned with Balor. I think, if the three of us concentrate on MacDougall, it is possible that I may be able to transport us to wherever he is. It is certainly worth trying."

Alan saw them stand in a huddle, their eyes closed, with Nuada's hands resting on the shoulders of his two companions. And abruptly the setting changed.

His pursuers were in the tunnel behind the last of the Anunnaki riders. Alan looked back and saw them standing and staring in momentary surprise at the spectacle of eight mounted riders; he heard an angry roar from Pryderi, barely audible amid the clatter of the hoofs. Then they were out of sight as the tunnel angled sharply.

Alan sent a quick thought to Taliesin. *"We're being followed by Nuada, Beli, and Pryderi. They materialized in the tunnel behind us, on foot, of course, and in the dark now. Nuada's powers are carrying the other two. Balor is supposed to be with them, moving on his own, but something went wrong and he appears to be lost. Nuada learned where we were from your mind while we slept.*

"I think the Anunnaki should be told so that, if the three catch up with us, they'll be prepared."

"Unfortunately, during sleep our guards are down," the Bard responded. *"But pursuit was inevitable, from both the gods and Scathach; it was merely a question of time. However, in the words of the great law-giver Hammurabi, 'Forewarned forearmed.'"*

"I thought Cervantes said that in Don Quixote,*"* Alan said quizzically. *"And you seem to know a great deal about very ancient times."*

The Bard looked at MacDougall. Even in the eerie green light Alan could see his broad grin and the twinkle in his eyes. *"There is nothing new under the sun—nor under the aurora. And I have been many things during many times. I shall tell Ashak."*

Alan directed his thoughts toward the three gods and now saw them seated on the flattened grass where he and Taliesin had slept. And even as he listened to their conversation, he realized in surprise that he had not called upon the serpent-gods for the power of such viewing.

"I want no part of that tunnel," Beli was saying. "And so long as he is on horseback there is no way we can catch up with him."

"At least," Nuada commented, "we know we can follow him. He won't stay in the tunnel or on horseback forever. In time, he'll be on foot; and if we keep trying, we'll find him when he's vulnerable."

"Who were the horsemen with him?" Beli demanded. "I think I saw Taliesin, but who were the others? Where did they come from? I thought this was an island of women. They had the two surrounded."

"I suppose," Nuada said, "they must be from the other end of the island, and the probable reason for Scathach's having an army."

"Whoever they are," Pryderi rumbled, "they won't stop me from getting my hands on him. Remember," he added viciously, "I get him first. I deserve it after what he did to me." Idly he tugged at his sword. When it slid from its scabbard his face brightened. "It's free!"

Instantly the others drew their weapons.

"The spell has been canceled by distance," Beli exulted, "or they've stopped casting it. I'll spit him like a pig!"

MacDougall cut off the vision as he saw a small circle of auroral light far down the tunnel. They must be reaching the end of their underground ride. He didn't find the pursuers' words informative or amusing.

The tunnel began a long upward slope that ended in the face of a low cliff. Beyond it lay a totally unexpected landscape, a scene that could exist only in this impossible Other World.

It was a desert, a gray, rock-strewn wasteland—not an expanse of Sahara sand dunes, but a desert of the American West, of sage, thorny mesquite, and cacti. There were cacti scattered among the hodgepodge jungle growths surrounding the Gate; but here were giants, some with arms projecting, manlike, at grotesque angles. Some were strange forms with stilettolike thorns, unlike any he had ever seen.

Even the sky had changed to harmonize with the unnatural landscape. There was always the black of starless space as a backdrop for the aurora; but here the red of the other half of the island had deepened to a maroon, shot through with slashes of crimson, sulphurous yellow, and murky green. All of it, land and sky, seemed to have been created as a setting for the twisted Anunnaki. It was a lonely, barren, depressing land.

The tunnel road continued its winding course across

the desert, and the demons kept the horses moving at the same even canter. Undulating like the land on the other side of the woods, this, however, was far more rugged, harsh, and jagged. At the top of the first rise, Alan looked back and saw in the distance the wall of forest, a green expanse stretching from horizon to horizon. As the miles passed, he continued casting an occasional glance over his shoulder, expecting his pursuers to appear. He saw them only once, and that for a fleeting instant, as they disappeared as quickly as they had appeared.

At length Ashak brought the horses to a halt at the lip of a wide bowl hollowed out of the desert floor. It was a great amphitheater, carved from the basic clay. Row after row of curved seats descended in graduating steps to the central arena. Seats and arena floor were covered by a layer of hewn stones. The road led down a ramp, through the arena, and up the other side.

"Here in the olden days," Ashak said, with a sweeping wave of an arm, "we held the games." Regretfully he added, "We wearied even of games. They ended when those of the Anunnaki who were permitted chose the Sleep."

At a walk they descended the ramp to the arena and again they halted. Ashak pointed to a square stone structure centered at one side, rising about twenty feet above the floor. A single stone seat, like a throne carved out of solid granite, occupied the roof of the block.

"There sat the God of gods, Amaruduk, and in the other seats were the watching Anunnaki. From the chamber beneath came the duelists. These were the captive warriors of Scathach who had to fight to the death, until only one survived. It was rare sport." Ashak chuckled. "The winner of all the bouts had to face the champion of the Anunnaki, who invariably won to conclude the games." He sighed heavily. "But when the wars stopped and the Sleep began, the games ended."

Revolted by the picture the demon had drawn, Mac-

Dougall exclaimed in disgust, "Rare sport, you call it! Bestiality, rather—"

He stopped short as Nuada, Beli, and Pryderi suddenly appeared in their midst. The red-haired giant at the instant of appearing reached up and wrenched MacDougall from his saddle and flung his arms around him in a great bear hug.

"Now!" he shouted; but as Nuada sprang to his side, a mass of the Anunnaki appeared out of nowhere, and clutching hands swept down upon them. Nuada never reached Beli in order to complete their planned kidnapping. During the struggle that began with the entry of the demons, MacDougall managed to wrench free and wriggle out of the mass of bodies.

"Well!" Ashak exclaimed with satisfaction. "I thought this might be a logical place to invite the attention of the pursuers, with reinforcements waiting for my thought. So now we shall have five guests to take to Amaruduk."

"Keep them apart," MacDougall warned sharply. "Only the white-haired one has the power to transport the others."

As if Alan's words were a signal, a storm of violence burst from Pryderi and Beli. Massive arms flung the Anunnaki left and right as ferocious growls burst from the jailer of Ochren. Beli fought in silence.

Now swords appeared in the hands of the demons and some found flesh. The voice of Ashak shrilled above the bedlam. "Do not kill them! They must go to Amaruduk." More and more of the Anunnaki continued to appear out of nowhere, and inevitably the weight of bodies had to overcome. The three gods were borne to the ground, completely buried under demons.

MacDougall, standing well back from the struggling mass, watched in fascination. Taliesin, still astride his horse, had moved away, as had Ashak and the other mounted Anunnaki. A sudden thought came to Alan from the Bard: *"Nuada—he's free!"*

Part of the heap of demons had collapsed and were groping for an opponent who was no longer there. A dozen feet away Nuada materialized, with two of the Anunnaki clinging to his arms. With swift violence, the King of the *Tuatha de Danann* flung them reeling to right and left, then whipped out his sword. With a triumphant shout, he charged into the pack, his glittering blade slashing.

He bore an invincible blade, Alan remembered!

Sudden bedlam prevailed as Beli and Pryderi responded to the cry by struggling erect, shedding demons. Nuada's fierce onslaught sent blood spurting, and the attack from behind them spread wild confusion through the demons' ranks. Pryderi seized three of the Anunnaki in his crushing grasp and squeezed, their screams ending in gasps; and Beli caught one by the ankles and swung him around like a flail. Shrieks of agony rose from the wounded.

All this had happened in seconds.

As MacDougall instinctively drew his sword, a sharp denial came from Taliesin. *"No—on your horse!"*

Swiftly Alan swung into the saddle; but even as he did so, a tremendous voice roared, "Stop!"

With the single word echoing through the arena, Amaruduk appeared on the stone throne overlooking the conflict, and all of the battling Anunnaki, including the wounded, vanished. For a split second, the three gods froze. In that instant, a sharp cry came from Amaruduk. "Namtar, Ushabshi, Luenna! Possess!"

Three of the demons swung swiftly from their saddles, collapsing lifelessly as their feet struck stone. At the same instant, vaporous black clouds enveloped the heads and shoulders of Beli, Nuada, and Pryderi.

Strangled cries burst from the three, and their arms flailed wildly around their heads, swords dropping from flaccid fingers. Then, after only moments, an appalling silence fell on the scene; the writhing struggle of the three became all the more dreadful because they made no sound. Watching in horror, MacDougall lived again those times when he had choked under the onslaught of possessing demonic spirits.

Time froze in this timeless world. None of the remaining horsemen moved. Paralysis seemed to grip even their mounts. Then the arms of the three gods fell limply to their sides, and the dark vapors vanished. Simultaneously the recumbent Anunnaki were gone.

"Welcome, Alan MacDougall, to the land of Marduk." The familiar voice of Amaruduk, alive with awareness of power, broke the stillness. "Will you dismount and join me on the dais? And bring your friend with you. I would meet this one who, I have been informed, wishes to meet me."

CHAPTER 9

The Land of Marduk

As MacDougall and the Bard mounted the steps and approached Amaruduk, Alan threw off, with a conscious effort, the spell that gripped him. The spectacle of Beli, Nuada, and Pryderi standing like so many robots awaiting animation was especially horrifying, but he thrust them from his mind, forcing himself to meet the hawklike gaze of the one-time god of Sumer, Assyria, and Babylon.

Calmly Alan said, "My friend is the Bard of Bards, Taliesin, a man to whom even the gods bow in Tartarus."

Amaruduk smiled condescendingly. "But still, he is merely a man, and the gods of whom you speak are such as these." He gestured toward the three. "Gods who are not gods. Gods now possessed by my Anunnaki."

Taliesin spoke with quiet self-assurance. "The name Taliesin means nothing to you. Yet I remember who you really are, Naqabel!"

The face of Amaruduk instantly became a study in incredulity. "Naqabel! Who are you? I have not heard that name for ages upon ages." His eyes burned into those of Taliesin. "Who are you? You must have been there during the Great Confrontation."

The Bard bowed, and his reply was solemn and subdued. "I was there, as were you. Do you recall Cheniel?" His expression grew grim. "We were there, Naqabel and Cheniel, among the Selected Ones who were given a choice, and we chose—unwisely."

The being the Bard called Naqabel stared with narrowed eyes. "Cheniel," he repeated. "But now you are a man. How can this be?"

MacDougall had been looking from one to the other during this strange conversation. They appeared to have forgotten he was there. "Will someone tell me what this is all about—" he began, to be halted by an impatient gesture from Amaruduk.

"We will pursue this further in more comfortable surroundings," Amaruduk said, and turned to the mounted Anunnaki. "Ashak, dress the prisoners' wounds, then bring all the visitors to me." As suddenly as he had appeared, Amaruduk vanished.

The Anunnaki inspected the injuries, none serious, and bound them with strips torn from Nuada's cape. Afterward the three gods retrieved their swords, strode to horses, and mounted. As Ashak also mounted, he spoke respectfully to Alan and the Bard.

"Sirs, we ride."

Wordlessly, MacDougall and Taliesin climbed into the saddle and took their places side by side in the procession. Although Alan's thoughts were occupied with the swiftly moving happenings that had followed the appearance of the three gods, the mystery of Taliesin's revelation dominated all else. He could see only one answer to what the Bard had said.

He had been present at the time of Lucifer's rebellion against the Almighty One. And this meant he must have been one of the Hosts of Heaven, an angel! He thought of the strange claims Taliesin had made at other times, references to places he had been, events he had seen, firsthand knowledge of things too ancient for him to have known. Alan shook his head. There was much he did not understand.

They were following a road through rough country, sparse growth doing nothing to dispel the desert desolation. The somber tints of the aurora served only to accent the gray gloom. Ashak led, with one of the Anunnaki directly ahead of Alan, and Taliesin came behind the possessed Nuada.

Despite his mental preoccupation, MacDougall cast occasional glances over his shoulder at two of the riders in the rear—Beli and Pryderi. Even though they were under demon control, he could not quell a feeling of uneasiness. Beli, in particular, was a being of tremendous strength, mentally and physically. How complete was the Anunnaki's dominance?

One of his glances caught Beli's gaze boring into his back. As if his look had triggered a reaction, a shout burst from the red-haired giant and he spurred his horse. The animal reared up on hind legs, and confusion spread like a contagion to the others. Alan clung to his reins, fighting to calm the startled stallion, too busy to note what went on around him. With the animal under control, he looked anxiously for Beli.

The god of Ochren's Nether World, like Nuada and Pryderi, was again enveloped in a black demonic cloud. Three motionless Anunnaki lay by the roadside; and as before, when the gods had been subdued, they and the dark vapors disappeared. Ashak smiled grimly at MacDougall.

"If two are not sufficient to control them, there is always room for another. In the Olden Times, scores would occupy a single host." He chuckled. "It became a game, a contest to see which group could crowd the most of us into a single body."

As they resumed their journey, Alan stared unseeingly ahead. He had always thought of demon possession as superstitious nonsense, but there was nothing nonsensical about this. What a hell of a place! At least, his concern about his enemies was dispelled in part.

There was little conversation between him and Taliesin, audible or mental; both were wrapped up in their own thoughts. After a time, the sameness of the dreary landscape flowing by mile after mile became oppressive and the trip interminable. There were hills and depressions, but even they seemed to assume a monotonous pattern after a time. He thought of Tartarus with its forest-cloaked hills, of the lovely valley to which the Troll King, Einurr Gurulfin, had led him, and of crystalline Falias. Truly Amaruduk must have incurred Lucifer's anger to be condemned to this. He thought of the dark island, Ochren. In retrospect, it was a fearsome place, but somehow less repellent than Marduk. Yet it was not the place, so much as its demonic dwellers, that bothered him.

When at last MacDougall saw a distant line of pale green, he felt a surge of relief. They must be approaching the stream, the southern arm of the watercourse that flowed from the Well of Darkness. Logically the Castle of Amaruduk would be erected near the water supply and with it, grazing for the horses. The Anunnaki could steal their own food from Scathach's warehouses or the harvesters, but they could hardly do the same for the animals.

The horses, seeming to sense their approach to food and drink, quickened their pace, soon reaching what suggested an elongated oasis with lush grass and trees several hundred yards wide lining both banks of the river. Surprisingly, scores of horses were visible among the trees, appearing to be unconfined and peacefully grazing. But why confine them? They wouldn't wander into the desert.

"Lord Enki," MacDougall asked curiously, "with the ability of the Anunnaki to transfer from place to place, why so many horses?"

"Because, as I told you, only the Anunnaki have the power," came the answer. "The Igigi do not. And as I surmised, most of the servants of Amaruduk are of the Igigi."

The road led up to the river's edge, where a branch split off to follow the stream, the main way continuing eastward across a stone bridge that arched to the other bank. The riders followed the branch. Ahead lay the ocean. Silhouetted against it on their side of the river rose two stone buildings, unusual to say the least.

The nearer of the two was a gray stone *ziggurat*, a smaller version of the one that had appeared in Alan's fantastic vision or dream. The Tower of King Etana of Kish had had seven levels, each smaller than the one beneath it; this had but three. All these were smaller, and there was another striking difference. There was no symmetry to the tower. It appeared to be the work of a tipsy architect and builder, with uneven walls and reeling stairways—or, as he knew it was, the creation of the same malevolent being who was responsible for the grotesque Fomorians, the surrealistic city of Lochlann, and the distortion of the demons of Marduk.

The second building was equally strange, but in a different way. Here was no grotesquery; quite the reverse, in fact. Like the *ziggurat*, it was wrought of gray stones, but these were smoothly tooled and symmetrically shaped. The building appeared to be square, about a hundred feet long on each side and about thirty feet tall. Another thirty feet above the roof rose a polished gold dome, casting back the panorama of auroral fires. There appeared to be great double doors at the visible corner, but there were no windows. The stately structure was completely out of character with the rest of Marduk.

MacDougall had time for only a cursory glance when

they reached the entrance to the *ziggurat* and Ashak called a halt. All dismounted, and the Anunnaki leader stared into vacancy. After moments, he addressed the demons possessing Beli, Nuada, and Pryderi.

"Go to your rooms in the Castle and remain there until you are summoned. Be on constant guard, for these are strong men and may attempt rebellion at any time." To the other Anunnaki, he said, "Care for the horses; then you are free." Finally he turned to Alan and Taliesin.

"I am to guide you to the Lord Amaruduk in his own quarters. Know that you are greatly honored. Follow."

As Ashak led them around the corner to the outside stairway leading to the second level, MacDougall noted that his enemies entered the Castle on the ground floor.

Climbing the steep stairs with their unexpected swervings was a minor adventure. On the second level, they moved around the back to the stairway leading to the third. Here they passed through a massive bronze double door that opened at their approach; and as they entered, the usual vaporous green globe appeared above them, lighting their way.

For the first time they saw indications of the splendor to be expected in the Castle of one who had been God of gods—a floor of smooth mosaic, intricately designed with intertwining patterns suggesting a Persian rug, and walls of smoothly polished lapis lazuli. But in all of it something was slightly askew.

Alan remembered a visit to an amusement park somewhere in his past and his wandering through a building where disproportion and distortion were evident in everything. So it seemed here.

"Lord and Lady, why this repeated crookedness?"

There was gloating in the Lady Inanna's answer. "Evidently the Lord of Light will not let Amaruduk forget his failure for one moment. He sees it everywhere. His offense in giving way to the Enemy through Ahuramazda had grievous results, and he is suffering the consequences."

At the end of the corridor, another bronze door barred their way; before it stood an armored and armed guard, one of the Anunnaki in whom there was no crookedness. He was handsome, impressive, and, as MacDougall saw at once, an example of skilled shape-changing. At their approach, he bowed deeply, and the door opened behind him.

Stepping aside, he said in a deep voice, "Enter. The Lord Amaruduk expects you."

As the door closed behind them, MacDougall held his breath and stared in fascination at a fantastic chamber. It was a large room, but not unusually so; it was the opulence of its furnishings that impressed Alan. Cloth-of-gold hangings covered the walls; a deep-blue ceiling was set with countless sparkling gems, reflecting the pale-green radiance of five floating lights; the floor was covered thickly with deep pile suggesting spun silver, yet of finest texture; there were great contour chairs, thickly padded, covered with velvety black fabric, and casual tables of carved ivory and burnished gold scattered about with artistic carelessness.

All this MacDougall saw in passing, his gaze drawn irresistibly to the far end of the room, where, in a wide alcove on a raised dais of lapis lazuli, stood a golden throne like something out of the Arabian Nights. Upon it sat the Lord Amaruduk, a regal Amaruduk sumptuously clad in a robe of royal purple, with a heavy gold chain about his waist and a white fur cape across his shoulders. A golden cincture encircled his head, holding his black hair in place.

Three Anunnaki in black robes sat on lesser thrones at floor level, one on either side and one directly before their monarch. There was no trace of distortion in their posture.

"Approach!" came Amaruduk's command.

As they moved through the breathtaking room, Mac-Dougall thought, This is too much! It was theatrical, overdone, like something out of Hollywood—and even the movie makers would not go this far.

"Taliesin, do you see what I see?"

"Yes—the same fantastic illusion. This is in a class with that of Amaethon and his Roman village in Annwn, the musicians and dancers and the many other dwellers in Manannan's Caer Pedryvan, *your own fracturing of the dome and the flooding of Lochlann. Look, really look, at the room."*

MacDougall exerted the power that penetrated illusion to see in ghostly imposition a plain room with stone floor and walls and plain, spare furnishings, even to the seat on the gray stone dais, as well as the seats of the three Anunnaki. As for Amaruduk and his acolytes, they were clad in gray, and their twisted forms had returned.

Halting about ten feet away from the central demon, Alan relaxed his vision, accepting the illusion. It was easier on the eyes.

The one-time God of gods studied MacDougall and Taliesin intently before he spoke. "The three Anunnaki before you are my lieutenants or administrators—Marsili, Shutarna, and Habiru. They serve as my advisors on occasion. But for what we are about to discuss they will not be needed."

He paused; as if receiving a command, the three vanished.

Amaruduk stared at Alan and frowned. To the Bard he said, "Should he be here, or should he join my helpers?"

"I strongly favor his being here," Taliesin replied firmly. "He already knows much and he may well add substantially to our conversation."

"Very well." Amaruduk stood up and descended a small stairway at one side of the dais. "We will find comfortable seats and relax with some very fine wine. There is no need for haste."

Even as they seated themselves, the wall hangings on one side parted and three beautiful maidens entered. Like slave girls, again out of the Arabian Nights, they were striking creatures with their straight black hair, eyes darkly outlined, small breasts encased in gold-filigree breastplates, and short, gold-colored kirtles. Their feet were bare. Another striking illusion, Alan thought, hiding twisted Igigi. They moved small tables up to the three chairs; as they left, three others entered, carrying wine decanters and golden goblets. They poured and withdrew, all in silence.

Amaruduk held up his goblet. "This is Scathach's finest. We appreciate her skill, or that of her Druidesses, as the case may be. They are master vintners, to my delight. May your visit be fruitful."

They drank, and Alan instantly recognized the liquid dynamite, sipping sparingly. "The Sorceress introduced me to this most delightful beverage," he said casually, placing the goblet on the table. "There was one other I enjoyed even more."

As he spoke, one of the serfs reappeared with a second goblet and decanter and smoothly replaced Alan's wine.

"That," the Lord said, "is my second choice." Deliberately, he took another drink, then placed his goblet beside him.

"You have had a glimpse of my vast domain," he said with an ironic smile. "All, that is, that lies above the surface. The Igigi have their quarters underground. The Anunnaki occupy the first level of this tower. There are not very many of them awake; most are asleep awaiting the call of the Master."

"Also underground?" MacDougall asked.

"No—in the outer courts of the Great Hall, which you saw. Under the dome lies the Temple."

"Will we be able to enter it?" Alan asked, thinking of the Crystal Temple in Falias where he had sat on the Stone of Fal and had received his near-fatal wound.

"No," Amaruduk answered curtly. "If you have no other questions—"

"Oh, but I do," MacDougall persisted. "These buildings, who erected them? The Anunnaki and the Igigi?"

Amaruduk looked annoyed. "We did not build them. They were here when we came, just as you see them. The dome and Temple, even the racks and compartments for the Sleepers; though their use was not made clear until long after the coming of Scathach and her women, all were here. Then instructions came for most of the Anunnaki to enter the Long Wait until the Day." The Lord added, "Even the underground dwellings for the Igigi were already here."

"What about the tunnels? That must have been a tremendous undertaking. Or were they here, too?"

Amaruduk smiled grimly. "My Anunnaki had merely to oversee the work. We simply used the free labor that Scathach supplied. Not willingly, of course. The warriors worked quite efficiently when it meant food and water as an alternative to the lash." He shook his head with mock regret, then sipped his wine. "They did not live too long, but there were always replacements."

As MacDougall appeared to have another question the demon raised a hand. "Enough." He spoke directly to Taliesin.

"So you are Cheniel and you once knew me as Naqabel. That was very long ago and much has happened since then."

"Indeed," the Bard responded. "Yet I have never forgotten the Lovely Place; and I have never ceased to regret the choice I made. But when Lucifer, the Archangel of Archangels, in all his splendor set himself up as equal with the Almighty—yes, would surpass Him—I was among his legions who were bedazzled by his radiance.

When we were told to choose to follow one or the other, I chose wrongly. From the moment we were cast from the Presence I knew, I knew how wrongly."

"But you are a man!" Wonder and doubt filled Amaruduk's voice. "Never in all the ages have I met another angel who became a man."

"Nor have I," Taliesin-Cheniel answered with deep solemnity. "And again and again have I wondered why I was given a chance to make a second choice. But I was so chosen. Time beyond reckoning had passed; and I had followed the Dark Master, always on the edges of those who served him, never free of regret, seeing much of this universe and worlds beyond, and reluctantly doing as I was told.

"Then, during a time of deepest despondency One appeared to me, One without a trace of darkness, a true Angel of Light, who said in words I remember well, 'Your lament has been heard, and I have been sent by the One whose Name cannot be spoken. He foresees a time when you may serve—if you choose to become a man. Consider well. Now for you there is no death, though in the fullness of time there will be—reward. As a man, death will come with its fear and pain, though life thereafter will follow.'

"'There is nothing to consider,' I answered; and a weight as of worlds rolled from me. I who had always been Cheniel became Taliesin."

"But," Amaruduk-Naqabel protested, "what of the power—the glory? The pleasure of power unlimited, the glory of adulation from multitudes, the power to change worlds, and the glory of godhood?"

"Where is that power and glory now?" the Bard asked quietly. "You, who were God of gods, are confined to this little island of Lucifer's creation."

Obviously shaken, Amaruduk fell silent. Then as if to change the subject, he bent piercing eyes on MacDougall.

"How is it that you, a man, alive to the Other World, alien to this, could repel me?"

As MacDougall hesitated, Taliesin said quietly, "Tell him, Alan. It is well that he should know."

Deliberately MacDougall removed his cape and jacket and bared his right arm, exposing the two-headed serpent armlet.

"Not I," he said with a faint smile, "but the prisoners in this jewel. You once had dealings with the two gods of Sumer, Inanna and Enki."

"Inanna and Enki!" Startled, Amaraduk half rose, then sank back onto his chair.

"Yes, Amaruduk," Inanna responded triumphantly, her thought open to the three, "we are here with Mac-Dougall. He is our host. And I took great delight in teaching you the lessons you so richly deserved."

Amaruduk was struggling to grasp what he had just been told. "It seems incredible that you are here." His face brightened at a sudden thought. "It took the two of you—"

"Not so," Enki's thoughts protested angrily. "Inanna needed no help. Had I participated, you would have known it. You would never have made a second attempt to possess MacDougall. One lesson would have been sufficient."

"Why could I repel you?" Inanna's voice asked. "First, MacDougall was a most unwilling subject who resisted with no mean strength. I, who once was Tiamat, have greater power than you, for now you are alone. So possessing Alan MacDougall for your possible return to the other world is impossible." After a pause she added, "I suppose you are not aware that my sister Ereshkigal is on this island."

"Ereshkigal!" the demon echoed in astonishment. "Here in Marduk?"

"No—in Scathach's Castle imprisoned in the image of

Lamashtu. And she has been there through all the centuries."

Amaruduk gasped, then forced a laugh. "First came the news that Taliesin was Cheniel, who knew me from the beginning, then your presence with MacDougall, and now Ereshkigal as the power behind Scathach. Is there more I should know?"

"Tell him, Lord and Lady," MacDougall suggested, "that if he were able to pass through the Gate in his own form, death would come quickly. He did not believe me."

"MacDougall's word is true." The serpent-gods spoke as one, and Inanna added, "The doorway for you to return to the Other World is closed."

Amaruduk stood up; moments later, MacDougall and Taliesin followed suit. The Lord of Marduk said quietly, "I have much to think about. You will be conducted to rooms on the first level and food will be brought to you. You may wish to have it served—"

Abruptly he stopped, seeming to listen; then incredulity and anger appeared on his face.

"How dare she!" he exclaimed harshly. "Never before—"

The object of his wrath suddenly appeared above the three, the projection of Scathach.

"At last I have found you," she said triumphantly to MacDougall, ignoring the others. "How long will it take you to see that you cannot deny your destiny? There is no place on Scath, including Amaruduk's tunnels and his Castle, that is hidden from me."

"Destiny, hell!" Alan exclaimed in disgust; but his words were lost in the louder shout of Amaruduk.

"Know, witch, that this time you have gone too far. Never before have you dared to pry into Marduk—*not* Scath, as you know—and you will pay."

A ringing laugh came from the Sorceress as her image vanished. "I can see you just as clearly and hear you just as well without appearing. Nothing of yours has been concealed from me, nor ever will be." Her face reappeared. "What have you done to the visitors from the other islands? Not that I care, but they seem as docile as cows."

Beside himself with fury, Amaruduk groped for appropriate words. Scathach continued speaking, addressing the Bard. "You must be Taliesin. Manannan spoke of you. Apparently I have you to thank for the visit of the troublemakers, since through you they learned of Scath. But then Alan would be at fault, since he called you. No matter."

She cast one last barb at Amaruduk: "See that no harm befalls MacDougall. I will hold you accountable. Now I go."

Had she really gone? Alan wondered.

Enki answered his silent question. "She has."

When the Lord of Marduk finally spoke, his voice was cold and expressionless. He was obviously holding himself under rigid restraint.

"She shall be attended to. Now you will be shown to your rooms."

With the words, an Anunnaki appeared at the door, leading them into the corridor, the ubiquitous green globe of light appearing above him. It vanished as they left the building to descend the crooked stairways, reappearing when they reentered the tower on ground level. Moving through a hallway of gray stone without any sort of ornamentation, they passed numerous plain wooden doors, as usual without visible locks, and were shown to neighboring rooms.

As MacDougall entered his, the green light appeared, hovering just below the ceiling. Alan had wondered about illumination in the windowless building, and as the guide turned to leave he asked,

"What about that light when you leave?"

"It will remain there, maintained by one of us, until

you depart." He added, "Food will be brought and water for washing." The door closed behind him.

Curious, MacDougall asked the serpent-god, "Lord Enki, can you explain the light?"

"Yes. It is a concentration of the energies all around us, a power possessed by the Anunnaki and those of a higher level. The ability is now denied us since we no longer have control of what you might refer to as cosmic energies."

Alan grinned ruefully to himself. His knowledge had not increased. He dropped his cape and jacket on the bed and looked around.

His room was small and bare, the furnishings a low, very narrow bed, a small table, and a straight chair. Rough boards screened off one corner, concealing a basin fastened to the wall and a hole in the floor with the sound of running water far below.

As bad as the cell in the prison of Ochren, MacDougall thought with distaste. He would not be here very long. His door opened and Taliesin entered.

"And I complained about Tartarus! Awful rooms," he said.

Alan sat on the bed, leaving the chair for the Bard. As they waited for the food to arrive MacDougall commented, "I can't understand the disparity between the conditions of Scathach and Amaruduk, or, for that matter, between the gods of Tartarus, or even Ochren, and Amaruduk. All the gods-who-were-men live in comparative luxury. Here, stripped of illusion, is nothing but bare subsistence. The serpent-gods have been imprisoned for ages, as against the relative freedom of Scathach and the others."

After a thoughtful pause, the Bard answered, "The solution seems quite clear. The gods who once were human were sent here by one Master, the Supreme One, whom they disobeyed; the rebellious angels were sent by another Master whom *they* displeased."

"That raises another question. I have thought of these islands as Lucifer's creation, a part of his domain. As such, I assumed all who dwelt here were under his control. But if the Almighty sends some here and Lucifer sends others—"

"But don't you see? The Dark One sends those who are his, the rebellious angels, and the Almighty those who are His! As for control, Lucifer exercises command, but within limitations, since the Supreme Being must be in supreme control. I have wondered—might this not be a place of waiting for a time of final judgment?"

"You mean Purgatory?" MacDougall used the English word.

"I know not the term—"

The Bard was interrupted by the arrival of two Igigi, one with a supply of dried fruit and nuts and the other carrying a pail of water, which he took into the corner closet. As they left one said, "We have placed food and water in the other room."

Taliesin rose to leave. "After the ride through the tunnel and across the desert, washing will be welcome. And a bit of rest after eating will do no harm." Alan agreed and they separated.

As MacDougall poured water into the basin, he noticed a wooden plug closing a hole in the bottom. He chuckled. Underneath was no pipe; releasing the water sent it to the floor where a slope carried it to the opening. Primitive, highly unsanitary, and crude! He grimaced and used what was available.

While he washed, he thought of Taliesin's revelation and the Bard's once having been one of the Host of Heaven. Alan had begun to suspect something of the sort, but the knowledge was a shock none the less. Cheniel! He wondered if it had a meaning. This suggested that Enki and Inanna must once have had angelic names. Forget it, Mac! Things were sufficiently complicated without that.

Later, as he ate the familiar fare of Scath and drank from his canteen, his thoughts dwelt on recent events, especially the appearance of Scathach and her seeming to do everything possible to infuriate Amaruduk. It made no sense at all. What could she gain? Almost, she seemed to invite attack.

His hunger satisfied, he unfastened his sword belt, placed the weapon on the floor beside the bed, and stretched out on the hard surface. He closed his eyes.

"Lord and Lady, I want a conducted tour of the building next door. From what I saw, it appeared to have escaped the distortion of Amaruduk's tower. I'd like to see the Temple and the Sleepers. But first perhaps you should put a spell on that door. With Beli and the others so close, though demon-possessed, I'll feel safer with the door solidly locked."

"It has been done" came Enki's response. "We begin your tour with the Temple. Fortunately it is occupied, so there is light."

MacDougall seemed to be looking down into a great, round room with one entrance, a wide, arched doorway framed by a band of intricately tooled gold. The floor, saucerlike, sloping gently to the center, was made up of black stone slabs, smoothly polished and carefully fitted together. About midway between the walls and the center rose seven pillars of bloodstone, carved as were the surrealistic monoliths Alan had seen in the underground chamber and the Grove of Spirits, extending as supports to the golden dome above.

Gray-clad Anunnaki, all with gold chain belts and swords, stood in small groups, engaged in subdued conversation. Others were entering in a steady stream, swelling the assemblage.

The most striking feature of the chamber itself was the continuous circular wall, broken only by the wide doorway. At first Alan thought it was covered by a tremendous mural painting, the creation of an artist of surpassing skill, the colors as fresh and vivid as the moment they were applied. But as he studied the fantastic scenes depicted, he realized this was an incredibly fine mosaic stretching from the floor to the edge of the golden dome. The artistry and the infinite patience of those in a long-gone day who created this masterpiece in glass and gems were beyond belief.

It took the form of a vast montage, scene after scene blending smoothly into the next. It began with a titanic struggle between a godlike man and a mighty, scaled monster of the deep. It continued with the god-man's bloody triumph, his elevation to a royal throne; battles between multitudes, and triumph after triumph, always centered about the same god whom MacDougall now recognized as Amaruduk. It ended with the god cast down before a single sphere of bright, clear light; in the final scene, the same figure, now crooked and mis-shapen, lay prone before a perfect depiction of a blood-stone monolith.

As he studied this fantastic spectacle, Alan sensed a fringe thought of Inanna, annoyed and disdainful, "That creature is not at all like Tiamat."

Alan could have spent hours studying the wall, but the steadily growing crowd demanded his attention. Moment by moment more and more of the Anunnaki poured into the great chamber. They entered and stood there, moving only to make way for others.

A startling idea occurred to MacDougall. "Lord Enki, let us see the Sleepers!"

Instantly the scene changed, and his wild idea was verified.

The Sleepers were awakening!

The long corridor encircling the Temple led past endless tier after tier of bronze racks reaching from floor to ceiling. These held transparent oblong boxes, reminding Alan of the crystal coffins in the top level of the Hall of the Dead at Falias that held the ethereal bodies of the

Daughters of Lilith. These racks held gray-clothed An-unnaki—all except the bottom level, empty as far as Alan could see from his vantage point. The bodies were gone; and from both directions, meeting at the doorway and entering the Temple, came those awakened Sleepers.

Why? Alan asked himself in wonder. Twice he had been told the Long Sleep should last until the Day, whatever that meant. Could this be the "Day"? It seemed unlikely. Fascinated, he watched the unbroken line of demons flow into the Temple until the startled thought of Inanna erupted in his mind: "Balor!"

MacDougall's eyes flew open to see the god of the Fomorians towering above him at the end of the bed, his long sword clutched in both hands and raised above his head. Even as it swept down Alan reacted too rapidly for thought, rolling off the bed to the floor and vanishing into invisibility. He heard the thud of the weapon striking, and a frustrated roar burst from Balor.

Alan had landed on his sword, but it was covered by his jacket and cape, and there was no possibility of his grasping it. He kept on rolling until he touched the wall. The Fomorian god had followed, leaping to the side of the bed, then halting, apparently listening. Stealthily, MacDougall stood up and leaped to one side as Balor again swung his weapon, barely missing his target.

Thus began a deadly game, the god swinging his weapon wildly at random about him, MacDougall trying desperately to stay behind him. Blows that could decapitate a man or inflict a grievous wound whistled through the air. Alan wanted to shout for help, but the sound would have shown where he was.

Taliesin! Mentally he called the Bard. *Get help! Balor appeared in my room!"*

He could spare no thought for elaboration, needing total concentration to stay alive. But help suddenly came. An Anunnaki materialized, and an instant later collapsed as a dark cloud formed about Balor's head.

The god uttered a startled howl, his arms flailing the air. Wildly, he fought the formless thing, writhing and twisting, his arms swinging aimlessly. MacDougall instantly reappeared and caught up his sword.

A waving arm sent Balor's heavy weapon flying through the air just in time to strike broadside the chest of Amaruduk, who had suddenly appeared. The Lord of Marduk reeled back, tripped over the overturned chair, and sprawled on the floor.

Swiftly he scrambled erect, his face livid with anger. He swept up Balor's sword and sprang toward the black-bearded giant. Just before striking he caught himself.

"Who is this?" he demanded hoarsely.

"The god of the Fomorians. Balor is his name," Alan answered, breathing heavily. "He and Nuada came from the island of Tartarus, the other two from the second island, Ochren. All were gods of an island now called Britain in the Other World. They came on a magic coracle with a fifth god and another of lesser powers, as well as four Druids. Balor left Scathach's Castle with the rest, seeking to capture me and attempting to transfer himself by his own ability, a power he once had. Apparently he bungled and got lost. He finally caught up, appearing here in my room, immediately trying to kill me."

"Very well," Amaruduk exclaimed. "You have a sword. Kill him."

MacDougall shook his head. It was a tempting prospect, but he couldn't do it. "I could not kill one as defenseless as he now is. He died once in this world and was given another body. He deserves to lose this one, but not by my hand."

At that moment there came a sharp rap on the door. "Alan," Taliesin called. "Let me in."

A thought flashed to Enki, and the Bard burst in as the locking spell ceased. At a glance, he took in the situation. "I see ample help came."

"Yes," Amaruduk responded. "Your mental alarm

was heard." He added decisively, "I have decided. The four so-called gods will be returned to Scathach as they are, under the control of my Anunnaki. They will not be released until they are on their coracle, returning whence they came. If they cross my path a second time, there will be no mercy.

"You, Alan MacDougall, and your friend Taliesin will be guided on horseback to the end of the large tunnel that brings you closest to the spot where we met. This should be near the Gate, so that you may return to the Other World. From the tunnel end, I suggest you ride through the grass to the forest edge and the cart-path close to the Gate.

"Feel no concern about Scathach's following you. She will have her mind occupied with other matters." There was a malevolent note in his voice, a cold certainty that left no room for doubt.

Things began to happen with the speed and dispatch possible only where telepathy prevailed. While MacDougall put on his jacket, sword, and cape, Balor walked docilely into the corridor, to be joined in moments by Beli, Nuada, and Pryderi. There was no greeting, no conversation. While Amaruduk stood by, calmly overseeing, the four silently formed a tight circle and suddenly vanished.

An instant later the demon Ashak appeared in the corridor and spoke to MacDougall. "The horses are being prepared and will be awaiting us outside the Castle. We have a rather long ride ahead of us, so a parcel of food will be on each horse. You will wish to refill your water receptacles."

Most thoughtful, MacDougall told himself.

Amaruduk uttered a final word. "It was an interesting meeting and it will produce surprising results. Scathach will be *so* pleased at the help I am giving you. *So* pleased when she learns I have helped you return to your own world." He looked intently at Taliesin.

"Cheniel," he said solemnly, "you have awakened memories long buried under the weight of ages, happenings I have tried to forget. The brightness of the power and the glory has dimmed. Would that I had been given the same chance to make a second choice." With regret he added, "But I suppose I would not have changed my mind." Their hands met, and Amaruduk disappeared.

On the paving outside the *ziggurat*, horses, ready for the ride, were waiting. The three mounted. Led by Ashak, they went to a cistern where they filled their canteens, then started on their way.

They followed a road running parallel with the stream, just beyond the edge of the turf. It created an interesting contrast. On one side was the thickly growing pale-green vegetation; on the other, the bleak, repellent desert. But MacDougall's thoughts were not of the landscape; rather, they centered on the most recent turn of events, the abrupt termination of their stay with the Lord of Marduk. Quite suddenly he had been eager to be rid of them. Then there was Amaruduk's scarcely veiled threat against Scathach and, most startling, the awakening of the Sleepers.

Taliesin broke in on his thoughts. *"Alan, tell me about Balor's coming."*

MacDougall told him, starting with his viewing, through the serpent-gods, of the interior of the Temple and what it revealed; the waking of the Sleepers, and finally his opening his eyes at Inanna's warning just in time to escape Balor's sword.

The Bard's response revealed grave concern. *"I see a storm brewing. The awakening of the Anunnaki at this time is most assuredly not according to any master plan. It can only have one purpose, a major attack on Scathach. And in view of her open defiance of Naqabel, this could be the bloodiest war ever to strike this island. I can't see what she had to gain by doing what she did."*

For a mile or two there was no communication between them; then Taliesin mentally announced, *"Alan, like Amaruduk, I have decided. I am going with you into the Other World."*

The sudden statement, totally unexpected and without warning, shocked MacDougall beyond measure. He turned and stared incredulously at the Bard riding at his side. Aloud he exclaimed, "You can't do that! And you should know it better than anyone."

Ashak turned in his saddle and looked back in surprise. "What did you say?"

MacDougall forced a laugh. "Silly of me. I was thinking of something I should have said to Scathach, and it slipped from my tongue."

To Taliesin Alan directed a mental question. *"What do you mean? You know that means death."*

The Bard smiled faintly as he met Alan's gaze. *"You forget, death is not instantaneous; and the other Gates are in your tower, with access to Tartarus or Ochren—or perchance the island beyond the fourth Gate. A quick exit from Scath and perhaps one last glimpse of the Highlands—these are worth the risk."*

"As you wish," MacDougall responded. The Bard was never foolhardy; if he thought it could be done, it probably could.

The miles slipped by without incident, and the woodland loomed ahead when they reached a ramp leading into the tunnel. As before, a globe of green radiance appeared above them and moved with them. Their way seemed to veer to the left, but, except for occasional weaving and winding, the way was smooth and progress steady. After a time, they began passing numerous branching tunnels, opening to east and west, but all these seemed smaller, not large enough for a horse and rider. They came finally to a leftward branch and they followed it. At last, they reached another ramp. At their approach, a double trapdoor opened overhead, and they

rode into the auroral light. They were again in the middle
of a stretch of tall grass.

"Here I leave you," Ashak announced. He pointed
directly ahead. "There lies Scathach's village. A short
distance to the left of us, you will find the cart path leading to the woods—the way, so the master tells me, that
you followed when you first came to Scath. It will take
you where you wish to go." He turned and rode down
the ramp, the trapdoor closing behind him.

They followed directions, riding through the waist-
high growth, and in due course came to a rutted road.
MacDougall halted and looked toward the tower of
Scathach, little more than a smudge on the horizon. A lot
had happened there. He thought of some fascinating revelations that had been made, if revelations they were: the
"dream" in which Vollmar, bastard son of King Vortigern, supposedly his preincarnation, fulfilled a statement
of Ahriman the Lieutenant of Lucifer, concerning his
royal descent; the pact that had been made which promised him world rulership; and interesting sessions with
Scathach the Sorceress. Now all had to be put behind
him.

"Should we not be going?" Taliesin asked quietly.
"There is nothing to be gained by our tarrying here."

Alan turned his horse. "Of course." Then quickly he
glanced back and gave a second hard look. "What's
that?"

Rising slowly along the horizon, like billows of black
smoke, starting in the area of Scathach's tower, they
could see a vaporous black wall forming. As they
watched in fascination, it spread ponderously to east and
west, mounting higher and higher, a barrier reaching toward the aurora.

MacDougall thought of that first fog which Taliesin,
with Danu's help, brought into being to hide their entry
into Murias. Was this another magic spell?

The Bard answered his unspoken question. "It's the

work of the Druidesses. Why I cannot say. I recall that there was a King in the Olden Times named Loegaire, who was persecuted by the early Christians. He had his Druids send thick darkness upon the priests. If thick fog, why not thick darkness? If Druids, why not Druidesses?"

By this time, the wall of black had grown to huge dimensions, stretching east and west as far as the eye could reach, and seeming to merge with the sky.

Excitedly Alan exclaimed, "Let's see what is happening behind that wall. The Sorceress must have a reason for having it created. Through the armlet, maybe we can find out what she has in mind. You concentrate on me and both of us shall see."

Of the serpent-gods he asked, "May we see the Druidesses in action?"

In both minds appeared a panoramic view of the Groves of the Druidesses. Everywhere sat gray-cowled women, heads bowed, eyes closed, as still as stone. "In action" was hardly the term.

"There must be someone directing. Let us see the Daughters of Calatin."

The scene shifted to the interior of the Witches' apartment. The three crones crouched over a small table, the top of which was a slab of polished black stone. Centered on the table, modeled in raw clay, was a crude but recognizable model of the island with the tower, the guards' village, and the groves, all in position. And like a narrow band just beyond the buildings, stretching from shore to shore burned a smoldering band of fire. From it rose heavy black smoke to form a vaporous wall. The eyes of the Witches were closed, and their lips moved in silent incantations.

"More is happening." Enki inserted the thought. The view shifted to the open space between the corral and the moat. This was filling with warriors, fully armed, extending down to the seashore. And in an unbroken line they were flowing along the southern edge of the village!

"Unbelievable!" MacDougall exclaimed. "There aren't that many warriors in the whole village. Where can—" He stopped short as sharp lances prodded his back. He turned sharply to see a score of Amazons on horseback, hemming them in, some with lances and others with arrows aimed, bowstrings drawn back.

"Queen Scathach said we would find you here," one announced, "and we should bring you. There were no restrictions."

For a split second, in a sudden surge of fury, Mac-Dougall almost spurred his horse in an attempt at flight, but reason prevailed. Taliesin's calmly uttered "Careful, Alan" helped. Though inwardly seething at his own carelessness, at Amaruduk's baseless assurance that he need fear nothing from Scathach, and at the persistence of the Sorceress, he said in disgust, "Very well. Let's go."

CHAPTER 10

The Battle of Scath

Alan MacDougall watched as three of the guards dis-
mounted and stood close together, facing each other,
eyes closed, holding their lapis lazuli pendants. They
were reporting to Scathach, he thought bitterly. There
was no trace of relaxing among the others, who still held
their weapons poised menacingly.

In moments the amorphous gray circle appeared
above them, and the image of the Sorceress appeared.
There was a harried expression on her face as she said
impatiently, "I see you have caught MacDougall and his
companion. Good! Bring them and lock them in separate
cells in the dungeon until I have time to deal with them.
See that they do not escape or you will greatly regret it."
The projection vanished.

Hmmm! I no longer rate top attention, MacDougall
thought. She must have a lot on her mind.

As they rode slowly toward the vaporous black wall,
with the guards intent on their task, Alan sent a disgrun-
tled thought to the Bard. *"I am becoming weary of all*

this. Flattering though it may be, this popularity is not appreciated. I have had more than enough of Scath-ach."

"*Well,*" Taliesin responded, "*in view of what is coming, I believe the safest place we could find in Scath is the inside of a well-locked dungeon cell. The battle I foresee will not be ours. I would not side with Scathach or Amaruduk or Beli."*

They arrived at the barrier, and the lead rider hesitated, then rode into it. It was an eerie sensation, MacDougall thought, as the blackness closed about him—utter blackness, as dark as the depths of a lightless cave. They passed through it, emerging to face a wall of Guards, bows at ready.

"*Look at their eyes,*" came the Bard's shocked thought.

Alan gazed intently at the nearest warrior, then at the next, and looked hastily away. Like the eyes of the soulless Daughters of Lilith, dwelling in the trees of the Grove of Spirits, the eyes of the warriors were without expression, utterly blank.

All the riders dismounted. Completely boxed in, the pair of captives were led through the mass of Guards to the moat, then in single file across the bridge and the maze, and into the Castle. Here, too, was the hubbub of preparation, with the normal staff of Guards greatly increased.

The center of sudden attention, the two were led down the spiral stairway, descending to the second level belowground, where the steps ended. Here only a few gas burners on the wall gave meager light, deep shadows prevailing everywhere, the air heavy with musty dampness.

Massive bronze doors with thick bars across their center marked the individual cells. Great triple bolts secured them. There was no magic here, only the most primitive—and effective—locks. With difficulty, the bolts were slid aside and the doors opened on hinges that squealed in protest. MacDougall and the Bard were thrust into neighboring cells. Vigilance had never relaxed, the prodding lances being ever against their backs. The bolts shot home, followed by the clatter of boots on the stairs. The prisoners were alone in semi-darkness.

Alan drew out his flashlight and swept a beam around the cell. It was a square cubicle of damp and moldy stone, without windows and with only one door. Vents in the heavy planks that made up the side walls and the space between the bars provided the only semblance of ventilation. Massive bronze chains, green with age, dangled from the walls, ending in what appeared to be heavy metal collars. A low stone barrier stretched from side to side along the rear wall; after a glance behind it, MacDougall turned away in disgust. Heaps of blackened refuse with here and there suggestions of whitened bones filled the space. One consolation was that the deposit appeared to be of ancient origin. Except for a low plank bed, raised a few inches from the stone floor, the room was empty. MacDougall sank to a seat on the stone barrier.

"To think that Brendah had to spend sleep after sleep in a hole like this. How could she stand it?"

"These women are tough," the Bard answered absently.

"If only there were some way for us to reach her," Alan continued. "I'm sure she would try to find a way to release us, would take delight in helping us escape. But how—"

"Alan," Taliesin interrupted, his voice expressing unbelief. "It seems impossible to me that Scathach is doing what she is doing. You cannot realize the enormity of her offense. She is meddling with the normal procedure of what you call the Halls of the Dead. I can't see how she could do it—how she *dared* bring these soulless bodies out of their stasis. For that is what these warriors are. It violates every instinct. Would your serpent-gods be able to tell us?"

"We'll find out." MacDougall grasped the armlet. "Lord and Lady, how did Scathach arrange to have these warriors animated?"

"Not the Sorceress," Enki scoffed. "It is entirely the doing of Ereshkigal. Remember, she once was the goddess of the Nether World, with countless dead as her subjects. Dark powers were hers, and evidently some still remain. Perhaps Scathach expressed the need, asking for some way to defeat Amaruduk, but that is a guess."

"You heard, Taliesin?" Alan asked. Then, at a burst of noise and feminine cries echoing down the stairwell, he exclaimed, "It's started! Lord Enki, let us observe. Taliesin, stay with me."

In their minds' eyes they saw the scene on ground level. For an infinitesimal moment, it seemed to be a tableau, frozen like a single frame of a film. There were five gray-clad Anunnaki, swords in hand, and facing them were three rows of warriors who were guarding the main entrance. Evidently they had just spun around at some alarm. The back row, now closest to the demons, were archers; and in that split second they pulled back arrows against taut bowstrings.

As one, they released their arrows, which sped unerringly into the breasts of the five Anunnaki. As they crumpled to the floor, they vanished.

Instantly a second group of ten demons appeared; an instant later, masters of shape-changing, all became replicas of the Guards and charged the archers with slashing swords. The unprepared women fell under the onslaught, blood spurting; and wild disorder ensued as other Anunnaki poured into the tower.

Carefully deployed warriors in three rows, swords, lances, then bows, guarding the staircase and the other entrances, were thrown into complete confusion. As the false Guards multiplied, there was no distinguishing friend from foe.

Appalled, MacDougall sent the thought: "Outside, Lord Enki." Instantly the setting changed. They were viewing a spectacle of unparalleled carnage. The confusion of the Castle interior was multiplied a hundredfold, with an added factor, the newly animated zombielike warriors. Where natural prudence and instinctive fear motivated women and demons alike, the unnatural recruits fought with frenzied abandon. Not only was there no fear, but their bodies literally had to be hacked to pieces before they stopped fighting. The resulting bloodflow was like that of a slaughterhouse.

Alan shut off the view. Scathach! What of her? With the thought they were looking down into the interior of the room of mirrors with the Sorceress at her post. Before her on the large screen was a perfect view of what Alan and the Bard had seen mentally.

Now Scathach sent the image moving along the inside of the black wall to the end of the village, and everywhere the same ghastly picture appeared, the same senseless slaughter. The wall of darkness was totally ineffective in barring the attackers. It should have been obvious, Alan thought, that it would not stop the Anunnaki, who could materialize wherever they wished.

"Not the Anunnaki," Inanna interjected, "but there had been too few of them to be a menace. The Igigi, who had made up Amaruduk's forces, had not that ability. Only his awakening the Sleepers made this debacle possible."

Their attention turned to the Sorceress, a picture of frustrated fury. Her eyes were glaring, her jaws clenched, her fists doubled, and her knuckles white. She glanced at other mirrors, showing a view of the Druidesses still immobile in their concentration; beyond them was a wall of protective fighters in furious conflict with the demons.

Suddenly the scene changed to the Daughters of Calatin, still hovering over their smoky wall. The projection of Scathach appeared above them.

"Spread the darkness in a cloud over this end of the island," she ordered. "Quickly! The attackers cannot fight if they cannot see. Hide everything with blackness."

Responding instantly, the three crones waved their long fingers through the black vapor, spreading it over the model of the field of battle. And as the miniature vanished under the blackness, so disappeared the scene of carnage revealed on the several mirrors.

MacDougall's thoughts turned to the visitors from Ochren and Tartarus; and in tune with his wish, the serpent-gods revealed a gathering in the torture room on the third level. Nuada was speaking, obviously influenced, as Alan and the Bard were aware, by his demon possessors.

"It is suicidal for us to remain here in Scath. Our quest for MacDougall has failed, but if he remains in this world there will be other opportunities. We have seen enough of this island. We have no part in the war between Scathach and Amaruduk, so the quicker we are aboard the *Wave Sweeper*, the better."

Manannan shook his head stubbornly. "I agree that this is not our battle, but I will not bring my coracle to shore while this madness is in progress. It would not be safe for the craft."

"But there should be no need for that," Beli growled. "We can transfer ourselves to your ship where it now floats. After all, the four of us came back together from Amaruduk's tower."

The sea god was not convinced. "True, the four of you did so, but there are ten, and five of the ten have not the power." A gleam of savage anticipation came into his eyes. "I suggest that I whip up a storm that will sweep these fighters from the field of battle and roll them like balls across the flattened grass. And before they can recover, we walk out of here and get aboard my coracle, which will be waiting at the tip of the island."

"The five of us should have no trouble carrying the others," Balor rumbled. "Combined, our strength is doubled and more."

Manannan looked doubtfully at the god of the Fomorians. "I understand you got lost while trying to find Mac-Dougall. Would we be safe—?"

Pryderi interrupted impatiently, "Why all this chatter? I say let those who will get aboard. Manannan may play with his storm and do it the hard way. In due time he will join us."

As one, the four under demon control, with full agreement, stood up, clasped hands, and disappeared. Startled, Manannan faced the others.

"Mathonwy, you and your Druids will join me in creating a spell the like of which the Isle of Scath has never seen."

MacDougall saw no more as he terminated his viewing. He spoke to the Bard.

"Taliesin, somehow we must get out of here. This place is going mad. Manannan's storm will clear things so we can get free of all this, providing we can get out of these cells. There must be a way—"

"I have thought of a possibility," the Bard responded. "Kindazi, the Anunnaki I spoke with in the Grove of Druidesses, might help. If I can reach him and explain to him what Amaruduk intended for us, I might persuade him to open these doors. In seconds, he could transfer here, slide the bolts, and return instantly to whatever he is doing. But we'd have to fight our way through the madness above our heads."

Alan answered impatiently, "Better that than sitting here waiting for the stupidity to end. Frankly, I think both Scathach and Amaruduk are in big trouble and I don't want to be around when lightning strikes. Try, man, try."

Silence fell within the cells while MacDougall waited, silence except for the sounds of conflict from above, which continued unabated. For what seemed to be a long time, he received no word from the Bard. The first indication that anything had resulted from Taliesin's effort was the rasp of the bolts as they slid noisily from their sockets. MacDougall sprang from his seat on the bed and reached the door in time to catch a glimpse of a gray figure as he moved to the Bard's door. He thrust open his own door against the protests of creaking hinges to find the corridor empty and the Bard emerging from his cell.

"A reluctant helper," Taliesin said. "At first he tried to cut off my thought, but I persisted. Finally he consulted Amaruduk himself—and we are out."

"But not out of trouble," Alan said grimly. "As you suggested, this is certain to take some fighting. Even if Manannan's storm clears the outside, it won't stop the demons inside the Castle. If only you had a sword."

"There should be no trouble finding one on the floor above, and I do know how to use it."

"Strategy," MacDougall continued after a short pause. "Invisible, of course. The Castle Guards won't see us, but the demons will, and they will be our problem. We slide along the outer wall and head for the southern exit. Logically, the storm will come from the north, from the sea, with the god of the sea creating it, so the tower will shelter us when we get outside. We can't plan beyond that." He halted. "I'll check the situation above." He closed his eyes.

Mentally he viewed the scene on ground level. It was sickening, strewn everywhere with bodies of slain or badly wounded Guards and atrociously hacked zombies. The outside entrances stood open, and both Anunnaki and newly animated women choked the entrances, fighting to get in.

Hurricane winds whistled and howled past the openings; the supernatural storm was at its height. Coinciding with the typhoon, down the stairwell came sounds of conflict. A quick extension of Alan's vision revealed a mass of armored soldiers filling the stairwell, descending inexorably. Illusion, but real enough to kill if one believed.

MacDougall switched his viewing to the outside. Utter chaos met his gaze. Mingled with the blackness created by Witches and Druidesses were the gale winds of Manannan, with lightning flashing and thunder rolling out of a lacerated aurora. Now the blackness weakened and fluctuated, seeming to be losing the fight against the storm. No warriors, so far as he could see, remained erect. To the north he saw the sea whipped into white frothing fury, sweeping up the river channels and over the ramp with mighty combers.

He shut off the view and turned to the Bard, drawing a deep breath and scowling blackly. "Impossible situation."

"I saw," Taliesin answered. "Are you sure we should try to leave?"

"Certain," Alan answered stubbornly. "Once outside we'll find a way out of this mess. Let's go."

Invisible, they climbed the winding stairs; Alan had his sword drawn. There was no need for stealth; as they approached the scene of action they could not hear their own footfalls. Taliesin procured a sword with no difficulty, as he had said, and they reached the corridor before one of the Anunnaki, outwardly an Amazon, detected them.

Instantly they were the center of attack, five demons charging as one. Backs to the wall they fought, the Bard revealing uncommon skill. Alan's blade seemed to have a will of its own, sending sword after sword slithering away. "Lord Enki—" he thought desperately.

"I'm doing my best. And I'm trying to reach their minds—"

As if he had suddenly been stricken deaf, there was a cessation of all sound for Alan MacDougall, and with it the loss of normal sight. It was not a darkness, but a blurred, universal gray. The Anunnaki were gone; the corridor had vanished. Alan felt a vague sensation of flight at infinite speed, an internal twisting, and a jarring halt, all of it ending the instant it began.

He became aware of heavy breathing and realized it was his own; he felt his pulse racing. His sight suddenly cleared, and he was staring into a gold-tinged expanse of dancing aurora. The silence about him was a tangible thing after the bedlam he had just left.

Dazedly he stared around, instantly recognizing the golden room of Ahriman the Persian, unseen and unrecognized ruler of the islands; Alan stood in the round chamber at the very top of the tapering, cylindrical Golden Tower. Luxurious gold-colored rugs covered the floor; the heavily upholstered furniture was of the same hue; and even the walls and ceiling were metallic-appearing gold, opaque from the outside, transparent from within. The room seemed to be thrusting into the very heart of the waves and streamers of the ever-changing, rainbow-tinted aurora. Twice before he had been in this enchanted and enchanting chamber with the Persian. Now he was alone.

Of course! He could picture Ahriman in a lower room, perched on a gold-railed platform above a three-dimensional, jewellike replica of the divided island of Scathach and Amaruduk. On his head must be the translucent dome with its strange spectacles, and in his hands the fantastic padded forceps that had plucked Alan MacDougall from the uneven conflict in the Castle of the Sorceress and placed him here. He himself had used those tongs in a rash moment to drop the Druid Semias on the roof of the Hall of the Dead at Falias, destroying his reason and leading to his plunging a knife into Alan's back.

MacDougall dropped into one of the chairs, feeling suddenly drained. So much had happened in so short a time that there finally had to be a reaction. He knew he wasn't made of the stuff of heroes, but he'd certainly been trying to play the part. He pictured that final duel in the corridor. Reluctantly he had to admit that Ahriman probably had saved his life.

Yet—damn it—he resented the interference. What was the Persian doing now? Probably meddling in the muddle created by the Sorceress and her ages-long foe. He scowled. Again he was forced to admit that, if anyone could do anything about the stupid conflict, it was Ahriman.

What about Taliesin? The thought hit him like a blow. What must the Bard think of his sudden desertion? Alan thought of attempting to reach him mentally but hesitated. If he were still fighting—

At that moment Ahriman appeared before him, and instinctively MacDougall sprang to his feet. As always, the presence of the Persian was overwhelming. He was a powerful man, fully six inches taller than Alan. The gemlike blue eyes, full, deeply red lips, ivory complexion, square jaw, and full-cut black hair, all were as Alan recalled them; but now the usually grim features were contorted by barely contained fury.

Alan forced himself to meet the piercing gaze with expressionless face and, he hoped, without revealing his sudden apprehension. What had he done to incur such wrath?

As if reading his thought, the Persian forced a smile and said quietly, "There is no reason for you to stand; and you are not the object of my anger. I have just been dealing with Scathach, Amaruduk, and Ereshkigal."

Relieved, MacDougall sank back into his chair, while

Ahriman seated himself in another, facing him. The Persian sat there, drawing deep breaths until he had regained complete control of himself.

During those moments Alan kept his eyes lowered, taking in Ahriman's surprising apparel. He was dressed entirely in white, a loosely fitting, high-collared blouse and free-flowing trousers, gathered at wrists and ankles. These were woven of a silken fabric with a delicate tracery of metallic gold threads forming an intricate oriental design. His only ornament was a large oval pendant of Imperial green jade suspended from a massive yellow gold chain.

Finally Ahriman spoke. "And what do you really think of the war in Scath?"

"My honest opinion? It is silly, childish, and stupid. All warfare is stupid, but this is asinine. What are they fighting about? They can have no good reason."

The Persian smiled faintly. "I admire your restraint. But then, you could hardly understand the full impact of what happened. Amaruduk's wakening of the Sleepers and Ereshkigal's interfering with the normal cycle of the replacement centers and bringing out animated bodies to be butchered—these acts carry serious consequences. Scathach cooperated with the dark goddess and will share in her punishment, after I report to the Master.

"Be this as it may, I stopped the war."

"You *stopped* the war?" MacDougall exclaimed in vast surprise.

"Yes. It required the display of powers I rarely resort to, but it could not be permitted to continue. The Anunnaki have returned to their slumbers, and the soulless warriors who survived have started the long walk back to what you call the Halls of the Dead. Even the visitors from Ochren and Tartarus are aboard the *Wave Sweeper* on the open sea."

MacDougall regarded Ahriman with amazement.

"You accomplished all that in the very short time after you brought me here?"

The Persian nodded and smiled faintly. "A very short time for you in your inactivity; but you have forgotten, as Taliesin told you shortly after you first entered this world, time here has no constancy; time is a variable."

"Taliesin!" Mention of the Bard recalled Alan's concern. "What has happened to him?"

"I returned him to the safety of his cell where he awaits the next act in the drama." He shook his head disapprovingly. "There was really no reason for you two getting involved in that last conflict between Scathach and Amaruduk. Needless exposure to danger—"

Impatiently MacDougall interrupted, "I know. My own curiosity and carelessness made it necessary for you to lift me out of trouble a second time. I suppose I should thank you for this rescue and for thrusting my unconscious body through the Gate after Semias stabbed me. I've wondered why you stopped at the Gate."

Ahriman frowned. "There are limits to the scope of the device. For reasons that should be obvious, it cannot operate outside this world of the islands."

"Surely you are not suggesting that your influence does not extend into the Other World!" Alan's boldness had returned, overriding his instinctive awe of Lucifer's lieutenant. "What about that attack in the Cameron bedroom? I know now what I suspected then; that was a demonic attempt to possess my body. You had nothing to do with that?"

"No entity from this world made that attack," the Persian said evasively.

"When I tried to dispose of the armlet," Alan persisted, "or when I planned to leave Scotland before I visited Ochren, I encountered strong mental resistance. Then a false message, supposedly from Taliesin, followed by an illusionary vision of the Bard through the second Gate, led me into the dark island. After my near death and slow recovery on the Cameron farm, the nightmarish demonic attack and its threat to Elspeth Cameron brought me into Scath against my will. You had nothing to do with any of this?"

Ahriman's cold eyes met MacDougall's, but his face remained expressionless.

"You have an excellent memory," he said quietly, "but you seem to have forgotten something I told you during our first visit. I recall the exact words: 'Anything Lucifer introduces is his, under his control.' You were introduced into Tartarus through the armlet; and although you are a reluctant participant in the affairs of this world, you are nonetheless a participant."

MacDougall felt a momentary stab of dread at the implication. Vehemently he protested, "Would this mean that my searching for my brother Malcolm in the Highlands, my finding the armlet, my passing through the first portal—all were under Lucifer's direction? I don't believe it."

"Belief or unbelief cannot alter facts." The Persian paused, then continued, "May I suggest that it would be, shall I say, unwise for you to continue your association in the Other World with this Highland woman who is totally unsuitable for you and your future greatness? After all, as you yourself have observed, misfortune often befalls those around you."

Alan bristled at the obvious threat, his face flushing with anger. "What I do in the Other World is my concern. And in this realm, as well. I will not be manipulated into mating with such as Scathach. I could see your hand behind my every contact with her, like her telling me she recognized me and knew me in former lives, when of course you had informed her of my coming, or like the dreams, or whatever they were, with my supposedly recalling former incarnations in which she always figured. There was even one adventure putting me in the royal line and involving me in a prophecy of promised rulership of the world! What nonsense!

"Oh, the visions were beautifully planned and most convincingly presented, but they were slightly over-drawn, going just a bit too far. It will take more than this to convince me that I am the one referred to in that in-fernal scroll."

MacDougall expected a strong response from Ahri-man, but the Persian did not change expression as he commented, "You are certainly difficult to convince. Even after the crying out of the Stone of Fal and all these other evidences, you still will not believe. Well, there is still the fourth Gate before you."

That was hardly news, Alan thought, though this was the first time an open statement had been made. He had expected to go through that final portal. But that legend-ary Stone of Fal, a steel-gray cube with fused edges that had cried out eerily when he sat on it, as a reputed sign of royalty, did trouble him.

"How was that sound produced? Magic, I presume."

Ahriman ignored the question. "You have learned all that is needful from your visit to Scath, so I shall return you to the third portal for your exit."

"Why not the Tartarus Gate, since all end at the same place?"

"Because there is one small act still to be performed," the Persian answered patiently. "The stage has been set, and it is necessary that you view the performance."

"Of course," MacDougall cried recklessly. "All your puppets are in place save one; and before you begin pull-ing strings, that one must assume his position. Another proof—"

The lieutenant of Lucifer suddenly looked the part as he glared at Alan; and again MacDougall felt the stab of fear. Ahriman's tones were frigid when he spoke.

"You grow overly bold, young man. If it is your pur-pose to irritate me, know that you are succeeding. I suggest greater prudence in the future. You are not beyond chastening." He stood up; Alan rose as quickly, now silent.

"Prepare to return, and I suggest you be invisible."

Hastily, MacDougall assumed invisibility as he had done so often. At the same instant, Ahriman was gone. Tensely Alan waited for what he knew must follow. He pictured himself dangling from the tips of giant tongs, being whisked at fantastic speed through the air from the Golden Tower in Tartarus to the jungle in Scath. His heart began to race in anticipation.

Then it happened, and again he felt that impossible blending of sensations—an end to sight and sound, incredible flight, a sort of vertigo, and instant cessation. Senses began to function, and he realized he was standing on the very edge of the portal, seeing a ghostly outline of the Highland *broch*. A step, and he would be in his own world.

He stood motionless as remembered sounds and scents poured in upon him from the jungle that was his introduction to Scath—the humming as of countless bees, the rustle of myriad leaves, stirrings in the thicket, and a cloyingly sweet scent. There flashed into his memory a sensation of evil permeating the place, and he realized that prolonged exposure to this impression had dulled his awareness of it.

There was something else. Through the heavy undergrowth a score of feet away, he saw a row of Scathach's warriors, backs turned toward him. His gaze followed the line across a wide curve; and as he slowly turned, making a full circle, he realized that a tight though irregular ring of guards completely surrounded the Gate. Obviously they were there to prevent his reaching it.

During his turning, Alan had noticed a change. The area of the jungle floor between the trees he had marked with his sword had been cleared. The cleared stretch continued in a swath, weaving in and out between the trees, roughly following the course he had struggled through with the help of his sword as a machete.

So that was how they had found the position of the Gate! Brendah, of course, remembered where she had captured him and had simply backtracked. Then she should be visible here, if only the warriors were facing him; there was a sameness about bare backs. But Brendah should show lash marks—and he saw them, a tracery of welts that had not yet fully healed.

She was one of three standing side by side, tightly together in the cleared path; and between them Mac-Dougall glimpsed a broad, darkly dressed figure. He caught a glimpse of a fringe of thick white hair topped by a bald head. Taliesin! It had to be. Excitedly he sent a thought.

"Taliesin, I'm behind you, standing directly in front of the Gate. Ahriman picked me out of that fight and took me back to his Tower. After we talked, he placed me here."

Alan saw a stirring in the little group, the Bard turning his head, ostensibly to say something to Brendah.

"I see you," came his delighted reply. *"Good to know you are safe. I thought Ahriman was the answer to your vanishing; and he had to be behind the fantastic happenings that followed."*

"What brings you here?" Alan asked. *"Part of this apparent trap?"*

"I am the bait, the decoy. I am supposed to lure you here. You have arrived just in time for the completion of the arrangements. The Sorceress should be here at any moment. Of course, you need not wait; you can leave when you wish. But remember, I plan to join you, so don't close the portal."

"You haven't changed your mind?" MacDougall asked. *"You, if anyone, must be aware of the danger of disintegration within a very short time. Even if you re-*

turn promptly to Tartarus, who knows how your body will be affected? Is it worth the risk?"

"I have not changed my mind." The Bard's thought was resolute. *"And after you have left, I will find a way to follow."*

There was a stirring in the forest beyond the circle of guards, and around a curve in the rough path came Scathach and her retinue. She was seated in a sort of litter, called a palanquin in the Orient, Alan remembered; it rested on long poles, borne on the shoulders of four stalwart Amazons. Five of her Guards led the way and five followed.

Watching, MacDougall saw a rounded cloud of gray mist hanging over the Sorceress, with three ugly faces clear against it—the Daughters of Calatin, each looking in a different direction, alert for any movement.

Alan grimaced. They really wanted to capture him. But they had no chance with his freedom a step away.

Just outside the row of Guards, the Queen's carriers halted and lowered her to the path. The fourteen ranged themselves evenly around the circle. A way parted and Scathach walked regally through the ranks of the Amazons and moved to the center of the area with the marked trees. MacDougall watched her approach with a queer feeling, but she ignored him. She stopped about two feet away and looked around, evidently examining the white slashes on the surrounding trees. She took her place precisely at the center, in position to pass through the Gate, though of course without realizing the fact, then turned her back on MacDougall and the portal.

Motionless, she held the position as if for effect, a striking picture in purple and gold, never more beautiful. She wore a gold circlet across her forehead and around her black hair, gold breastplates, the inevitable lapis lazuli pendant, a short purple cape over her shoulders, a pleated full-cut skirt ending above her knees, and high cloth-of-gold boots. Finally she spoke, her voice ringing clearly through the woods.

"Alan MacDougall, hear me! If you are watching— and I am sure you *are* watching—I know this is the gateway to your world. Though I know it is not permitted that I pass through, so also are you barred. As I bar the way, so shall it remain until my warriors find you. You cannot escape. Reveal yourself now and I will be merciful. Delay and take the consequences."

Enough, MacDougall told himself; he'd heard the same threats from her before. For an instant, he thought of reappearing just before he stepped through, but decided against it. Let them search.

Crouching, he stepped into his own world.

About to turn to watch the rest of the action in Scath, he caught a hint of motion and a flash of light from the far side of the *broch*.

"Alan! Can it be you?" It was Elspeth's voice, filled with wonder. The light the beam came from was her flashlight.

"Darling—you here!" Alan dashed across the flagging and caught the girl in his arms. "What brings you to the tower?"

"You left just a week ago, and I thought— But you appeared out of nowhere—"

"Let me show you." Swiftly MacDougall flung off his cape and jacket and bared his upper arm, exposing the twin-headed serpent. Putting his arm around the girl, he raised her hand to touch his armlet.

"Oh," she exclaimed, then held her breath as she saw what he saw, the scene beyond Gate three. He led her to within a foot of the portal. Scathach was still speaking, and her words came clearly to their ears.

"The three Daughters of Calatin have assured me that you are still in Scath. They will scan the island from end to end until—"

She stopped in midsentence as Brendah, from her po-

sition in the circle, whirled, leaped like a tigress, one arm
thrust stiffly before her, and caught the Sorceress
squarely on the chest. A single startled scream burst
from Scathach as she reeled backward and sprawled
awkwardly on the floor of the tower.

At Brendah's first movement, MacDougall had instinctively leaped away from the Gate, bearing Elspeth
with him, barely avoiding the plummeting form of the
Sorceress. For an instant his eyes were held by the
drama in the Other World.

Brendah, with sword held high, shouted triumphantly,
"Gone is the witch! Not again will she order lashings—"

Then the other Guards swept down upon her; and at
Alan's feet the startled Scathach scrambled erect.

Wide-eyed, she stared at MacDougall and the girl,
then darted glances from side to side like a caged animal,
awareness of her position slow in coming. Suddenly, terror transfixed her features as realization dawned. Her
mouth gaped, her lips drew back, and her hand clutched
her throat as a choking scream burst forth. She seemed
paralyzed with fright.

At that instant Taliesin sprang into the room, barely
missing the Sorceress. She scurried to one side, halting
before the fourth Gate. The Bard straightened up and
looked around.

The positions held for dragging moments. Action had
followed action with such speed that everything seemed
to have happened at once. Alan had his eyes fixed on
Scathach, so he saw her next move, totally unexpected.

She had halted a step away from the open fourth Gate
with its idyllic scene, smooth lawns, winding white
paths, and distant marble castle. He heard her murmur:
"*Caer Sidi*, the Perfect Place!" Suddenly she darted
through the portal and raced across the lawn as if fearing
pursuit.

"An interesting development," Taliesin said quietly,
"but not surprising." MacDougall realized that he spoke

in the language of the Other World, but Elspeth's hand was still pressed against the armlet, so he felt sure she understood. He watched as the Bard stepped to the Gate to Scath and closed it. "I believe we have seen all we wish to see of the land of Scathach and Amaruduk." Smiling faintly, he looked at Elspeth with a twinkle in his eyes.

"And who is the lovely maiden you hold so tightly?"

MacDougall grinned in slight confusion, but did not release the girl. "This is Elspeth Cameron. If I let her go, she will not understand you, and for her the portals will vanish.

"And Elspeth, this is the Bard, Taliesin, my only friend in the Other World." She smiled warmly and nodded.

Taliesin bowed deeply, then said, "Since my time here is very limited, may I see the other Gates?"

Alan led him to the first portal, Elspeth watching with even greater fascination. The Bard looked steadily at the tranquil landscape, the frosty aurora, and the rolling, pale-green hills, with distant Falias like a jewel on the horizon. He indicated the second Gate.

"And that, I suppose, leads into Ochren."

They peered at the gloomy spectacle of the dark island, its gray turf and dark sky, with its timid aurora. Alan felt Elspeth shudder as she whispered, "And you were there!"

"And now the land beyond the fourth portal," the Bard said quietly.

They halted at the last Gate, staring at the beautiful scene, the slightly undulating green lawn a fitting setting for graceful flowering bushes, stately trees, and noble pillars of white marble supporting domed silver roofs. The aurora overhead was at its most splendid radiance. The Sorceress was no longer in sight.

"How lovely," Elspeth breathed.

"Lovely to look at," Taliesin agreed, "but still part of

Lucifer's creation." He turned his head away from the portal for a moment, looking toward the silvery light framed by the entrance into the *broch*. He seemed to hesitate in momentary indecision, then suddenly he darted out into the mottled sunlight of the oak forest.

Alan felt Elspeth stiffen in his grasp as she murmured, "Where is he going?"

"Nowhere. Just outside."

In a few moments the Bard returned, walking slowly, with evident reluctance. He halted before the fourth Gate. His gaze met MacDougall's; and there was an unusual sparkle in his eyes, an enraptured expression on his face. His voice was hushed.

"A sight I never again expected to see, the blue sky of the Highlands. Air I never again expected to breathe, the clear air of the Highlands. What treasure is yours, my friend!" He looked at Elspeth with a warm smile. "What treasures! And now I must return." He sobered.

"When you decide to follow, you will find me waiting. Until then—farewell."

With a wave of his hand Taliesin stepped through the fourth Gate.

ABOUT THE AUTHOR

Lloyd Arthur Eshbach was born on a farm in southeast-
ern Pennsylvania on June 20, 1910. He still lives in Pennsylvania and has spent most of his years in the same area. He
began reading science fiction, and fantasy in 1919 with the
fanciful tales of Edgar Rice Burroughs, A. Merritt, and their
contemporaries in the pages of the Munsey magazines. He
wrote his first salable SF story in 1929 and in the 1930s became a "big-name" writer. He began publishing SF books as
Fantasy Press in 1947. Although he was not the first specialist publisher in the field, he was the first to present a full line
of science fiction titles. His own writing, always a spare-time
effort, included, in addition to SF, tales of fantasy and the
supernatural, mystery stories, adventures, romances, and ju-
veniles, some published under pseudonyms. With his entry
into publishing, his writing became quite sporadic, and his
last story appeared in 1957.

After the failure of his publishing venture—a fate met by
all of the SF specialist houses—he became an advertising
copywriter, a religious publisher, advertising manager of a
major religious publishing house, and a publisher's sales rep-
resentative.

In 1978, in retirement, Eshbach began writing again, his
first effort being *Over My Shoulder: Reflections on a Science
Fiction Era*, a memoir of his life in SF, concentrating on the
history of the fan hardback book publishers of the 1930s,
'40s, and '50s. This was issued in a limited edition in 1983.
He completed E. E. "Doc" Smith's last novel, *Subspace Encounter*, left unfinished at Doc's death in 1965, which was
also published in 1983. *The Sorceress of Scath* is the third
book in a four-novel fantasy that began with *The Land
Beyond the Gate* and *The Armlet of the Gods*.

THE BEST
IN FANTASY BY

Lloyd
Arthur
Eshbach
The Gates
of
Lucifer
Series